The Book of
STEVEN

The Book of
STEVEN

STEVEN T. STEVENSON *and* SHAH R. AZAD

iUniverse®

THE BOOK OF STEVEN

iUniverse books may be ordered through booksellers or by contacting:

iUniverse
1663 Liberty Drive
Bloomington, IN 47403
www.iuniverse.com
1-800-Authors (1-800-288-4677)

ISBN: 978-1-4917-5616-4 (sc)
ISBN: 978-1-4917-5615-7 (e)

Library of Congress Control Number: 2014922709

Printed in the United States of America.

iUniverse rev. date: 1/27/2015

For my Eternal Goddess, whose own light gave me
the hope and guidance to endure and believe.

Cast of Characters

Steven: Me, a.k.a. the universal idiot

God: The supernatural being who pulls all of the levers and makes life happen (may or may not be the same figure to everyone)

Jesus: The supernatural being who has also assumed a human role and who looks after all of us while we are trying to get it together (may have a different alias in some cultures)

Ted: Fucking Ted … I will get to him later

Others: To be introduced as the story goes along

PROLOGUE

In the beginning, there was nothing. Only darkness. And me. Steven, that is.

But there was no light and no sound.

There were no trees or dolphins or blue jays.

There were no books or pogo sticks or bicycles. No dance hoops.

No desks, pencils, or paper. No television. No radio. No Internet.

No virtual reality or pseudoreality.

No porno magazines. No nudie posters.

No drugs, tobacco, or alcohol. Not even a steak sandwich to dream about.

No mocking mirrors.

No marbles, no refrigerators, no fire extinguishers.

No dinosaurs, monkeys, or regrets.

No enemies, no disappointments, no great lost loves.

There were no moons and no stars, no supernovas.

And there was no one else. Only yours truly.

And emptiness as far as my spirit could wander.

At first there was nothing, and there was Steven.

Now, having absolutely no idea how to behave in such an absurd and oppressive situation, the panic set in, almost immediately …

The first thing I can remember saying was "Mmmmm ... mmmmm ... mmmmm ... aaaaah ... ohmmm ... haaaa ... waaaa ... heeel ... hell ... hey ... help ... hello ... hey ... haaaaa ... hummmm ... whaaa ... what are I ... why am I ... where ... what the ... where am I ... hey ...

"Hey! Help! Hello! Hello! Hey! Let me ... let me out of here! Oh shit! I can't move! *Help! Help! Hello? Aggghhh!*

"Oh shit, holy shit, oh my ... oh, holy shit, where am I? Oh Jesus ..."

And a calming voice said, "Steven. Relax. Do not try to move. Do not try to do anything. Find a place of stillness within you, and peace be with you."

I said, "Oh shit, oh lord, where am I?"

The voice said, "In heaven."

So I said, "Holy shit! Are you serious?"

The voice replied, "Yes. Now just try to relax. You will not be able to see for a while. You will not be able to move, either. Just try to relax. Focus on your breathing, and try to find peace."

"Oh, oh my, oh, okay. I, um, I uh, how, um—"

"How did you get here?"

"Yes."

"You died on earth. You came here. Now, just try to relax. Focus on your breathing, and try to relax. I will come back for you soon. You are safe, and everything is fine. Do not worry about anything. You are in our hands now. Peace be with you."

"Oh, oh, okay, I'll stay here and ..." *Relax?*

"Steven, if you need me, just call my name, and I will be here."

"Oh, ho, oh ... okay, thank you! Hey. Hello? Where did he go? Wait, who was that? Saint Peter?

"Hey, Saint Peter? Shit. Hey! Mr. ... oh, what the hell was his last name? It wasn't ... Peter, was it? Why don't saints have last names? Shit. Hey ... you ... guy, Mr. ... um, hey, hello!

"Guess not. Who else is up here? In ... heaven? How the hell did I wind up in heaven? Who else could that have been? I should have read more on this ... it's, um, it's ... oh, Jesus!"

And he said, "Are you okay?"

"Jesus, is that you?"

"Yes. Are you okay?"

I said, "Oh shit, oh sweet Jesus, yes, I'm okay. Sorry. I didn't mean to do that. I, um—"

In a soothing tone, he said, "Look, just try to relax, and I will come back for you when the time is right."

"Oh yeah, sorry. I didn't ... I mean, I wasn't trying to—"

"I know. Don't worry. I will come for you when your sight has returned and you can move around. Until then, if you do need something, you can call for me."

"Oh, okay. Yep, 10-4. Sorry about that. My mistake. Hey, so, um, what's the ... hello? Anyone there? Shit. He's gone already.

Okay. Relax. Just breathe. Whooo … ahhhh … whooo … ahhhh … whooo … ahhhh … whooo … ahhhh …

"Man, this is nice! I never spent much time just sitting and relaxing, thinking about my breathing and—whooo, ahhhh, whooo, ahhhh. In, out, in, out, inhale, exhale, inhale, exhale, expand, contract, expand, contract, ahhhh …

"Hey, I wonder how long you can hold your breath in heaven. Let's see … one Mississippi, two Mississippi, three Mississippi … Is heaven somewhere near Mississippi? I wonder if I'll get to find out. Wait, what was I doing? Holding my breath. Yeah, okay, one Mississippi, two Mississippi, three Mississippi …

"Wait a minute. I don't feel any different if I breathe or if I don't. My chest doesn't hurt. Hey, I can do this forever! I don't need to breathe. I can hold my breath, and nothing happens. Holy shit! That's cool! I wonder if this is how a fish feels. Wow!

"Wasn't I supposed to be doing something? Oh yeah … relax, breathe. Well, if he says to breathe, it must be for something. Okay. In, out, one, two, up, down, expand, contract … not too difficult so far. One and two and three and four and … Hey, what's the highest I've ever counted to? I wonder if I can count higher in heaven. Hey, what's infinity, anyway? What's eternity? I'll bet that I can ask someone that in heaven. Where the hell is heaven? Oh well, maybe I'll find out. One and two and one and two and … I wonder how long I have to lie here before something happens to me. Who knows? In and out and in and out and … hey, I think I can see a faint glimmer out of the corner of my eye. Is that … light, or … maybe I'm just imagining it?

"No, probably too quick, Steven, and you've never been quick at anything. One and two and one and—hey, maybe I'm in a coma and dreaming all of this. I heard that happens to some people. Yeah, maybe I'm just in a coma, and this is just what you do in a coma. You talk to people and lie around and breathe in and out, and one and two and … shit, this is pretty *boring.*

"But I heard him say heaven. He said heaven, so maybe I'm in heaven and not in a coma. I guess I'll have to wait here to find out. Hey, that does look like a bit of light. And … and … I think that I can feel my toes. I have toes in heaven! This is pretty cool! I think that it's getting warmer too. Ahhhh, glorious warmth! I wonder if we're close to the sun. Wait, Steven, why the hell would that matter? Close to the sun. You're an idiot. You think that they need sunlight in heaven? Shit, they probably just make warmth out of … hey, what do they make warmth out of in heaven? Holy shit. I don't know anything about this place. Was I supposed to learn something before I got here? Oh fuck, what if I am tested or something when I finally get to see and walk? I may be in real trouble!

"Hell, what do I know? I just got here. Steven, stop your ADHD for a second and just do what the man said. Breathe. In and out and one and two and up and down and … what is it that the Buddhists say when they're meditating? Ohhhhmmm. No, aum, yeah, that's it, aauumm, aauumm, aauumm. Hey, this feels pretty cool! I can feel it vibrating in my head! Aauumm, aauumm. It's like, um, like putting a tuning fork on your head. Steven, what the hell would you know about that? Aauumm. Okay, it feels like, um, like putting your head next to the dryer … aauumm. This is weird!

"At least I'm in heaven. This is awesome! I wonder how I got here. I wonder where *here* is. I'll bet that I get to ask these questions to someone. Shit, this is heaven! I'll bet that I get to ask any questions I want! When he gets back here, the first thing I'll ask him is if I get to ask questions to … wait, can I say anyone else's name? Does that cause the same problem? Ggg … Gggoo … okay, here I go … God. Hello? Anyone there? Anyone hear that? God? God? *God!* Nope. No problem.

"I wonder if I get to ask God anything I want. How cool would that be! I get to find out anything I wanted, and all I had to do was die. How did I die? I can't remember. I was … well, I was on earth, and then … what happened? Hey, how come I can remember how to count and how to breathe and how to talk but I can't remember how I got here? Oh well, I'll ask that too. What was I doing? Oh yes, aauumm, aauumm, one and two and one and two and up and down and in and out and …

"Oh fuck, shit, oh no! I killed myself! Now I remember! Holy shit, fuck, fuck, fuck! I killed myself. Fuck. Why did I do that? Holy … oh, oh, shit, I'm fucking screwed. Oh man, I'm fucking dead …

"Wait. I am dead. And I'm in heaven. I killed myself. What the fuck? How did this happen? I … I blew my head off! Why the hell did I …? Hey, I wonder if that's why I can't see anything. No, he said it was normal.

"Well, fuck. What am I supposed to do when he comes back? He must know. They know stuff like that, right? What do they know up here? It's gotta be everything. How could they not know everything? Oh shit, what do I do? What do sinners do in heaven? You're supposed to, um, uh, fuck … Why didn't I pay more attention in church? Why did I blow my head off? I wonder if everyone up here knows what I did. Fuck me. What the hell am I doing here, anyway, and how am I going to get out of this?

"If they find out, they'll throw me out of here for sure. Wait, why am I here in the first place? Maybe no one knows what I did. Maybe I shot myself on a day when no one was paying attention. Oh shit, oh shit! No, I know. They're just making me suffer right now. That's what they do to people like me. They just let you sit in blindness and shit yourself until they come back and tell you, 'Oops, sorry, we checked the books and Saint whatever-the-fuck-his-name-is screwed up, and you've got to go. Sorry, pal, you should have made it look like an accident. Yes, we have the denial of insurance benefits right here. Says the investigator concluded that it was a bona fide suicide. No accident. Sorry, bub, you've got to go.'

"Oh shit, what am I going to do? What a fucking stupid thing to do. Jesus …"

Jesus said, "Steven, are you okay?"

"Hey, um, hey, man! Oh yeah! I was just relaxing, breathing, trying to stretch out a little bit, you know. Just trying to get my bearings, no big deal. Did I? Oh, sorry, did I accidentally call you?"

"Yes."

"Oh, sorry. I don't have my sight back yet, and I can't really move, either."

"Well, don't try to rush it. It can take awhile to get reacquainted. Just relax, and try not to do too much. You may start to see a little light after a bit. But you should not try to move until I get back. If you need me, I won't be far."

"Oh yeah, no problem. Hey, Jesus, one more thing before you go."

"Yes?"

"I'm in heaven, right?"

"Of course you are. Where did you think you would end up?"

I chuckled nervously. "Heaven. No, I knew it. I just wasn't sure that's what you said. You know, I'm still a little disoriented, that's all."

"As I said, it can take awhile to get reacquainted. All answers will be forthcoming. I have to go now."

"Oh, sure, sure, I'll see you later. Don't worry about me. Thanks."

"Is … I think he's gone again. Whew! That was close. Steven, try to remember not to say the *J* word too much until you figure out what the hell you are doing here and how the hell you are going to get away with the stupid fucking thing you did. Shit.

"Okay. Start at the beginning. I'm in heaven. Good so far. I'm supposed to relax, breathe, and get reacquainted. Wait? Reacquainted? What the hell does that mean? He must mean re— … oh, hell, I have no idea what he means. Maybe they speak funny up here. Didn't they speak funny in the Bible? Was I supposed to read that? Fuck. Well, at least Jes— … that guy seems to speak my same language. That's good. I hope that everyone else does too.

"But what the hell else am I supposed to do? Back to breathing? Oh well, might as well try. One and two and up and down and in and out and …

"To hell with this breathing stuff. What am I going to say to him when he gets back? There must have been some mistake. How do they make mistakes in heaven? There must be some kind of quality control guy up here watching out so shit like this doesn't happen. Then how did I wind up here?

"I did it. No question about that. I remember it. Thirty-fourth birthday. Went to the store. Bought a gun. No waiting period. *Thank God for that.* Went back to my crappy apartment, locked the door, sat down in the chair, and blammo. Fuck.

"Now what? I'm in heaven and can't see and can't move, and I don't know how the hell I am going to get away with this. How could they screw up like this? Let me think …

"So I shot myself. I don't remember anything after that. Well, duh, dumb shit. Why would you remember? You blew your brains out. Did it right too. Blew the melon clean off, I'll bet. Gee, Steven, at least you finished one thing in your life. Start over.

"I shot myself, I landed in heaven. But how? Maybe they buried me in the wrong grave? Maybe I was put in the grave of someone else who was supposed to be here, and instead that person is rotting in hell somewhere where I'm supposed to be? Shit. I should probably tell someone that I don't belong here.

"Hey, maybe they buried me in the right grave, but they accidentally put me in the wrong part of the cemetery? Like in the Jewish part or the Catholic part? Is there a religion that lets you kill yourself? Fuck. I should have paid more attention to these things. Don't some parts of the cemetery guarantee you a trip to heaven? Yeah, maybe that's what happened!

"Steven, that's the stupidest thing you've ever said. How could that possibly work? You think that if you were in a certain part of a cemetery, it would keep them from knowing what you really did? Come on.

"Anyway, who would have done that? My family was all gone by then, weren't they? Who the hell would have buried me? Who would have taken the time or even cared that I'd died? Oh shit, I wonder who found me after I shot myself. I didn't tell anyone I was going to do it. I didn't leave a note.

"Maybe my landlord found me after I didn't pay the rent for a while. Maybe one of the neighbors heard the shot. Oh crap. I must have looked horrible sitting there in that chair with my face blown off. That was probably pretty terrifying for someone to walk in on. Maybe someone called the cops. I hope a cop found me. They're supposed to be used to seeing stuff like that.

"I wonder if it was my downstairs neighbor Emily. I sure as shit hope not. I didn't look very good when I went home that day. Hadn't shaved for a week, torn sweats, and my apartment was a fucking mess. I hope it wasn't her. I hope my blood and brain parts didn't seep through the floor and, like, land on someone. Or get into the water supply.

"Man, Emily sure was gorgeous! Nice, too, I think. Oh hell, how would I know? I talked to her, what, like twice in four years?

"So, what the fuck am I doing here? Jesus, I wish I knew."

Alarmed, Jesus said, "Steven, are you all right?"

"Oh yeah." *Shit.* "Hi! You back again?"

"Steven, didn't you just call my name?"

"Did I? I'm sorry. I keep forgetting about that."

"Is your vision back?"

"Oh … er … um, let me check. No, not quite yet."

"That's okay. It can take some time. In the meantime, you don't have to do anything. Just relax. Everything is okay. After your vision comes back and you regain the ability to move, I will take you to see him."

"Who?"

"Him. You know, God."

I gasped so hard that I almost choked myself. "Oh yeah, sure, yeah, that'll be, um, great!"

"I have to go now."

"Oh, um, Jesus?"

"Yes?"

"I have one question for you."

"Yes?"

"We're in heaven, right?"

"Yes, we already went over this."

"Yeah, yeah, I know. But how did I get here?"

"You died on earth; you came here. Didn't you hear me last time?"

"No, yes, of course I heard that. But what am I doing here?"

"What do you mean?"

"Well … I … er, I mean, you know …"

Flatly, he said, "Are you asking this question because you killed yourself?"

Air raid sirens went off in my head. "Yes … I … um … yes. So … you know about that?"

"Of course. Is that why you are asking?"

"Yes."

"We don't keep suicides out of heaven. Everyone is welcome here."

"Whew! I mean, oh. That sure is nice of you. Thanks for that."

Jesus said, "Anything else?"

"Nope. I'm good. I'll just hang out here and, you know, breathe and relax and stuff like that, and I'll let you know when I can see. And I won't accidentally call you again like I did.

"Hello? Are you there? He's already gone again. Oh well."

"Steven, what the hell have you gotten yourself into now? Sure, he says that they let all suicides in, no problem. But what do they do with them? I'll bet they make the suicides the bottom of the trough up here. Slaves. Whipping boys. You know, the real bottom of the whole pile. I'll bet that I have to do the worst of the worst of the ... whatever it is that goes on here. What a mess. Christ ..."

Impatiently, Jesus said, "Steven?"

"Oh ... up ... did I, oh shit. That works too? I'm sorry about that. I was just, you know, talking to myself, and I guess I accidentally called out your name. I'm sorry about that. It won't happen again.

"So, who else have you been ... hey, hey? Whew! He's gone again. Steven, quit doing that. You know the rules. No *J* and no *C* while you're in here. But I can say God. God. *God*! Nothing. At least that's a relief.

"But shit, Steven, do you remember what he said? He is going to take you to see *God*. You are totally fucked now! Sure, Jes— ... I mean, he says that everything is fine and not to worry and just to breathe, but I'll bet that once I go to see the Big Guy, it'll be a different story.

"Why did they send him to see me first, anyway? Probably because he's the nice one up here, that's why. What did he do again? Oh yeah, he died for everyone's sins. Well, duh, of course he's going to be all nice to me when I get here. He already bought the big one so that I could … wait, it can't work that way. He bought the big one so that I could get away with shooting myself? That's crazy. How could that even be true? He died like a long time ago, and I just bit it very … hey, I wonder how long I've been up here? Oh well, just one more thing to remember to ask.

"Anyway, so he's the nice guy they send in to get you all buttered up for the big talk. Well, I'm not going to fall for that routine. I'll keep my trap shut, or at least as much as I can until I can get out of here and talk to some other people. Maybe some of the guys who were around before him. The guys who went out and kicked ass and did all of that other stuff. I'll bet that they'll tell me what the score is.

"Wait, what was I doing? Oh yeah, breathing. In and out and … oh, fuck, the breathing thing is stupid. I just wish that I could see something. I do see a little bit of light coming in, but I still can't tell if it means anything.

"So I have to go see God, and I'm not being punished, so far, for killing myself. But what am I supposed to say? What am I supposed to be doing here? I really should have read more of this shit when I was alive. Let me see if I can remember anything. There was God, and there was … that guy, and there were a bunch of angels doing something or another, and … what else? Ten Commandments. Yeah, what about those? Let me see. The first commandment is not to … kill. What the hell does that mean? I killed myself. And I'm here. Maybe it meant not to kill others. And I'm okay on that one … oh, wait. oh fuck! Now it's all coming back. Oh, Jesus …"

He snapped at me. "Steven!"

"Oh shit!"

"Steven? Can you see?"

"I … er … I … yep, yes, I sure can."

Dubious, he said, "Steven, can you really see yet?"

"No, I can't. But I'm really sorry about that. I was just thinking, and I happened to blurt out your ... you know."

"Yes, I do. Look, Steven, I don't mean to be rude, but I asked you to do one simple thing, and that was to wait until you could see again before you called me. Now, you have to understand that I have a lot of things to do up here and a lot of souls to attend to. If you keep calling me before you are ready, it does not do us any good."

"Oh, no, I know. I am very, very sorry. Hey, wait, I can see more light now. No, I can, I can almost make out your figure in the room. And I can see a wall behind you, and—"

His voice faded as he walked away. "That's good, Steven. Just keep working on that, and call me when your sight has returned."

"Right-o. Sorry about that again, J— ... er, Chief.

"Hey? Hey? How does he do that? Anyway, he's gone again. But I am fucked when he finds out about my family. My family ... my whole family. They all died in the car accident, and I was driving. I wasn't watching the road, and we hit that elk, and they didn't make it. How the fuck did I make it? Who knows? Mom, Dad, my little sis, all dead when we flipped over. And I made it out. Holy shit. I can't believe I didn't remember that right when I got here. Oh boy. Steven, what the hell are you doing here, and how the hell are you going to explain your way out of this? First, you fuck up and kill your family in an auto accident. Then, oh ... in a flash of brilliance and redemption, do what? Blow your own head off. Way to go, Ace!

"Oh fuck. Fuck me! This must be some kind of a trick. Maybe that's how it's done. They send you down to hell, and it's made to look like heaven, and they send in this fucking caretaker who answers to ... his name. And then, just when you can see and you can move, all of the memories of all of the fucked-up shit you did come back to you, and that's when they hit you with it. 'Sorry, Steven, now that the smelling salts have done their job, here is a shovel and an eternity of shit for you to move around to pay for all of the fucking worthless things you did when you were alive. Oh, and to boot, we're going to turn up the thermostat on you a bit. Hope you won't mind.'

"What the hell am I doing here, and what the hell am I going to say once I can move and have to call him back in here?

"Well, now I can see some light. And I can see something that looks like a wall. And I, well, I still can't really move my head. I wonder what the hell that's all about. You'd think that they could make this whole process a lot easier. Oh well, I guess I'll just sit here and figure out what I'm supposed to be saying once I get to talk to the Big Kahuna.

"Let's see, what did I learn about heaven while I was living? Don't do some things, *do* do others, be kind to your neighbor, respect your elders, eat your vegetables, look both ways before crossing the street, and … hey, I think it *is* getting warmer in here! And I *can* see something. I see a wall, and another wall, and it does … this place looks just like the room I had when I was a little kid! Holy shit! That's awesome! But there's nothing here … well, at least I can't see anything. The walls that I can see look the same as they did in my old room. Painted the same and everything. And … well, if I could turn my friggin' head, I could find out if there was anything on the floor. There's nothing on the … let me see … on the ceiling. But this is the same room I grew up in! How awesome is that? Hey, I wonder how they knew what my room looked like.

"Duh, Steven, they know *everything* up here. Crap. What else did I do wrong that I'm going to have to cover up for? I … well … I, I never cheated on my taxes. I never shot anyone else, I never …

"Well, fuck it. I can see now, so I might as well just get it over with. Hey, Jesus?"

Cautiously curious. "Steven?"

"Yeah. I can see now. I can't move or turn my head, but I can see."

Jesus stepped into my view. Smiling, he said, "Hello, Steven. I'm Jesus. Welcome to heaven. I'll bet that you have some questions, and I will try to answer anything you ask. However, some of your questions you might want to save for God. He will answer anything you ask him."

"Wow! You look exactly like the guy in the pictures!"

Frowning, he said, "Which pictures?"

"Oh, well, I don't know which ones. But I mean, the long hair, the beard, all of it. You look just like ... well ... you!"

Flatly, he said, "Oh. Thanks. I get that a lot."

"Wow. Okay. Anyway, I wanted to ask you something."

"Yes?"

"So ... do you ... um ... or, does he ... um ..." *Chickenshit.* "Um ... why ... or, how come I can't move?"

"We put you in a suit when you get here that simulates the body you had back on earth. It is a bit hard to get used to at first. But trust me—you wouldn't want to start out feeling what it's like not to have a body. Everything else is strange enough at first. You wouldn't want to have to deal with that."

"Oh gosh, thanks! That's great! So, um, why can't I move it?"

"You will learn how to. It takes time. Just like getting your sight back."

"Why couldn't I see when I got here?"

"Well, the journey you take covers a great distance, and when you are traveling, if you could see, it would be traumatizing to you. So your sight just goes away when you depart from earth, and it comes back slowly after you get here."

"Well, that's good. It wouldn't be, I guess, very good to have people traumatized on their way up here." *That probably comes later.*

"Exactly. So, your sight comes back slowly, and then you get used to the suit we put you in, and then you can move around a bit. However, Steven, there are a few ground rules in heaven that I need to tell you about."

Oh fuck, here it comes. You rotten egg. Your shovel weighs sixty-five tons, and we have another suit for you to wear—full of burning daggers and scorpions.

"First, this is your room. It is only your room. No one else can come in here but me. I will not come in here unless you call me or if there is something that we need for you to do."

"Oh … oh … okay. Wow, that's nice! I get my own room in heaven! Thanks, Jesus."

"Don't mention it. Everyone has his or her own room here. So, as I was saying, I will be the only person who comes in here other than you. And you cannot go anywhere in heaven unless I am with you. So—"

"Wait, why not?"

"Well, it is a little hard to explain. You are in a room right now with a bed and walls. Outside of here, there are other things, and you would get lost if you went anywhere without me. So I have to take you to wherever you need to go."

"I guess that makes sense."

"Trust me—it's the way it has to be. If you want to go anywhere, just call me, and I will take you there."

"Oh, okay. That's nice of you."

Continuing unfazed. "Don't mention it. The other thing to know is that this is your room. We try to make it look familiar to you so that you are more comfortable up here. Did you recognize it when your sight came back?"

"Yes! Yes, I did! I looked at the walls and the ceiling and said, 'Holy shit, this is my old room!' Oh, sorry. I'm probably not supposed to curse up here, right?"

"No, that's okay. Don't worry about that for now. Anyway, this is your room, and right now, there is nothing in it but you and your bed. You can bring things into your room, however, as you see fit."

"Bring things in? How do I do that?"

"Well, we do things a bit differently up here. You don't have things just yet, but you can make things appear if you want them to. So if you want to have a book or a basketball or a kite or whatever, all you have to do is imagine one that you had or read or played with when you were alive, and you can have it in your room. I will tell you that it is hard to get the hang of at first, so just start with small things, and then you can work your way up as you get better at it."

"Holy shit! Oh, sorry … again. I mean, wow! That's really cool! I can make stuff appear in heaven. Okay, I will … um, I will start slow and get used to it, and then I will … well, I will—"

Moving away from the bed, he said, "Steven, don't think too much about it right now. Just know that that is one of the things you can do up here. First, you need to focus on getting used to the suit you are in so that you can move around a bit. After that—"

"Hey, now that I'm awake and seeing things and remembering … stuff, don't you think it would be okay for me to just drop the fake suit and … um, I guess—"

"No. Trust me, Steven—you are not ready for that. You will stay in the suit, and after a while, it will work just fine for you up here."

Great, thanks.

"When you can move around a bit, you can practice bringing some things into your room, just so you can get a handle on it. I have to go, but you can call me again when you can walk and are ready to go see God."

"I will. Thanks! And I will start with small things. And I will make sure not to bring anything in here that I don't really, really need." *They must be frugal up here, right? Puritan way and so on?*

Still walking away, he said over his shoulder, "That's fine. And please do remember—"

"I know, I know, don't call you until I'm ready."

Then he faded into mist. "Wow, that guy really moves! Okay, so now I'm in my room in a suit that I still can't work right, but I can see, and they gave me my friggin' old room! This is awesome! What do I want to have in here with me? Let's see … what did I like playing with best when I was on earth? Hmmmm?

"A bicycle? No, still can't move. A book? No, who reads books in heaven? A basketball? No. Um … uh … well, I obviously can't get any porno magazines up here. Let's see. How about my old desk? Yeah. Let's get some more furniture in here. That way, it will look like my old room. My old desk and my old chair. I'll get those in here, and then when I can get up, I will be able to sit at my desk and … oh, who the hell knows?

"Anyway, let's see how this works. I'm concentrating, I'm thinking really hard, I can see my old desk, I can see its contours and color and shape and …

"Holy shit! There it is! Hey, I can turn my head a bit more. That's awesome! Okay, so there's my old desk. Sweet! Now focus on the chair … and there it is! Wow, this is really cool, and really easy too! Desk and chair. Check. Now if I could just figure out how to get up. I wonder what the hell the suit is for, anyway. He didn't have a special suit on. I wonder why I need one. Oh well, I'll probably find out later.

"So desk, chair, that's a good start. What else did I have in my room? Oh yeah, that fucking sweet-ass poster of … holy shit! There it is on the wall! Oh fuck, I'm going to get killed for putting a poster of her up on the wall. Look at that. She's barely wearing anything at all. Oh, fuck me!

"Now how do you get rid of stuff? Go away! Go away! Get off my wall, you big-breasted monster! Go! Shoo! Get. Fuck, it's not working.

"Oh well. I guess I'll figure out how to explain that one later. Now let's see.

"What else do I need? Hey, I can move my leg. Wow! It's friggin' heavy. I wonder if I'm in a lead suit or something. No, wait, he said rubber. Did he say rubber? Who knows? But my leg is really heavy. Wow.

"What else. Let's see, chair, desk … Candy … Candy, get the fuck off my wall before I get in trouble! Move it! Go!

"Nothing. Shit. What else? Hey, I had a picture of my family on my wall. I'll get that back up there, and maybe I can talk about that and he won't notice the other one.

"Steven, what are you talking about? Like he's not going to ask about the poster just because you're talking about your family. After all, you killed them. I'll bet that doesn't get you any special privileges up here. Fuck. What am I doing here?

"Oh, to hell with it. Show me a nudie mag!

"Fuck. There it is. Sitting right on top of the desk. Great. And you still can't move and can't get out of the bed. Steven, you moron, what are you going to do when he comes back and you can't get up to hide that thing under the bed?

"Jesus Fucking Christ, you're dumb!"

Alarmed, Jesus reappeared. "Steven?"

"Oh, hiiiyaaaaaa … hey, there, how's it going?"

"Steven, can you move yet?" he asked, annoyed.

"No. Sorry, it's very hard to get used to things up here." *Enter clever Steven.* "I've been trying to focus on moving in this suit and trying to learn how to make stuff appear, but I keep goofing up. See, I used to have a picture of my dog … um, Mandy, on the wall, and I tried to make that appear, and I … um, I guess I screwed it up because now I've got that … thing stuck on my wall, and I can't get rid of it. And I was trying to … um … get a sports magazine I used to read, you know, for when I can get up and read and move and stuff, but that one accidentally showed up. And, um …"

"Steven, that's fine. Can you please just do me one damn favor, though, and try not to call my name again until you can move and you are ready to go see God? Is that too much for you to deal with at this point?"

"No, no. Sorry. I just, um—"

Poof, and he was gone again. "Way to go, Steven, you've already pissed off the only person you know in heaven. This is going great so far. I'm sure that you will be elected president of this place in no time. Yep, you are going to make it big up here.

"Shit. I forgot to ask how you get rid of stuff. Oh well. Hey, he didn't even yell about the poster or the magazine. Do you think that he bought my story? No, no way. Maybe he's got a lot on his mind? I guess I'll find out later."

Knee deep in a disheveled pile of junk, I said, "Stupid conjuring mess. Thanks for the instruction manual, guys. Hey, can I get a helper in here with arms that actually work? 'Steven, you're never going to get this room cleaned up in time to go to see Grandpa.' 'Thanks, Mom. How about lending a hand instead of just sitting there like a ...' Man, what a fucking mess!"

"Steven?"

"Oh shit. Hey, Jesus!"

Accusingly, he said, "Steven, what have you been doing in here?"

"I um, I was just trying to make the place look a little more like it used to."

"Why is half of that poster ripped off the wall?"

Because I was trying to take down Ms. Big Tits, but my fucking right arm doesn't move, and my left one only reaches up about halfway. "Um, I was trying to take it down to replace it with the one I really wanted to have up there, and I guess my suit doesn't work very well. I can't raise my right arm, and my left arm only goes up about halfway."

Annoyed again, he said, "Steven, look, don't worry about that right now. I told you to call me when you could walk."

"I … um … yeah, I was going to, and then I kind of lost control when I was practicing bringing stuff into my room and—"

Surveying the room with a frown, he demanded, "Why do you need all of this stuff up here?"

"Oh, I don't. Like I said, I kind of lost control, and things just started appearing out of the blue, so to speak. The desk is still nice and clean, though." *I hope he notices that I hid the porno mag and replaced in with a Bible.*

"Look, Steven, this is the only room you have up here. You can't get rid of this stuff, so be careful. You won't have any room left if you keep it up like this. Anyway, are you ready to go?"

"Go?"

"Yes. To see God."

Ice cicles formed on my back. "I … um, I'm not sure that I'm really ready to do all of that. Like you said, I haven't gotten the whole conjuring things down yet, and my right arm still doesn't move, and my left arm isn't very good, and my left foot doesn't seem to respond very well, and … um … I think I have a fever too."

Grabbing me by the arm, he said, "Steven, you can't have a fever in heaven."

Trying to dig in my heels, I said, "Well, my stomach hurts pretty bad. Is there a bathroom up here?"

"Your suit does not have a stomach in it. The rest of that stuff doesn't matter. As long as you can move enough to get out of bed, you can go and see him."

Pit of Hades, here I come.

As Jesus escorted me down a long corridor, he scolded, "Steven, stop tripping. And try to stand up straight."

"Well, it's a little hard to walk in this suit. Anyway, hey, Jesus, why did you ask me earlier what picture I had seen you from?"

Absently, he said, "What? Oh, as part of the welcoming program up here, we are always trying to make sure that the image I project in heaven resembles what people are familiar with down there."

"Really?"

"Yes. It is a tremendous help to most people to see a familiar face when they first get here."

I'll bet. "But you don't know what you look like in the pictures down there?"

He looked down at me annoyed and said, "Steven, I am pretty busy up here. I don't have the luxury of flying down to earth to check every time someone sees my face in a piece of toast."

As we passed through a radiant doorway, I exclaimed, "Holy shit! Is that him? Hey, he looks like … like … hey, Jesus, is that my grandpa? Is God my grandpa?"

He said, "No, Steven. We try to make him look like the person who meant the most to you down on earth. It is all part of easing the reentry process."

Smiling deeply, God said, "Hello, Steven. Welcome back."

I leaned in and whispered, "Jesus, what did he mean by 'welcome back'?"

Jesus said, "Steven, we knew you before you were born."

So I said to Jesus, "Oh, that's nice."

And tentatively to God, "Um, hello, Grandpa … or … er, God. Should I stand or kneel or sit or what?"

God gestured. "Steven, why don't you try to sit over there on that bench?"

I said, "Oh good. Thanks."

And God began. "So, Steven, we are glad to have you here, and we are very interested to know what you learned down there."

What the fuck? I said, "I … what I learned down there?"

Expectantly, God said, "Yes. What was your favorite part? We are always anxious to learn that!"

You have to be fucking kidding me.

Jesus whispered to God, "Boss, Steven killed himself on earth. Committed suicide. Shot himself in the face."

Appearing very concerned, God asked, "Are you sure?"

Jesus produced a stack of papers and replied, "Yes. We have the insurance documents right here. Says no accident, intentionally self-inflicted death."

Fuck me … here we go! Sorry, Steven, mix up at the funeral home. Pack your bags and get ready to sweat a lot.

Leaning in and narrowing his gaze at me, God said, "Steven, come a little closer to me. Oh, now I see it."

"See what?" I said defensively, turning away.

God raised back up frowning and said, "Never mind, Steven. I must say that this is very troubling. You have committed a very serious sin, and it is going to take a lot of work to make up for it."

Groan.

Leaning in again sharply, he demanded, "Steven, do you mind telling us why you killed yourself?"

Oh shit, oh shit. I was supposed to be thinking about this earlier.

God said, "Steven, look, this isn't a test. We are not here to punish you."

Right.

"However, it is very important for you to know why you did what you did, and we are here to help you understand that."

Trapped like a rat.

Panicked, I offered the quickest answer I could come up with. "I um ... I don't think that I can I really know how to explain it at this point. This whole process has been a bit traumatic for me, and I think that I need some time to go back over my thoughts and come up with the right words to tell you."

God settled back again and simply replied, "Okay, Steven. We will do it that way."

Whew! Dodged a bullet on that one! Wait, do what?

"Jesus is going to take you back to your room. I want you to think about why you did what you did and come back to tell me about it."

Are you fucking serious?

God said firmly, "Steven, this is very serious. We need you to come back here ready to work on your problems so that you can move on."

Move on where? Do they make you spend time writing the bad things you did on a chalkboard before they send you to hell? Oh, this is all going to suck big time!

He pointed toward the door. "Steven, go with Jesus now."

Clutching the bench and unsure of what lay in store for me, I said nervously, "Hey ... wait ... um, sir. Listen, I understand that what I did was very bad, and I am very sorry for having done it. Can I ask you a few things before I go away?"

He replied, "Well, Steven, the most important thing right now is to work on understanding what you did, and everything else can wait. But go ahead."

I continued, "Okay, um, so Jesus told me a while ago that we're in heaven?"

"That's right."

"And ... um, he's Jesus, right?"

"Yes."

"And … um … I … um, sorry for asking this but, who are you exactly?"

Almost proclaiming, he said, "Steven, I am God."

"I … um … yes, that's obvious, and nice to meet you again, I guess. I didn't expect you to … um, look like my grandpa."

He said, "Steven, I can appear to you in any form I like or in any form you would like. We usually like to present you with things that you are familiar with from down there to aid in the transition process and—"

Waiving a hand, I said, "Yeah, yeah, Jesus told me that part already. I just … um … I thought that I'd find someone or something … well, a bit different."

Pausing briefly, he said, "Look, Steven, as part of the reentry process, we have to do certain things. We have to talk to you. With most souls, we talk to them about what they learned and what their favorite part of the experience was. With you, it is a little different, because you shot yourself in the face. So we have to do other work, but that still involves sitting here and talking with you."

In disbelief, I said, "So you, God, are just going to spend all the time in the, well, I guess the universe, talking to little old me about what I did?"

"Steven, I am not just talking to you. I am talking to 108,000 souls right now in fifty different languages. I initially appear to each of them as someone from their life down there. Now, if that is uncomfortable for you, I can appear as people most often think of me."

And before me sat the old guy with the long, white beard. "There, Steven, is that better for you?"

"Um … yes, I guess that's good enough. Thank you for all of those answers."

And then God said, "Steven, go with Jesus now, and think hard on the sins you have committed, and be ready to come back to talk with me about them."

Fucking fuck, fuck. I actually replied, "Okay. Thank you … um, sir."

IV

When we got back to my room, Jesus shook his finger at me and scolded, "Now, Steven, I want you to stay here, and you can't come out until you have done as he commanded. Think hard about what he said, and you can call me when you are ready to go back and talk to him."

Feeling a bit insecure, I said, "Hey, where are you going?"

He replied, "I too have many souls to attend to up here. You will be fine. You just need to search within yourself, and all of the answers will be forthcoming. Now remember, don't—"

"Yeah, yeah, I know. Don't call you until I'm ready." Poof, gone again.

"Well, Steven, this fucking sucks. It looks like you haven't landed in a very good spot, and now you have to go back and explain to the big guy in the beard why you killed yourself. I'll bet that there is a huge fucking punishment waiting for you, no matter what you say.

"Let's see. How is Houdini going to get himself out of this one? What is the best excuse for shooting yourself in the face? I could tell them that I was diagnosed with some awful disease and only given a few months to live. No, that won't work. They probably know that I wasn't dying of anything. I could tell them the whole story about killing my family in that auto accident and how the accident was all my fault.

"No, that won't work, either. That was too long ago, and besides, you'd just be drawing attention to another one of your colossal fuckups.

"Wait, my family is dead. They must be up here somewhere. I wonder if I can find them. Why didn't ... um, the J–Man say anything to me about them when I got here? Must be some kind of suicide hazing ritual ... isolation and all until you go in and fess up and ask for forgiveness. Yeah, that must be it.

"So what the hell do I tell them? Let's see ...

"Hey, where'd that porno mag go? Oh yeah, I put it in the bottom drawer of the desk. Jesus didn't even think to check for it. But he didn't notice the Bible I put on the desk, either. What gives? Holy shit. Was I supposed to be reading that thing up here? I wonder if there are any clues in there about how to get past the Big Guy? I wonder if there are any good excuses for killing yourself written in there.

"Seriously? Where's the fucking index to this thing? Oh ... I have to start at the beginning? No way. Forget about it.

"I'll never get out of this room at this pace. And I don't care what he says, my stomach is killing me! I wonder what that's all about. Fuck.

"Okay, work through it, Steven. So I killed myself. What was I doing when I killed myself? Sitting in my room. Well, that's no surprise. I had been sitting in my room a lot back then. Why the fuck was I doing that? I never went out, never did anything. Just sat there surfing the Internet and ...

"Holy shit! Can I get a computer in here? That would really help things. I'm sure that if I could look this stuff up, someone must have touched on the subject of killing yourself and going to heaven. No ... no fucking way. But if I had a computer, I could look up other cool stuff. Hey, I wonder if it's still football season. How the hell long have I been up here, anyway?

"Okay. Show me a computer.

"I said *show me a computer!*

"What the hell? I have every other damn thing in this room, from a bicycle that I can't ride because I can't figure out how to lift my feet more than two inches off the ground to a stupid fucking toy zebra that just appeared when I was thinking about that hot-ass dancer who used to wear zebra-skinned tights. And every other goddamn thing in between, but no computer.

"I've got to ask someone about this. But I can't get out of here again until I come up with a story. Okay, let's see. Sitting in my room … alienated, yeah, alienated from the outside world … yeah, that's good. But why? What was I doing back then? Watching a lot of Internet porn and jacking off. Okay, that probably won't sound very good. I was … um, alienated and detached from everyone around me, because I was all alone, and … um, I was what? I was disgusted with the outside world. Yeah, that's it! I was sick of watching all of the pain and horror around me, all of the death and destruction and sickos and perverts and, yeah, and it drove me to hide out in my place. I had … what do you call it? Agro, no agoro, that phobia thing about going outside. Shit. I wish I had a dictionary.

"Hey, look a dictionary! Agoraphobia. That's it. Thanks, little red friend! I wonder what it says about suicide in here. Let's see …

"'Suicide. The act of killing yourself because you do not want to continue living.'

"That's stupid. Why else would you kill yourself? I can't go back to them with that. 'Hey, God, sorry, but I didn't want to go on living. Place sucked, and the paint was peeling and all, and … ' No, I'll stick with the agoraphobia and go from there.

"Anyway, thanks for nothing, Mr. Dictionary. I'll just put you here right next to Mr. Big Book, and you guys can be friends.

"Okay. Agoraphobia. They can't test for that, right? I mean, if I say that I was afraid to go out because of all of the awful stuff on the street, they can't know the truth. Well, Steven, you sure seemed able to go out long enough to buy that gun and … shit!

"But I was desperate. Yeah, really desperate. So I did it that one time. Wait a minute, you had a job. You went to work every day. Crap. I did. Okay, agoraphobia won't work. But the whole disgusted thing will. Yeah, too many murderers and rapists and filanderers … wait, how do you spell that? There it is. Philanderers. *Definition.* Interesting. Why didn't I do that? Oh … have to have a wife. Missed that one.

"Okay, so I'm all alone, working in a dead-end job, alienated, sick of humanity, and whammo. Yeah, that's gotta work! It will show them how sensitive I was to the woes of the world. Let's see, how do we really sew this all together?

"Aha! That's it! Man's fall from grace! I read that shit somewhere. Yeah! That was it. I was sick of seeing the rest of the world tear itself to pieces, I could really see how far we had all fallen, and instead of some asshole who goes around shooting other people for how bad their lives are, I just couldn't take it and got out. Yeah, that's gotta work! Now let me see. I've got to memorize some Bible passages about this shit so I can really wow them over. Okay, where is all of that stuff in here …

When Jesus and I entered God's throne room again, God said expectantly, "Welcome back, Steven."

Tentatively, I said, "Hey, *hello* again. Glad to be back here." *And not yet burning in a pit somewhere.*

"Well?" he prodded.

Raising my hands to ward him off, I said, "Listen, so first of all, I need to seriously apologize."

"For what?"

"Well, for everything. I mean, I know that I'm not here under the best of circumstances, and I'm sure that I'm not the most splendid new arrival you've ever had up here, and I know that I did some awful stuff, and I'm really sorry about all of it."

God leaned toward me and said, "Steven, I asked you to go back to your room and think about why you killed yourself."

Still deflecting, I said, "Yeah, yeah, I'm getting to that. Look, I probably was supposed to have a speech prepared when I first got to heaven, but I don't. So sorry about that too."

He just stared at me blankly. Nervously, I lowered my hands in my lap and continued. "Anyway, what I did while I was in my room, see, is I thought a lot about my life and where it had gone and where it had gone wrong and why I did what I did. I also spent a good deal of time reading through the Bible, and … hey, which one of you wrote that?"

Both of them were now staring blankly at me. "I mean, one of you wrote all of that stuff, right? It's really good, you know."

God said flatly, "Steven, we are not much in the book-writing business up here. And those are supposed to be instructions about living life down there. Those passages cannot help you up here, especially after what you have done."

Shit.

God pressed impatiently. "So …?"

I continued nervously. "Um, yeah, so anyway, as I was, um, well, what I was reflecting on mostly about life down there and all and about my life was that, at some point, I really just got fed up with all of the people around me who, you know, seemed to have lost their way and all of the people who were not living good lives and all of the sinning and killing and the raping and murdering and all of that stuff I saw around me—"

God interjected, "Steven—"

My hands came up again. "Wait, wait. And what I came to at the point in my life just before I, you know, did myself in, was like this very real feeling of sadness about the whole earth and how nothing I could do could ever fix what was going wrong and how life just seemed pretty hopeless in light of all that was going on. So I shot myself."

After a long, thoughtful pause, God exhaled and said, "Steven, I want to tell you that I have been up here listening to stories for a long time, and I have never heard a line of crap quite like that. Did you put any effort whatsoever into thinking about what you were going to say when you came back?"

I tried to recover. "I … um … yes, of course I did. While I was in my room, I—"

God leaned in again, frowning. "Jesus tells me that you have a porno magazine in there."

Son of a bitch! I knew he was waiting to rat me out!

God said, "Steven, it seems that you are not really focused on what you are supposed to be doing up here. Down on earth, you committed a very serious sin, and now you are here in front of us, and we have asked you to do one very specific thing. Now why haven't you done it?"

I heard a deep rumbling in the pit of my stomach. "I … um … well, I guess you could say that I just have a hard time putting into words or thoughts or feelings what it is that I was thinking at the time that I killed myself. It … um, it just seemed like the right thing to do."

And God leaned back and finished by saying, "Steven, I want you to go back to your room now and spend time actually *thinking* about why you killed yourself. When you come back, I want to have a serious talk with you. Next time, it will just be you and me. Jesus will not stay with us, and you had better think long and hard about what you did and why you are here."

Why the hell am I here?

Pointing to the door again, he said, "Now, go back to your room."

Shit, I may need to phone a friend on this one.

Clutching the bench, I said, "Hey, wait, wait just a minute. I will, I mean, I promise that I will go back and think about what you told me to. But I … um, can I see my family members first? I mean, I know that they died before I did, and if I'm up here, I'm sure that they're up here and, well, I think that it would really help me focus on what I'm supposed to be doing if I could just talk with them for a little while, you know, to remember some of the things that I may have been going through back then."

And God said definitively, "No."

"What? Really? I can't see them?"

"No."

"Why not?" I exclaimed.

God replied, "Steven, we have a general policy up here that suicides are not permitted to talk to nonsuicides."

And my natural reaction to hearing that was to say, "You're shitting me? Oh, sorry. I mean, really?"

God said, "Yes."

"Why not?"

Calmly, he explained, "Well, Steven, there are two basic reasons for that. First, up here in the kingdom of heaven, nearly all souls are enjoying the experience of basking in the glory of creation and all the universe."

Really? That hasn't been shown on my tour yet.

"The rest of the nonsuicide souls up here are at peace and are living out their heavenly experiences. We found out a long time ago that letting the suicides mix in with them tends to ruin that experience, and so frankly, we made a policy a while back that suicides cannot talk to nonsuicides."

"Jesus!" I exclaimed.

And Jesus said, "What?"

So I corrected. "Oh, I didn't mean, like literally, 'Hey, Jesus.' I meant, 'Gosh, that sure is a harsh policy.'"

God said, "Steven, killing yourself is a harsh course of action to take. The second reason why we do not let you talk to other souls at this point is just a practical consideration."

I hazarded a guess. "What do you mean? Oh, because I need to be alone to focus on my crime and what I need to do to absolve myself of it?"

God said, "Not exactly. See, to us, it looks like you shot your face off."

And I exclaimed, *"What!"*

God replied, "Yes. You look to us just like a soul who shot his face off down on earth."

I shouted, *"Are you fucking kidding me?* Oh, sorry."

God said, "No. That is how you look up here, and anyone who sees you will see exactly what we see."

"Holy shit! That's ... um, well, that's a bummer. I ... well, then, I guess it's a good thing that I don't get to talk to anyone else. I ... um ... boy, I'll bet that looks pretty gruesome."

God said, "It does. Haven't you looked at yourself in the mirror yet?"

"No. How could I do that?"

"Do you have a mirror in your room?"

I said, "Mirror? Jesus, I—"

And Jesus said, "What?"

So I corrected once again. "Oh, shit. Sorry. I didn't mean to ... I meant, wow, it never occurred to me to bring a mirror into my room. I will do that when I get back."

God said, "Fine, Steven. But remember—"

"Yeah, yeah, I got it. I'll go back and think hard on what you said, and I will be prepared to talk about it when I get back here. And I'm sorry for not being ready this time."

My first thought when I got back to my room was "Man, this place fucking sucks! I can't talk to anyone, I can't go anywhere but here and in there to see God, and somehow I'm supposed to come up with a reason as to why I killed myself. And a believable reason at that. Where do you get those? Crap. I'm never going to get out of this.

"I'll bet that once I do give him the answer he's looking for, I'll get a fine pat on the back, and then it's straight to purgatory with a big fucking rock to tote up a big fucking hill. Yep, Steven, time to atone for your sins and pay the universe back for fucking everything up. Don't worry, we'll be here watching you drag an impossibly heavy rock up an unbelievably steep hill in your rubber space suit, which, by the way, still *does not fucking work right*, because I can't seem to lift my left foot more than a few inches off the ground, although I am now able to lift the right one higher. I can't raise my arms very high, and they seem to be extraordinarily short for this suit. Fuck, I feel just like a giant rubber T. rex doll. And I still can't figure out how to turn my head from side to side. Wait, what was that they said about my face? Alakazam, show me a mirror!

"Hey, there it is. Hey, there *I* am. My face, my face looks like … well, it looks just like it did when I was on earth. Same dimpled cheeks, same eyes set in dark sockets. Same heavy bags under the eyes.

What the hell were those guys talking about? There is absolutely no difference from how I looked before.

"And look at this fucking space suit! Hilarious! I look like a big puffer fish with arms and legs. Where the hell did they get the idea for this getup? Crap. Nothing works up here. Oh well. Nice going, Steven. You left a world where you were trapped in a body you hated in a time that you despised, only to come to a place where you are just as annoyed and trapped in a rubber balloon. Nice work, Ace.

"Man, was I ever fucking miserable on earth … okay, let me see. Let's work backward and try to figure out why I killed myself.

"Steven. Thirty-four years of age. Single. Thinning hair. Stuck in dead-end job. Stuck in apartment in crappy building living below loudmouthed fucking idiots. Parents dead from car accident five years earlier. Steven driving the car, only survivor. Sister died in the car accident too. She was nineteen at the time. Why the fuck did my parents have two kids ten years apart? Man, I barely knew that kid. She was so much younger than me. Seemed happy, though. Happier than I was. At least she was dating someone, or wait—was she engaged? No, not yet, just talked about it a lot. What did I do? I hadn't dated for years. One girl in college, ran away from her when she went crazy, and then nothing but a string of girls who seemed to get younger and stupider every year. Not a one of them worth hanging around sober.

"What happened with Emily? Nothing. You never said more than ten words to her. How old was she? How the hell would I know? You have to ask to find out information like that. You can't just stand in the elevator staring at your feet and hoping that she'll blurt out the answers to your prayers. She did always smile at me. And what a smile!

"Shit, I really should have taken a shot with her. What the hell? What would the risk have been? 'No, Steven, sorry, you're repulsive.' 'Okay, thanks, Emily, I guess I'll go upstairs and blow my head off.' At least you would have known one way or the other. Man, she was gorgeous! Classic punky look, dyed her hair a different color every other week. And those eyes …

"Fuck. Nice work, Steven. Now what? I have no idea. I can't point to any one reason why I killed myself. I just did it. Seemed like an easy option. Blammo, good night forever. I guess I didn't count on this. Shit, I wasn't thinking about any of this at all. I really should have weighed my chances. All I ever thought was that I was going to wind up sitting and having a really fucking boring conversation with some superbeing. But I didn't expect it to *actually happen.* And shit, now I've got to explain myself.

"I wonder if I can ask to be transferred somewhere else. Somewhere where they don't ask questions and you don't have to try to explain unexplainable things and where they give you *a goddamn fucking rubber space suit that actually works!* It is exhausting trying to think with this rubber monstrosity on me. Seriously.

"Well, I'm not going to sit here and come up with some fucking bullshit story. I'm just going to tell it like it is … well … like it was. I don't care what they do to me. I can't sit in here with all of this crap and do nothing anymore. Man, nice work, Steven. Real mess you've gotten yourself into.

"Jesus?"

Jesus entered. He seemed distracted, though, and simply said, "Yes, Steven. Are you ready to go back to see God now?"

I replied, "Not, not quite yet. I need to ask you a few things first."

"Okay, but make it quick."

"Um, okay. What's the rush? We're in heaven. Nothing else to do but hang out and talk, right?"

Still distracted, he said, "Steven, I already told you. I have lots and lots of souls to attend to. Now, don't get me wrong. You are all important, and I want to give you all equal time, but there are a lot of places for me to be at the same time, and I can't … shit, I gotta go."

"Fuck. Now what? Great. Really nice administrative planning up here. One Jes— … guy for the whole lot of us. Hey, what's the other guy doing? *God! God!* Your helper is too busy to answer my questions, and I'm stuck in my fucking room with nothing to do and a goddamn rubber suit that doesn't work, and by the way, you lied about my face looking like it was blown off. And this place *fucking sucks!*"

Suddenly, Jesus reappeared. "Steven."

Startled, I said, "Oh, shit, you're back? That was fast. Where'd you have to go?"

"Don't worry about that. What were you saying?"

"I said that I have some questions I'd like to ask you before I go back to see him."

Now his focus seemed back. "Oh, okay. Go ahead."

"First, he said that it looks like I shot my face off."

"Yes?"

"Well, I checked in the mirror, and I look exactly like I did on earth. Same features and everything. The only thing that's different is this suit I'm wearing."

In a matter-of-fact way, he said, "Steven, when you look in that mirror, you see yourself as you see yourself."

"Huh?"

"You see yourself as you see yourself. You can't see yourself as we see you. All you can see is what you expect to see there. You will understand better as things go along. But we do see you differently than you see yourself, and if you ran into other souls up here, they could see it too. So we have to keep you—"

"Yeah, yeah, okay. I got it. Steven is in suicide seclusion. Fine."

"Anything else?"

"Yeah. I … um … well, first, sorry about all of the crap in here. I got kind of out of control with the whole conjuring thing, and before I knew it, nearly every goddamn toy I ever played with as a kid was in this room. Shit, oh, sorry. I mean, darn, I probably shouldn't have wasted so much … hey, what's that stuff made out of, anyway? And what's this rubber suit for?"

Slightly annoyed, he said, "Steven, you are spending time asking about things that don't really matter and aren't important. We are in heaven. We can do anything up here. The stuff in your room, well, it's fake. That basketball isn't made of rubber. It is made of matter we borrowed from the universe, and up here, you can make it into a basketball just by thinking about it. But it's not exactly the same as what you had down there. Your suit? Well, we learned pretty early on that when souls come up here who have been living in human bodies, it really freaks them out if they don't have a type of body to move around in while they are up here. We had some people who really lost it at the beginning about being up here without a body to be tethered to."

"Oh yeah, I guess that makes sense. So if everything in my room is fake, and I can get anything in here I want, how come I haven't been able to make a computer appear? You know, I could really stand to plug in to the Internet and see what's going on down there."

"Steven, we don't have anything *that* fake up here. Sorry, no computers, no Internet. And before you ask, there are no radios or television, either."

Running out of options, I said, "Well, then, um …"

He cocked an eyebrow. "Yes, Steven?"

"What the hell am I supposed to be doing up here?"

"What did he ask you to do?"

Exasperated, I said, *"That's it?* I'm supposed to sit here and come up with a reason for why I killed myself?"

He replied slowly, "No, Steven. You are not supposed to come up with a reason. He wants to know why you did it. And if you do not discover the reason and tell him, you will never be able to get over it."

Still exasperated, I said, "Get over it? Get over what? It's done. I did it. I'm here now. Look, I'm really sorry for shooting myself in the face. I shouldn't have done it, and I know that it was a really, really big sin."

"The biggest, Steven."

Raising my hands in defense again, I said, "Okay, okay, I got it! Like I said, I am really, really sorry about that. I … um, I promise that I won't do it again." *Man, that sounds stupid to say.* "But look, don't make me do this! I'm happy to do chores up here or whatever it is that people do, or I can, well … just give me a giant rock, and I'll push it up and down a hill if that makes people happy. I'll do whatever I need to do to help out, but please don't make me sit here and think about this and have to go in and talk to him about it. I mean, look, it's fucking rough down there, and I just couldn't hack it. I quit. The world was a sucky place, and I had to get out of it. There."

Cocking his head in disbelief and glaring at me, he said, "Steven, do you have any idea who you are talking to?"

Fumbling, I said, "I … um. Oh shit, oh yeah, hey, sorry about that. I know that you had it pretty rough down there too. I guess I shouldn't be so insensitive."

"No, Steven, it's not that. You have to understand that … well, never mind. You just have to stay here and figure out why you really killed yourself, and you will have to go in there and tell him about it."

Fuck. "Look, don't you guys, like"—I gulped—"have my entire life on file somewhere? I mean, can't you just play back the tape and come up with a hypothesis or something? You can do that up here, right?"

"Steven, what point would there be in having us tell you the answer? It was your life. You ended it down there. You should be able to come up with the reason why that happened and tell him about it. Trust me, Steven. This is a very important part of the process. Look, I have to go now. Just do what he asked, and call me when you are ready to go back."

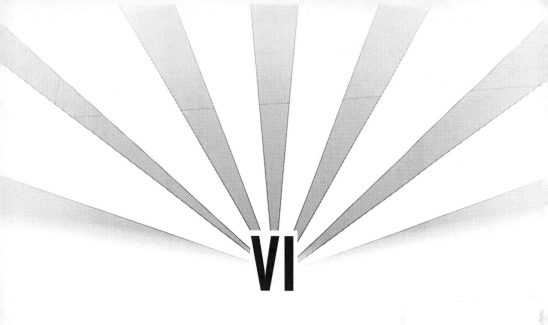

VI

"Great, Steven, now you're really stuck. How in the hell are you going to go back to God, the creator of all creation, and tell him that the world he designed fucking sucks? That it's a giant cesspool of selfishness and death and disease, and when your family dies in a car crash that was your fault and you find yourself all alone and sitting in a shitty apartment with nothing to look forward to except for the daily porn updates on the Internet, it can really seem like a good idea to just do yourself in? There's no way I can tell him that. What's he going to say? 'Gee, Steven, that's brilliant. Way to apply yourself, and thanks for stopping by to tell us. By the way, were you aware that my only son went down to earth and was crucified? At least he put forth some effort. You are just a waste of space. Oh, and to boot, we're going to keep you locked up in that shitty little room of yours filled with a bunch of crap that you don't care one bit about and let you meditate for eternity on what an asshole you were.' Fuck!

"And what's with this fucking space suit! I want out of this goddamn thing, and I want to … where could I go? I guess nowhere. I'm stuck. Shit. At least I could have been back on earth with … beer! Hey, now that could help to pass the time. A little buzz on! Yeah, why didn't I think about that earlier?

"Show me a sixer!

"Shit. Apparently there's no beer, either. Cigarettes? No. Marijuana? Nope. Crack? Steven, you've never done … oh, fuck it, beam me up, Scotty!

"What the fuck? So I'm stuck here, and the best thing I can get in this room is a stupid porno mag? Who cares? This edition sucked, anyway. Hey, wait, but I can get other stuff. There were some pretty damn graphic porno mags around by the time I bit it. Okay. Show me last June's edition of *T&A!*

"Nothing. What the hell? It worked last time. I said, *let's see some T&A!*

"Fuck. Oh, now I get it. Wonderboy came in here and found that magazine, and he turned off the porno switch or whatever they do up here. So I'm stuck with just this one magazine, and it sucks.

"What the hell, Steven? One magazine is better than nothing. You used to get off to the lingerie catalog back home, remember? Give it the old college try.

"Hey, hey? Where's my … what the … where's my dick? Don't tell me that they put you in a fucking huge rubber suit with no private parts? Oh, those puritanical bastards! That's it … Wait, go look in the mirror.

"Yep. Nothing down there. Suit just trails off into a pair of big fat legs. I do look just like a fucking marshmallow with legs! This sucks.

"Of course, Steven, why would they give you a dick? They probably know that you'd just spend time sitting in your room playing with yourself.

"Okay, Claus, I'm on to you. So it's to be a slow waiting game, eh? No frills, no drugs, no booze, no dick, nothing but me and this fucking room to deal with? Well, I can hold out longer than you can—believe me, buddy. Hey, I'll bet that I can just sit in here, and if I never call you-know-who's name again, they'll forget that I'm up here.

"Steven, that's fucking stupid. You think that you can hide under the bed in heaven?"

"Well, I'm going to have to do something. Now I'm getting hungry too. Hey, food! Yeah, I'll bet that you can eat in heaven. There's no sin against that, right?"

"Show me a steak sandwich!

"Nothing? Well, maybe they don't eat meat up here? How about a nice lemon meringue pie! Nope. Shit. Maybe no sweets. How about some pistachios? Nope. Nothing. Hey, can I get a slice of bread and some water?

"What the fuck? No food in heaven? At least in prison you get fed. Oh, this fucking sucks! Why the hell does my stomach still hurt if there is no food to eat up here?

"That's it! I don't care what happens to me after this. I'm not going to sit in this goddamn stupid room forever with no food and no Internet and nothing to do but hang around trying to find a good reason to tell him why I killed myself. Watch out, buddy; Steven's coming to tell you what's what!

"Jesus! Get in here!"

A bit warmer this time, God said, "Hello, Steven. Welcome back."

"I ... um ... yes, hello. And thank you."

Then he leaned in hard and said, "Steven, have you figured out why you killed yourself?"

And I leaned back. "I have. And ... I ... um, I'm going to tell you why I did it. And ... hey, where's Jesus going, anyway?"

Chuckling, God said, "Oh, don't worry about him. He is very busy and has quite a few places he needs to be in, usually at the same time."

Hardy-fucking-har ... I wish I had somewhere else to be right now too!

"So, Steven? What do you have to tell me?"

"I … um, well, you know, I was reading the Bible earlier and, you know, there are some really great parts in it."

"Is that right? Which are your favorite passages?"

Finding myself speeding downhill quickly, I said, "I … um … well, I don't recall them that well. You know, some people are good at quoting by, by, um …"

"Chapter and verse?"

"Yeah, that's it. I can't do that very well, but there sure were some comforting passages in there. And instructional too. Boy, oh, boy!"

God frowned and said, "Steven, you've never actually read the Bible, have you? You just have one sitting on the desk in your room for show."

How the hell does he know that? "I, um, well, I've looked through it and—"

"Steven, never mind."

Oh crap! Note to Steven: need to spend time reading the Bible.

"Steven, please pay attention."

"Yes, yes, sir."

"What is so hard about this? Why can't you tell me why you killed yourself? Tell me this: did you get married?"

"No."

"Have kids?"

"No."

"Work on a lifelong project?"

"No."

"Dedicate yourself to a cause?"

"No."

"Attend religious services?"

"No."

"So what did you do?"

And then the train derailed. "Look, pal, I may not have had the most glamorous life down there, but let me tell you, that place fucking sucks!"

Taking a deep breath and folding his arms across his chest, he said, "Steven. While you were gone, Jesus and I have been conferring about how you ended up—"

Oh, fuck me.

"And it is obvious that you missed something huge in your last life."

Panic-stricken, I said, *"Really?"*

"Yes. And, let me tell you, Steven, we deal with a lot of souls up here, and as we examined the thirty-four years that you were down there on earth, it was obvious that you were missing something time and again. It came around throughout your entire life, and you just missed it. And I think that may be the reason why you wound up quitting."

At this point, you could say that I blew up a bit. I really intended to go back and have a nice, calm discussion, but all of that stuff about missing something in an existence that was so painful to me that it felt like carrying a lead weight around for my entire life just got to me and I, well, I guess I may have been a bit upset at that specific moment. My particular response to him, I mean, what I actually said to him, may be a bit shocking to see, so be warned.

"*Oh, fucking-A fuck fuck shit bullshit*! I knew it! I knew that if I died, I would have to spend time having a fucking conversation with some asshole superdeity about the one thing that I missed in my life that would have made all the difference and which should have been totally fucking obvious to me if only I had been paying attention. Well, let me tell you, bub, you can't just sit up here on fucking high and judge people and tell them that some goddamn detail that passed through their lives while they were busy trying to survive and not get killed and not get thrown out on the street to starve in that fucking rotten cesspool of a place you have us all living in and should have been noticed by them. That's just not fucking fair!

"So tell me. What was it? No, wait, let me guess. Was it Brooke? That girl I dated in high school? Her dad had that great hardware business, and I'll bet that you're going to say that if I had not cheated on her and if I had spent more time paying attention to her, I would have inherited her dad's business and gone on to have a long and happy life filled with kids and joy and Sunday religious services and a whole bunch of other happy horseshit.

"Or was it the master's program I passed up? Yeah, so I had a chance to go and get a master's degree. So fucking what? Let me tell you, bub, you don't have to have a fucking advanced degree to have a happy life. And I don't give a shit if you think that I should have done it. I didn't fucking want to, and I still don't care, and I don't have to sit here and listen to you tell me that I should have gotten more education. So fuck you!

"Oh, wait, no, now I know ... oh, you bastard! You're going to say that I should have had a closer relationship with my family. That's it! Oh, fuck that! You have no idea what it's like to have to try to get along with a bunch of strangers living around you. My dad? Fuck, I barely knew the guy. He was always off traveling on business trips and taking my mom to exotic vacations in Europe, and they didn't always let us go, and I had no idea who the fuck that guy was. My mother? Fuck that. She was clueless. Just wanted to have a big, happy family and sit around and do nothing. I couldn't stand that shit. I hated her guts. And my sister? Well, she was a pretty good kid, but fuck, I couldn't stand how she was so happy all the time and liked spending time around my parents. That little fucking brownnoser. She'd bring her friends over to hang out *with* my parents. Weird, really fucking weird.

"Look, asshole, the world sucks, and I'm not going to sit here and listen to you tell me that I should have grown a sunnier disposition and learned to live with all of the bullshit and misery. It's shit down there! Total shit! And there wasn't a goddamn thing that would have ever, in a million years, kept me from blowing my fucking brains out!

"So, Mr. Fucking Big-Shot Superbeing, why don't you tell me in your infinite fucking wisdom what that one, one insignificant, moronic detail was that I missed?"

Opening his arms and pointing at me, he said, "You."

"Oh. Um ... I ... um ... well ..." *I think that I just shit myself.*

"Can I go back to my room now?"

VII

Safely back in my room and trying to get control over my breathing, I gasped, "Jesus, I don't think that I can take much more of this! What did he mean that I missed myself? How the hell can you do that? I mean, I was there. I lived my life. I hated it so much and knew, I mean *knew*, that there was nothing good at all in it for me, so I shot myself. I quit. I know. I did it. I gave up. But how can he possibly say that I missed *myself*? When I pulled that trigger, I could feel the infinite pain of my very being so acutely that shooting myself was the only way to make it stop!"

Calmly, he said, "Steven, you will have to talk to him, and he can explain further. What I can tell you is that we deal with a lot of souls up here, and we see a lot of people who have just come here from the earth. Sometimes we have discussions with them about whether or not they missed something about their lives or themselves down there that could have made the whole experience better. And with some of them, it can really be a lively debate.

"But, Steven, you blew your own face off. And we can still see that you blew your own face off. It is not very hard to conclude that you missed finding yourself down there. If you had found yourself, you certainly wouldn't have done what you did."

Fresh out of clever responses, I said, "Oh."

Resting a hand on my shoulder, he said, "Now, Steven, you are going to have to go back in there and keep talking with him until you heal. And we will know when you have healed, because we will be able to see your face again and not just something that looks like shredded hamburger."

"Jesus, look, I can't take this anymore!"

"Steven, you have to take this whole process very seriously. We need you to understand and really come to terms with what you did. You need to heal and get over this."

"But why?" I was actually sobbing at this point, if such a thing is even possible in heaven.

Stepping back, he said, "Because you have to return to earth."

My jaw hit the floor. "You are shitting me."

Calmly again, he said, "No, Steven, we don't do that up here. You are going back to earth when you have finished healing up here."

Still shocked, I said, "How ... I mean, how is that even possible, and—"

"Steven, you didn't complete your last life. You opted out. You quit. You threw in the towel. You have to go back and complete a life before—"

Suddenly, a glorious ray of light poured in! "Wait. So you're saying that I can get out of here?"

"Of course. Well, you have to heal first, but—"

"But then I can get out of here!" I jumped out of bed and threw my arms around him. "Oh, thank you, Jesus, thank you, thank you, thank you!" *I did get away with it! Porn and beer, here I come!*

Jesus pushed me back to arm's length. "Steven, you will have to understand that you missed yourself first, and—"

Bouncing up and down a bit, I said, "Roger that! I will. Missed myself—10-4. I've got it."

Gently pushing me down on the bed, he said, "No, Steven, you don't get it. But you will. Now, just sit here and think about what you did in your past life, and when I come back, you should be ready to start the healing process."

Still bouncing, I said, "Okay, okay, I will, I promise. I'll sit here and be good, and I won't do anything but think about what you and he said. And I'll go back and talk to him about anything he wants, and I'll heal, and I promise to make you proud of me!"

Moving toward the door, he said, "That's fine, Steven. Look, I have to go, and I'll be back in a while."

"Hey, before you go, can you … I mean, can I get a new suit? This one doesn't work very well, and I think that I might have—"

"Steven, you don't need a new suit. That one will work fine for you once you get the hang of it."

Thanks, pal. "Well, you can take this magazine with you. I don't need it. I probably should have been focused on more important things than that, and I'm sorry for conjuring it up in the first place."

Continuing to walk away, he said, "That's okay, Steven, I don't need to take it. It's yours while you are here. We will get rid of it and the rest of your stuff in here when you are gone."

"Oh, okay, I guess that makes sense. But I really don't need it, and I'm going to really think about what I've done and—" Then he was gone again.

Expectantly, God said, "Welcome back, Steven. How are you feeling today?"

"A lot better than I was before! How are you?"

He just sighed. "The same as I have always been."

"Oh, I guess that makes sense. You never go anywhere, do you?"

"No. There is really nowhere for me to go. But that's not important now."

"Oh, I know. Boy, do I know. Jes— … um, he told me that I have to go back to earth because I was a suicide, and I quit on my life and all. And I'm really sorry about missing myself in my last life and all of the things that I didn't do that I could have done, and I'm going to do better and really make it a good one down there.

"And I'm sure that we have some things to talk about before I go. However, before that, could I … I mean, could I just see my family members? I know that you said that suicides don't get to talk to nonsuicides up here and all, and I'm sure that is a very well-thought-out policy and should be in place, but I … um, well, I happen to know that my family is up here, because they were all in a big car crash where I was driving, and no one else survived but me. I think that the accident was my fault, although I was never charged with anything or had to pay restitution or anything like that. And I'm really sorry about the car accident, and I hope that my family is doing well up here and finding everything they want and that you enjoy talking with them. They were all great people, and I'm sure that they are better at this whole talking-to-you thing than I am."

God said, "Steven, we know all about the accident with your family."

"Oh good! I mean … whatever. But I was really worried about talking to you about that on top of the whole suicide thing and all. I figured that if I had too many strikes against me, that might muck up my chances to, you know, go back down there and try again."

"Steven, that does not make a difference. However, we cannot let you see your family."

"Oh, come on, just once! I … look, I don't have to talk to them for long, and if you want, I won't say anything about killing myself or getting to go back."

Obviously the reason why they don't let suicides talk to nonsuicides is not because of that fib about my face looking like it was blown off but rather because suicides get to go back to earth, and they don't want to make everyone else jealous!

"And I promise that I'll keep it short, and, gosh, I'd love to say hi to my little sister too, and—"

Plainly, he said, "Steven, they are all gone."

"*What?*" I exclaimed.

"Yes. They are gone already. That car accident was years before you got here, and they have already been through heaven and are now back on earth."

"You are shitting me."

"No, Steven, we do not do that up here."

Stunned, I said, "Oh, I guess that's right." *Readers, I checked earlier, and I had not in fact shit myself.* "Sorry about saying that too. So they're gone? I mean *gone* gone? Back on earth? Is that what happens? Everyone goes back to earth?"

He said, "Yes."

Dumbstruck, I said, "But how … why … I mean, I've never heard of that before. I'm sure I never read it, and, well, I guess I thought that when people died, they just got to hang out up here with you and do … well, whatever people do up here."

"Steven, your soul is energy in the universe. Energy can never be destroyed, and we need souls and energy down on earth. Once a soul has had an opportunity to come up here to visit with us and regroup, we send that soul back."

Excited a bit, I said, "Oh wow, now I get it! That's why everyone is so delighted when a new baby is on the way! It is literally a life coming back to earth! A … wait a minute, so that's a whole previous life who is then being born again, and the parents are—"

He brushed my thought from the air and said, "Steven, don't worry about any of that. We still have a lot of work to do up here, and as I told you, you cannot see any of your family members who were up here, because they are all gone already."

"Wow! I mean, wow! I had no idea. Obviously, I just had no idea. Hey, can I find them when I go back? I mean, are you going to send me to the same place they are? I'm sure that you send family members to the same, what … like state or at least the same country, right? I mean, I don't speak any other languages, and I think that I'd feel a little weird if you dropped me in China or something."

"Steven, I think that you would have a hard time finding them when you went back."

"Why is that?"

"Well, let's see. Your little sister is a dolphin currently swimming in the Pacific Ocean, and your mother is a blue jay flying around somewhere in Canada."

Indignant, I said, "Wait, wait, *wait just a goddamn minute!* Oh shit, I guess I shouldn't say that here. Sorry about that."

A deep frown spread across his forehead.

"Anyway, are you telling me that my family members—I mean the members of my family who were humans with me down there last time and who died in a car crash with me—have gone back as birds and fish and things like that?"

"Yes. Well, not your dad. He went back as a human."

"Oh, so I could go and find him, right?"

He said, "Probably not."

In disbelief, I asked, "Why not?"

"He wanted to go to Italy when he went back, so he is there now."

"You are shitting me."

He was still frowning.

"Oh shit, sorry about that again. I mean, are you joking?"

"No, Steven, we do not do that up here, either."

Bursting with excitement now, I said, "Wow! This is all, I mean this is all just absolutely crazy. I had no idea that a human life that died down there, I mean, I guess you don't die if your soul is immortal, right? And well, anyway, someone who stops living on earth can come up here and then go back to earth and relive as something else. This is all just crazy information!"

He explained, "Steven, life is life. And there is no death. Only a change of worlds. Down there, it takes a soul to make a human or a cat or a tree or a mosquito or a patch of grass or … Didn't you know about any of this?"

Shocked at the mere notion, I replied, "Of course not. How could I?"

"Haven't you ever seen a human with animallike characteristics?"

"No."

"Or an animal that behaves like a human?"

"No."

"Have you ever seen a cat that acts a bit squirrely?"

Sheer excitement took over at this point. "No, but I mean, do you have any idea how *fucking incredible* this all is? Wow! So the universe, or I guess at least heaven and earth, are just one huge recycling factory for souls, and souls can go from one form of life to another and go down there and die and come here and talk to you and go back and do it again and … Hey, what's it like to be a tree?"

"During the day, when the sun is shining down, a tree feels exactly like you do when you first wake up in the morning and reach all of your limbs out to stretch."

"Wow! That's a great sensation! I loved that feeling! And at night when the sun goes down?"

"The tree feels sleep the same way you do."

"Holy shit, that's incredible! But wait, you said that my sister went back as a dolphin? That clever little kid! She always was really sharp! I'll bet that dolphins have really fun lives, I mean, swimming around and diving and jumping out of the water and doing backflips and ... Hey, wait, don't they have to fight with sharks too?"

"That happens sometimes."

"Wow ... I sure hope that she's okay. I mean, I hope that she at least gets to live longer as a dolphin than she did as a human. Geesh, I feel so bad about that whole car accident and ... Hey, a bird! Wait, let me guess. Soaring through the clouds and shitting on everyone! Boy, that would be great! Just like Mom too! Hey, why the hell don't you tell people about this whole going-back-to-earth thing? If I had known that, I don't think that I would have killed myself."

Dubious, he said, "Is that right, Steven?"

"Goddamn right, that's right! Oh shit, sorry about that again."

"That's okay, Steven."

"But, well, anyway, this is great news! Hey, where's Jesus?"

Jesus suddenly appeared. Unassumingly, he said, "Yes, Steven?"

"Jesus, have you heard the good news? Life is eternal! And you can go back to earth and live again and it's great and ... oh, wait, you probably know all of this stuff."

Then Jesus started frowning.

"Anyway, what a great fucking setup you guys have! I mean, really terrific stuff! Nice job on the whole heaven thing and the eternal life thing and ... Hey, can you take me back to my room now?"

Jesus said, "Sure. Boss, we'll be back."

Still on overdrive, I said, "Yeah, boss, um ... er, God. We'll be back when I'm ready to go. Just need to think really hard about what kind of life I want to go back as. That's so awesome! I'm going to go back to my room and read a whole encyclopedia of life and get ideas for all of the cool things that I can be and, I mean, this is going to be so much fun! I could be a … no, I guess you can't go back as a pterodactyl. They're extinct, right? Well, something cool like that, maybe a hawk or a grizzly bear or, wow, I need some time to think about all of this."

VIII

Walking back, I started bouncing up and down and pulling on Jesus's arm. "Jesus, I mean, this is some incredible stuff! What a great universe you guys have got here. Humans going back to live as nonhumans and one great big circle of life and, I mean, this is really awesome! Wow! Hey, who handles all of logistics of talking to all of the souls and getting them to and from where they want to be down there and all of that great stuff?"

"God and I do."

I leaned back. "Really? No one else helps? Surely you have, like, someone assigned to the mammals and someone else for the fish and someone else for the birds and—"

Sighing, he responded, "No, Steven, it's just he and I."

"Wow, that's a lot of work to do!"

"You're telling me?"

Entering my room again, I said, "Oh, right. Sorry. Wow, I'll bet that you are super, super busy. Geez, I'm sorry, I have probably already taken up too much of your time. Go ahead and do whatever it is that you need to do, and I'll be here, and I promise not to call you until I'm ready to go back."

Standing by the door, he said, "Steven, that's fine, but there is one thing that I should tell you before—"

Gently pushing him away, I said, "Jesus, really, don't worry about it. And don't waste any more time on me. Please go and talk to whomever you need to, and I'll be here and ready to go when you come back. Really, I got it, and I'll do what I need to do and be ready to go when the time is right."

"But, Steven—"

"Seriously, just go. I'm sure that someone else needs you right now, and I'll be just fine."

"Okay. See you in a while."

Alone again, I said, "Holy fucking shit! What a great ... I mean, who would have ever thought that these guys ... I mean, they really have it right up here. I get a nice room where I get to play with all of my old things, and ... well, they weren't really interesting to me, but it did make things sort of nice and cozy. And even though I killed myself and killed my family members, everyone is okay, and they all got to go back and do whatever they wanted, and life goes around and around, and I mean this is just all terrific!

"I'll bet that there were fucking clues to all of this that I just didn't see when I was living. Shit. I really should have paid more attention. Wait, Je— ... he said that thing about a room in my father's house, and this is my room. Wow, cool! And ... well, I'll bet that he said something about eternal life, and I just missed it.

"Fucking hell. I absolutely tortured myself down there, and I had no idea that that universe was this wonderful. I mean, earlier, I wanted to get out of here as fast as I could, but that was just because things were so boring, and I couldn't get my suit to work right, and I couldn't get any porn or drugs up here, and ... but now I see how incredible everything really is, and I get a second chance to go back and ... Wait, is this my second chance? If life is eternal, then maybe

I've had lots of past lives. I'll have to ask one of those two about that when I get ready to go.

"But first, Steven, you must *choose wisely*. You get a chance to go back and do anything you want and go anywhere you want, and you'd better be careful about it. You don't want to get yourself sent somewhere where you'll just end up in a can of tuna in twelve seconds or wind up getting chopped into firewood. Wow, there are really a lot of dangerous things that you can get yourself into. Let's see, what is never killed? Lion? King of the jungle! They seem to be pretty safe. Wait, no, fuck, I see those programs on television all the time about lions being tranquilized and put into cages and … oh, fuck that. I'm sure that's what would happen to me.

"How about an eagle? Yeah, they're fierce, and can fly above everything, and wait … are also an endangered species, which means that they get killed a lot.

"Oh fuck. This is pretty tough. Hey, what about a shark? Nothing gets to sharks. Well, I guess sharks get killed too. I could wind up as shark fin soup. I could also wind up accidentally eating my sister, and I'd sure hate to do that to her after the whole car wreck and everything. Shit, I guess I need to take some time and think about this. Hey, what about that encyclopedia? Johnny, show me the encyclopedia! And there it is! Okay, Steven, take your time. Don't fuck this up. Let's come up with something good that won't cause you to get killed prematurely and so you can live a long, fun, kick-ass life …"

Rocking back in his chair, God said, "Welcome back, Steven."

Sitting down to deliver my grand speech, I said, "Hey! Okay, I've spent a long time in my room thinking about this, and, well, first off, let me just say that the world is full of an incredible diversity of life, and you guys really have an amazing thing going on down there. I mean, the number of species is just staggering, and the different places they all live in the world is … I mean, wow! Hey, really excellent job on the whole universe thing!"

"Thank you, Steven. But—"

"Wait, wait. Look, I really appreciate the way that you guys do things up here too. I mean, all of those souls to look after and all of the different places you send them to and the different types of lives you have to deal with and talk to and, I mean, this is just an awesome place!"

"Thank you, Steven. But—"

"Wait, wait. So okay, I realize that what I did last time was an incredibly big sin, but I now see what a wonderful place the universe is, and well, I'm really sorry for what I did and, you know, it's just because the place I grew up in was pretty tough, and I didn't really get along with my family. Well, I guess I didn't know them very well, and I always felt like a bit of a stranger at home, and … well, anyway, I didn't do a very good job at being a human, and I'm sorry for giving up on that whole thing, but you do have to know that it is very tough to be a human down there."

"We do."

"Well, so I'm sorry about all of that. But you know, I may not have been ready for all of that, and so I've thought long and hard about this, and I've done a ton of reading about everything, and I know exactly what it is that I want to go back as, and—"

"Steven, we are sending you back as a human, and we are sending you back to exactly where you were when you killed yourself."

I jumped to my feet. *"You have got to be shitting me!"*

"No, Steven, I am not. Didn't you hear Jesus? You have to finish what you started last time, and there are no exceptions. Suicides all go back to where they were when they quit last time.

And you have to make it through to the end, or we will just send you back again."

Fucking hell!

"I, um … can I go back to my room now?"

"Yes, Steven, and when you come back here, we will start again."

IX

It felt like I was back in my apartment waiting to die. At some point, Jesus opened my door and said, "Steven, what are you doing?"

"I … um, nothing, I guess."

"Why are you hiding under the covers in your bed?"

"What do you mean?"

Pressing me, he said, "Why are you lying in bed and hiding under the covers? You were supposed to go back to talk to God. How long have you been in here?"

Devoid of all hope, I said, "For an eternity, it seems. Look, Jesus, I … I just can't."

"What do you mean, 'can't'? You have to."

Pulling back covers with a sigh, I said, "I can't. Look, I'm sorry. I'm all alone up here."

"We're here!"

"Yeah, *great*. Sorry, Jesus, I am apparently just a waste of space and no good to the universe. And it's hopeless, and I'll never make it next time. Why don't you just go on without me?"

Concerned, he asked, "Steven, why are you so down?"

Glaring sharply at him, I said, "Because. I killed a lot of people. And ... well, I killed myself. And then I get here to find out that it's *okay*, that I'm not going to be boiled in oil, that I have not caused the universe to split in two, but instead that you are just going to send me back to do it all over again. Well, that all sucks!"

"Why do you say that, Steven?"

"I ... well, why the hell don't you guys do something up here? I mean, look, get with the program! Don't you have a ray gun or something to zap me into oblivion?"

He just stood there blinking.

"Can't you throw me to some wolves?"

More of the same.

"Isn't there a cross that I can be nailed to or something?"

Putting his hands on his hips, he said firmly, "Okay, Steven, now that's personal. Stop it. Just stop it. Look. Like it or not, you are part of the universe. Your soul is eternal, and you have to go back and do what you originally set out to do."

"What did I originally set out to do?"

"I can't tell you that."

"Really?"

"No. I can't. You have to go talk to him to find out."

"But I mean, why am I not—"

"Chained to a rock at the bottom of a pit of fire?"

"Yes!"

"What good would that do?"

"Well, there's got to be some punishment for killing people, right? And for killing yourself? Come on! I feel like I'm just being buttered up for something sinister, and I can't talk to anyone else to find out how to get out of here."

Comforting me, he said, "Steven, death is a part of life down there. How it happens certainly matters, but we don't chain people to rocks up here. And anyway, we can let you talk to other suicides."

Lifting my head up, I said, "Really?"

"Yes. But not yet. First you have to—"

"Oh yeah, right. I have to heal so that it doesn't look like I shot myself in the face. Fuck."

Pulling the covers away, he said, "Yes. Look, why don't you get out of bed and come with me? Go talk to him, and he will answer all of your questions. And you will start to feel a little better."

"I seriously doubt that."

"Steven, your new life down there is going to happen whether you like it or not. All you are doing by lying there is making the process take longer."

Fucking hell!

"Steven. I promise the whole trip gets better from this point on."

Frailly, I said, "You swear it?"

"Yes. Look, don't you have any questions you want to ask?"

"Questions? I don't know. What's the point?"

"Steven, you are here to learn and heal. Asking questions helps with the whole process."

Sounds pretty fucking useless to me. Shit. But what else can I do? Finally, I said, "Well, maybe I could think of a thing or two to ask. Just to help pass the time."

"That's the spirit! Come on, things do get better from here on out. Trust me."

Right. "Okay, maybe this won't be so bad. I'll come just this once, but after that, if things really aren't better, I'm going to stay here and not come out until you let me talk to some strangers so I can get the skinny on this place."

"Sure thing, Steven. We'll start there."

Crossing his hands in his lap, God said, "Welcome back, Steven. How are you today?"

Sitting down, I grumbled, "I'm fine, I guess. How are you?"

"About the same as always."

Reluctantly, I said, "Great. So what's on the training table for today? Oh, wait, before we start, I guess that I should finish my apology."

"What apology?"

"I was apologizing earlier for what a shit I was, and, in the middle, I guess I said some pretty rotten things to you, and I probably shouldn't have."

"That's okay. I deal with that a lot."

"So … you're not mad at me?"

"Steven, I do not bother getting angry. When you see everything as I do, anger is just wasted energy."

"Oh, I'll bet that's right."

"Anyway, so J—"

Helpfully, he said, "I call him Junior."

"Junior?"

"Yes. As you may already know, if you call him by his true name, he will come to wherever you are. That works everywhere up here, so we try to be mindful and not to call him unless he is needed."

Acridly, I said, "That sucks. How the hell did he get stuck with that rap? Oh shit. Sorry. I guess that up here everyone is glad to do what they're supposed to be doing and—"

Waving me off with his hand, he said, "Steven, don't worry about him for now. He is just fine and perfectly content where he is."

That must be nice.

"Did you have anything you wanted to talk about today?"

"I … um, did I have anything … oh yes. J— … uh, *he* said that I'm supposed to ask you what it was that I set out to do last time."

Raising an eyebrow, God said, "He did?"

"Yep."

Then he just stared at me.

Shrugging, I pressed. "So what did I set out to do last time?"

"Live as a human."

"What?"

"Live as a human."

"No, look, I get that. Or at least I think I get that. I have been born more than once, and I was a human in my last life, and I missed myself, and I committed this great, terrible sin, and now I'm here. But what I wanted to know is, what did I set out to do last time?"

God cocked his head and looked at me puzzled. "I don't understand your question."

Annoyed, I said, "You what? How is that possible?"

He said, "Steven, it's not a very good question."

Oh fuck. This is going to take awhile.

"*Why did I go back to earth as a human?*"

"Steven, there is no need to raise your voice up here. I can hear you just fine."

"Oh shit. Sorry. Did I just do that?"

"Yes."

"Sorry. So why did I go back to earth as a human?"

"Why wouldn't you?" he said almost rhetorically.

"Why … why … why wouldn't I? That's a good question. I guess I would, except that the last round was so hard, and now I'm stuck going back as a human again."

Raising his eyebrows, he said, "So do you want to go back as something else?"

"*Yes!* I mean, yes, I do. I did a lot of research on this, and I made very careful notations of what I wanted to be, and—"

Then he yanked the rug out. "But you can't."

"No. *Shit. I know.* You told me that. Look, how about if you just send me back as a dolphin? Like my sister. That would be great! I could hang out with her and swim around, and we could get to know each other better than we did the last time."

"No."

"Why not? What's one dolphin, more or less?"

"Steven, dolphins do not commit suicide."

"So?"

"So right now you are in a high-risk category for committing suicide again."

"So? I mean … really? That's certainly one concern, I guess. But even if that's so … so?"

Raising a lone finger, he said, "Steven, we have never had a single soul in the universe commit suicide more than once."

I said, "No shit?"

Ominously, he said, "No, Steven. And if that happens, we are very worried that all life as you know it may come to an end."

"Seriously?"

He replied. "Yes. What you did is extremely troubling to us, and we have to make sure that you do not commit suicide again, for the sake of all of the other lives down there."

"Are you fucking kidding me!" I exclaimed.

"No, I am not."

"Shit! Wow! So … well, then, why don't you send me back as something that doesn't commit suicide? Like a dolphin?"

"Because, Steven, you have to *want* to not commit suicide. It does not do any good if we just trick you into not committing suicide in your next life."

I threw up my arms. "Okay, that's it, fuck this place. Jesus!"

Jesus strolled in wearing an Argentina sports jersey. "You rang, Steven?"

Coming quickly to my feet, I said, "Yes, yes, I damn well did! I … Hey, are you wearing a soccer jersey?"

"Yes. Why?"

"Where the hell did you get it?"

"At the soccer game."

"The what?"

"The soccer game."

"Oh, well, anyway, never mind that for now." Grabbing his arm, I said, "Take me back to my room, now."

X

We traveled back in silence. I was fuming. When we got to my room, Jesus sat me down on the bed and said, "Steven, what's wrong?"

"Well, first of all, do you know what he just told me?"

"No."

"Really? Don't you guys share notes on things?"

"Not really. Why?"

"Well, oh, never mind. He just told me that I have to go back to earth as a human, because I have to make it to the end next time without killing myself, or else all life as we know it is in jeopardy."

"That's right."

"Fuck! That sucks. That's a pretty heavy burden to bear."

In disbelief, he said, "Steven, do you have any idea who you are talking to?"

"Oh shit, sorry, I guess I should—"

"Look, never mind. Yes, what he said was true."

"Well, how is that possible?"

"Why don't you go ask him?"

"Why?"

Standing up, he said, "Because I'm pretty busy."

"You're … you're *busy*? Doing what? Oh, I forgot—soccer. Let me guess: everyone in heaven gets to play soccer except the suicides."

"Well, yes, that is true. But I was at a game in Argentina."

"Argentina? You mean, like, on earth?"

"Yes."

"What the hell were you doing at a soccer game in Argentina?"

"What do you mean?"

"Aren't you supposed to be taking care of souls up here?"

"Steven, I go wherever I am needed. Argentina is playing Brazil right now, and before the game, the players started praying, and—"

"Oh, fuck. I get it. They called your name, and you went."

"Yes."

"Wow. How the hell do you find the time to … never mind. I don't care. So, what, you were favoring Argentina?"

"No. Why?"

"The jersey. You're wearing an Argentina soccer jersey."

"Well, I wore the Brazil one last time."

"Oh, fuck. I don't care. Look, why is my little soul threatening to destroy all life?"

"Steven, you will have to go ask him. I'm busy. I have to go now, and when you are ready to go back and talk to him, let me know."

When he left, I screamed at the top of my lungs, *"This place really fucking sucks!"*

Entering again and surveying the recent carnage, Jesus said, "Steven, what the hell did you do in here? Why did you smash up all of your things?"

Because I hate you and everything else up here, and I want you to throw me out of this fucking place!

"I, um … I just didn't like any of those things anymore. So there."

Picking up a piece of glass, he said, "You smashed your mirror. Now you won't know when you have healed."

The damn thing didn't work, anyway, and I looked just fine, thank you very much.

"Jesus, I doubt that it's going to happen. I'm not getting any better."

Moving toward me, he said, "Steven, you're not even trying. Now, get up, and let's go back in to see God again."

Meekly, I said, "Are you going to stay with me?"

"No. Why would I? I have things to do."

Smiling at me, God said, "Welcome back, Steven."

Groan.

"What would you like to talk about today?"

Getting the fuck out of here.

Slumping down, I said hollowly, "Um, was there a reason why I went back last time, other than to be a human?"

Opening again, he said, "Yes, of course!"

Sitting up a bit, I said, "Okay, now we're getting somewhere! What was it? Oh, wait, I'll bet that it was some awesome idea that I just didn't get to because of … well, because of a lot of things we don't need to repeat or talk about right now. So what was it?"

God shrugged and said, "I have no idea."

"*What?* How can you not know that?"

"You made that decision the last time you were up here, before your last life."

"So?"

"I have only looked at what you actually did with your last life."

"So why don't you look at what I did up here last time?"

Tilting his head, he asked, "Steven, why would we bother with that?"

Raising my voice, I said, "So I can find out the fucking answer to what I was supposed to be doing!"

"Steven, from the available records, it appears that you went back to kill yourself. Anyway, that is how it ended up."

Shrinking away a bit, I said, "Yes, yes, and, again, sorry about that. But I must have wanted to go back and do something great!"

"Why do you say that?"

"Because! Why the hell would anyone go back as a human *except* to do something great?"

"Steven, billions of people who die and come up here decide to go back as humans. A lot of them go back just to go back. They say that they missed something last time, or, well, we have one guy who said that he wanted to go back last time just to fuck off some more."

Wow, God curses!

Leaning in, I said, "That's all very interesting. But I mean, aren't we supposed to be doing something more, something greater than, um … just fucking off?"

Shrugging gently, he said, "To each his own, Steven."

Bolting upright, I said, "No shit? Wow! That's a pretty great policy! Well, it applies to everyone except suicides, apparently."

"No, Steven, we apply that policy to suicides as well. But they also have to go back and finish what they started."

"So what did I start?"

"How should I know? That is for you to know and do."

Fuck.

Folding his hands in each other, he said, "Is there anything else you wanted to talk about today?"

Slumping again, I said, "Um ... well ... why the hell can't I remember what I set out to do? And why the hell can't I remember being here last time, or my last life ... you know, the one before that last little thing that happened?"

God smiled knowingly and said, "Steven, forgetfulness is all a blessed part of the process."

"Like hell it is! Do you know what I could do if I could remember all of my past lives and what I set out to do and everything that I learned?"

"No, Steven, what could you do?"

"Well, probably something *spectacular*, which is probably what I set out to do last time, and I got hung up and lost my way because of this fucking problem with remembering past lives, and that's where things went wrong."

Innocently, he asked, "So that is why you killed yourself?"

"Um, well, that's probably part of the reason."

"Steven, if you did not know what you did not know, how could it cause you to shoot yourself in the face?"

Frustrated, I said, "Fuck. I don't know. It's just a bad glitch in the process, and you guys should do something about it."

"Steven, that cannot happen at this point."

"Why the hell not?"

God settled comfortably in his chair and said, "Well, Steven, forgetting your past life is nearly as old as life itself. You see, in the beginning—"

If you have made it this far, I should warn you that when you ask a simple question to God like 'Why the hell not?' much like talking to your actual grandfather at times, you do not always get a direct answer. Don't get me wrong. They have come a long way since parables and all of that other shit, but the roundabout nature of answering questions is still a big problem. And I don't know if it will get better anytime soon.

"Well, back then, we were on the far side of the moon."

"You mean the dark side of the moon?"

"The what?"

"Never mind. Please continue. Wait, where are we now?"

"Behind the universe."

"No shit? Wait, how do you get here?"

"Through a black hole."

"No shit?"

"No, Steven. Anyway, we were getting ready to send an innumerable number of lives down to the earth for the first time, and—"

"Where'd they come from anyhow?"

"Me. Steven, stop interrupting. You will understand better when I am done."

"Oh shit, sorry."

"So we had everyone here and ready to go. And I said, 'Are you all ready to experience this?' And in unison, a sea of voices all cried out, '*Yes, yes!*' Steven, I can tell you, it was a pretty terrific thing to experience."

"I'll bet it was. Then what happened?"

"Well, we had high hopes for the potential of what was about to take place—"

"Wait, who's 'we'?"

"Junior and I. So we flung them down into the watery earth and waited."

"Wait, where did he come from?"

"I had an affair with a supernova. Look, Steven it is a little hard to explain everything in the universe to you at the same time. So please try not to get distracted, and I promise that I will answer anything you have to ask me in due course."

Yeah, except why the hell I went back last time ... and that last question ... but I'm keeping track ... shit, I wish I had a pencil.

Trying to find a comfortable spot on the bench, I said, "Sorry, please continue. And then what happened?"

"Well, nothing at first. And then most of them exploded."

"Exploded?"

"Yes. You have to realize that at that time, life on earth was supported by little more than air bubbles in the water. As it turns out, you cannot keep the kind of energy that makes up a soul contained in just water bubbles. The energy tends to exceed the structure it is placed in and, well, kablammo."

"Wow! Then what happened?"

"The ones who blew up came back up here, and we sent them back again. Little by little, the structures holding life grew stronger, and those souls were able to stay down there for longer periods of time."

"How did they grow stronger?"

"By going back time and again. The water mixed with life, and the life mixed with the sediment from below, which was being churned up, and eventually it all created, well, you can think of them sort of like double-walled air bubbles."

"Huh. So after life was able to sustain itself for longer periods of time, then what happened?"

"Problems."

"What problems?"

"Well, you see, at the time that we first introduced life onto the earth, there was nothing down there. Nothing but water covering everything. It seemed like a good place to deposit life to see if it would grow. The problem with starting from scratch, however, is that there was nothing extra down there for life to sustain itself with.

"So while these little beings were paddling around in the water and trying to figure out where to go and what to do, they suddenly became aware that they were growing weaker, feeling faint, and that is when the fear started.

"We could see it from up here. The first one down there started to feel afraid that something bad was happening, something that he had never felt before, and the only thing he knew was that he felt life draining out of him. So he started to swim faster and faster, searching everywhere for something, anything to get rid of that dreadful feeling of wasting away. But as I mentioned, there was nothing else down there except for a sea of little beings just like him.

"At the last moment, right before he felt like he was at his end, he panicked and swam right into the being next to him. The collision killed the other one, and his soul came back up here."

"And what happened down there?"

"The first one saw that he had killed someone else, and, things being what they were at the time, he felt a great deal of shame about having done it. But he was still expiring, and down there was a fresh carcass. So he ate it."

"*He ate it?*" I exclaimed.

"Yes. Well, technically, he just absorbed the nutrients, but for all practical purposes, he ate it."

"Well, why didn't he eat, you know, like the burst air bubbles of the past lives?"

"I do not know. It never occurred to anyone that they needed to eat. It sure didn't occur to us."

"And then what happened?"

"He rejuvenated. It was like getting a second life. He felt great and swam and swam and dove and jumped out of the water and felt like a new being again. And then the hunger came back."

Leaning away, I said skeptically, "Wait a second. Are you telling me that life on earth started out by cannibalizing itself?"

Blinking innocently, he said, "Steven, what do you think happens today?"

"Oh shit, oh holy fucking shit! Um, oops, sorry. I ... am I supposed to be working on that?"

"Steven, don't worry about it for now. You have bigger problems than your limited creativity in expressing yourself."

"Life eating life! Wow! You're right. I can see it now. But what happened to the being, you know, the first one who was killed?"

"He came up here. And he said, 'Hey, I was swimming around and having fun, and then this jerk ran into me and smacked the life out of me.' And I said, 'Look, that was bound to happen. Try not to get too angry about it.'"

Waiting for the punchline, I said, "And ...?"

"Then he asked if he could go back and try again. And I said, 'Of course you can.' So I sent him back."

"And what happened to him?"

"He eventually starved to death and came back up here, and I sent him back again."

"And, well, okay, so I guess I get the going back down there to try it again part, but what about that first son of a bitch who killed the other one?"

"What?"

"What happened to him?"

"Oh, eventually someone ran into him and killed him. And he came up here and said, 'Hey, I was swimming around and having fun, and then this jerk ran into me and smacked the life out of me.' And I said, 'Look, that was bound to happen. Try not to get too angry about it.'"

"And …?"

"Then he asked if he could go back and try again. And I said, 'Of course you can.' So I sent him back."

Throwing up my hands, I said, "Wait a minute, whoa boy! Slow down! So you're telling me that the first act that a life took on earth was to take another's life, and all you said was *'Try not to get angry about it'*?"

"Yes."

Leaning on my knee, I said, "Listen, bub, you needed to get a little tougher on these folks. I mean, if the birth of life on earth was marked with nothing but killing, it's no wonder that things are so bad now. What you should have done is grab that first guy by the scruff of his … well, I guess they didn't have necks yet, right?"

"No, no necks yet."

Clutching the air with my hands, I said, "Well, you should have grabbed him by the whatever and said, 'Listen, pal, if you go off and kill one more thing down there, that's it. I'm going to end the whole thing, and you are going to burn in a pit of hell forever. So you just have to get used to eating scraps from expired souls, and you cannot take another living being's life.'"

He cocked his head and said, "Steven, what good would that have done?"

"God, you're God. You are the father of all life in the universe. If it is fucking up, you need to grab it by the shirt collar and say, 'Listen, get with the program, or you're going to be toast.'"

"Steven, you have to understand something first. I did not create life for my own sake. I created it for *its* own sake. Telling someone that he or she couldn't kill someone else would be the same as making life for my own sake. And that is not the point."

Stomping my foot sharply, I insisted, "But it *is* your life."

"No, it is not. The moment that those little beings said that they wanted to go off to test life on the earth, it became their journey, not mine. That was the whole point from the beginning."

Leaning back, I said, "Oh, fuck me! So you're telling me that what we're up against down there is not just people killing each other over sneakers and religious differences. You're telling me that we have to combat an eternity of life where killing has gone on and you haven't smited—or is it smoted … or what's the past tense of smite? Sorry, my dictionary is back in my room."

"Smote."

"Okay, where you haven't smote anyone to let all life know that killing is not allowed?"

"No."

Slumping down, I said, "Shit. There really is no hope for life on earth."

"Steven, that's not true."

"What do you mean? You just said that killing has gone on since the very beginning, and all you did up here was give the killers a pat on the back and tell the victims to try to take a more … meditative approach to the whole thing."

"Steven, I didn't say that. I said, 'That's going to happen; try not to get angry about it.'"

Exasperated, I said, "Well, what the hell good was that going to do?"

"It was meant to convey a message without imposing my own will."

"Fuck. *Like that's ever going to work.* Okay, I get it. So no one can remember his or her last life because of all of the killing that took place?"

"No. Well, not exactly. The memory problems didn't start until souls began inhabiting the bodies of other souls."

"What?"

"Well, this one particular being, he had been killed around a thousand times—"

Perking up, I said, "A thousand? Holy shit, that's a lot!"

"Steven, you have to keep in mind that most of this took place within the span of a few billion …"

"Years?"

"No, seconds."

"What?"

"Oh yes. It was all very short at the beginning. Life had not yet adapted to existing outside of heaven, and the lifespan of any one being was shorter than the blink of an eye."

"Well, why the hell didn't you send them down there with, like, battle armor or something? You know, like a shell or a capsule or whatever?"

"Steven, those things did not exist back then."

"I guess that's true. Wait, what were we talking about?"

"This one being who had been killed about a thousand times already."

I settled back in. "Oh yes, please go on."

"Thank you, Steven. So he came up here on the one thousand and first time and said, 'Look, life down there is pretty poor. And all we get to do is swim around and either starve or kill other people, and that's pretty nasty and brutish. And I'm getting a bit dizzy from having to go from here to there and back again. I mean, life's just too short. Can't you do something about all of that?'"

"And, I said, 'No, sorry. Do you want to go back again?' And he did. But he was apparently not heeding my advice, and he got quite angry at me. The next thing I knew, he had figured out how to split in two."

"No shit?"

"No, Steven. Somehow he had figured out how to replicate himself."

"Wow, that's great!"

"It was certainly interesting at the time. I had no idea that life could do that to itself."

"What do you mean?"

"Well, this was the first time for everything. I mean everything. No one had seen any behavior of any life anywhere outside of here, and at that time, there was nothing up here, either."

"So how did it happen?"

"I still do not know. Apparently, his anger about not being able to stay down there long enough—or to go longer without having to come back up here or to have more fun—was enough to make him angry, and he completely split in two."

Feels like that sometimes, I can tell you. "What happened to his double?"

"Nothing. There were no extra lives to fill it at the time, so it became just a hollow shell."

"And what happened to him?"

"He died. And he came up here and said, 'Ha, screw you! I figured out how to duplicate myself. Now send me back down there so I can inhabit that shell.'"

"And I said, 'Look, I can't. The shell is dead; you can't do anything with it. And, by the way, someone just ate it.'"

"So he said, 'Well, send me back, anyway, and I'll keep trying.' So I did."

"And then what happened?"

"Nothing. Well, a lot of the same for what seemed like an eternity. Souls killing and eating and killing and eating each other. I tell you, I had no idea that would result from how we started up here."

"What do you mean?"

"Steven, we started with a completely unified population of souls who were all delighted—dare I say enraptured—to be going off on a new adventure. Within a short period of time, that all changed to killing and eating. Some of them were even eating ten, twenty, fifty times what they needed to in order to survive."

"Why was that?"

"Apparently, they felt like I had trapped them into something, and to get back at me, they did what felt best to them, which was eating."

Suddenly there was a deep rumbling in my stomach. "Um, yeah, that sounds horrible." *I wonder if this is a bad time to ask about that steak sandwich?* "Wait, why do you keep referring to them as 'he' and 'him'? Were the first lives on earth males?"

"Of course not. They weren't anything. Different sexes had not been invented yet. But those beings that I was talking about eventually became males."

"Oh, I see. Wait, where were we?"

"Something else happening. Eventually, when something did happen, it was because a life was up here getting ready to go back, and that little guy down there was just about to start his splitting in two routine, and when I sent the life from up here, somehow it was able to combine with the other just at the point of division. And for the first time, there was something new down there?"

"What?"

"It wasn't much different. It was the same soul that was just up here, except that instead of being as fragile and weak as the other lives, it was slightly *more* robust. In fact, new life created in this manner lived twice as long as any of the other prior versions and never had to kill anyone to do so."

"Wow, so replication was a great improvement?"

"In some respects, yes. The main problem that the first new guy had was that the old guy, the one who had split in two to make the shell, well, he somehow got to believing that the new guy was really a part of him. That he had figured out how to duplicate himself for real—not just the shell part, but the life part too."

"And so what did he do?"

God shook his head. "It was truly awful. He tried to rule over the other one like it was his personal slave."

Sounds familiar. "That must have sucked."

"It did."

"So what happened? The new guy lived twice as long as his father?"

"Oh no. They wound up killing each other and had to start over."

Slapping my knee, I said, "Ha! Poetic justice, right?"

"No, Steven, that had not been invented yet, either."

"Oh, right. Wait, how the hell does this relate to why I can't remember anything?"

"That was the odd side effect of one being going down to inhabit the shell of another. Apparently, you cannot be born to another without dying to yourself first. Losing the past memories is part of that."

"Well, shit, that all sounds pretty awful."

"As it turns out, it was a great improvement. Souls who used to be mortal enemies down there started unwittingly benefiting each other by allowing life to progress with each new division. And because no one could remember what happened the last time, all of the past killings and collisions and everything else were forgotten."

"So everything worked out after that?"

"Of course not. The next thing they did was go to war against each other."

"Wait, I thought you said that—"

"Oh, Steven, you cannot kill hatred just by erasing memories. As it turns out, that was when souls first started to *teach* hate to each other."

Exasperated, I said, "Fuck, it's been around that long?"

Nodding slowly, he said, "I am afraid so."

Wow, we really are doomed. "So in the middle of all of this chaos, did any of them … um … um—"

"Kill themselves?"

"Yes."

"No, Steven, that did not start until much later."

"Well, why did you ask all of them if they wanted to go back?"

"That was at the very beginning of the beginning. We could have turned back at that point if we had wanted to and if enough lives had said that they did not want to go back."

Raising a hopeful eyebrow, I said, "Can we pull the plug now?"

"No."

Slumping down, I said, "*Great.* So what happened next?"

"The same thing that has always gone on down there—killings taking place for one reason or another and life trying to protect itself against the nature of the world."

"What did they do?"

"That was the birth of the second interesting development. Groups. Prior to that time, there was no concept of one group against another or exclusion of some for the benefit of others or anything else like that. Everyone down there was in it together, and they did not perceive any differences among them. When the war broke out, whole bands of lives got together in little groups. Safety was the idea, you see. They set themselves off in little areas away from everyone else. And then they started going out to ambush other souls who were not part of their group."

Frowning, I said, "That sounds awful."

"It certainly was. I never could have imagined how all of those souls could do that to each other."

"So we're all just rotten? I mean, we've been rotten from the beginning, and it's never going to change? That's it, isn't it?"

"No, Steven, that's not it at all."

"So why are you telling me this story?"

God threw up his arms and said, "I was trying to cheer you up!"

Great fucking idea. "Wait, was I down there?"

"Of course you were."

"What was I doing?"

"Pretty much the same thing as most everyone else. You were lying on the bottom of the ocean waiting for food particles to drop down to you."

Shocked, I paused a moment and said, "Really? That doesn't seem very ... um ... sporting, considering everything that was going on at the time."

Reflecting, he said, "You know, Steven, it is very interesting. You have always been an outlier, but ..."

"A what?"

"An outlier. You were on the outer part of the ball of energy that was the original formation for life. Some souls were packed on the inside, some nearer to the edges, and some made up the very outer surfaces. Like a ball, see?"

"Oh, I see."

"And you were near the outside, which typically produces a certain type of behavior—but in you, it never really did."

"Really?"

"No, Steven. In fact, you seem to have spent most of your existence on earth just lying on the bottom waiting for something to happen."

Shocked, I said, "Hey, wait just a second! That can't be true, is it?"

"I'm afraid it is."

"Why … well, I wonder why I didn't do anything. I mean, I've done things, right?"

"Sure, Steven, you have always done *things*. But in your last life as well as the ones before it, there has always been one consistent theme."

"What, missing myself?"

"Yes. You have never lived according to Steven and—"

Feeling myself start to overheat, I said, "Okay, wait just a g—, no, I guess that doesn't make sense to say at this point. Hey, what does that mean, anyway?"

"What?"

"You know, goddamn this, goddamn that?"

"How should I know? Most people tend to say that when they're mad at something, so I guess they think that I've damned whatever it is that they're talking about—or perhaps that I am going to damn it. I don't know for sure, but it's all pretty amusing to watch!"

"Oh, well, sorry, I'll try to stop saying that. Anyway, look, you've built a universe where the first act on earth was a murder—"

"I don't think that it was technically murder."

"What?"

"That first act. I don't think that it would meet the definition of murder. You know, the intentional killing of a human being with malice aforethought. Technically, it wasn't even a human. After all, you don't say that a deer was murdered by—"

"Okay, okay. Shit. I get it. But the first act of whatever the hell those things were ... hey, where is hell, anyway?"

"I can't quite answer that question."

"Why not? Is it, hey, is this all just a big joke and I'm already in hell? Fuck, I knew it!"

"No, Steven, it's not that. But what you think of as hell can be anywhere. Up here, down there, you name it. Right before you pulled that trigger, I'm sure that you would describe how you were feeling as something close to what has been described by others as hell."

"Boy, did I."

"And we have certainly had souls up here who felt like they were being tortured. You yourself weren't doing very well earlier."

I'm not much better now, bub.

"But do we have a specific place with a guy with a pitchfork?"

"Yes?"

"No. Steven, hell can be any place where your soul is prevented from fulfilling its purpose and where it is torn in two by the forces that oppose you."

"Well, how do I prevent that? And how do I know what my purpose is?" *Especially if you won't tell me.*

"That is entirely up to you. If you do not know yourself, hell can be everywhere, and you can find yourself dragged into it without even knowing it."

Man, I'll say. You should try wearing one of these stupid fucking suits. "So ... but we're definitely in heaven, right?"

"You are in the place people call heaven. Well, you are staying in the Suicides' Ward of heaven. We can't let you mix in with the other crowd, you know."

"Yeah, yeah, shit. I know that. Hey, where was I?"

"You were starting a lecture about the universe I created."

Climbing back up to my pulpit, I said, "Oh yeah. Let me tell you, when the first act of life is to kill other life and … hey, so those first lives were made out of what, exactly?"

"I told you. Air and water and a little bit of dirt mixed in."

"No kidding?"

"No. There was nothing else for them to be made out of."

"Oh, I suppose that's right. Wow! Little water bubble creatures smashing each other! That … well, that doesn't sound very tragic to me."

"Steven, those were still lives on earth."

Unimpressed, I said, "Oh yes, of course. And they had to come up here and talk to you and go back, and I'm sure that it was very, um, disruptive and all to be killed back then."

"It was. But you should have seen the sky."

"The sky?"

"Yes. It was spectacular! For eons, you could see a stream of souls at night flowing back and forth from heaven to earth. It was really magnificent."

"I'll bet. Hey, why can't you see that now?"

"There is too much artificial light down there, and the air quality is completely different."

"Yeah, I guess we've screwed things up pretty badly."

"I didn't say that. You just can't see the lights at night as well as you used to."

"But even if we screwed up the air quality on earth, why can't you see the souls from space?"

"You can. On the return trip."

My eyebrows raised. "Really?"

"Of course. When souls are fully recharged and leaving here, you can catch a glimpse of them. You just can't see them when they are leaving earth, because they are nearly used up. Haven't you ever seen the light emitting from a black hole?"

"No."

"Well, never mind, then."

"But if I shot myself, how did I have any energy left to get here?"

"Steven, you can never completely kill yourself. Your soul is programmed to come back here when a fractional portion of it is still left. So no matter what you do, you will not risk jeopardizing the return trip."

"But I mean—"

"No, Steven, we have never lost a soul in the universe."

Slightly relieved, I said, "Oh, that's good. Hey, can we look outside of here now? I mean, can we see the earth and everything else?"

"Yes, but you have to go out on the observation deck. From there, you can see everything."

Looking around excitedly, I said, "The observation deck? Where is it? Can I have Junior take me out there?"

"No. Sorry; we do not typically let suicides out on the observation deck. There is a risk of you jumping and all. You can understand, right?"

I was incensed again. "You have got to be fucking kidding."

"No, Steven, I am not. Sorry—rules are rules."

"Oh, this place fucking sucks!"

"Steven, don't feel so bad. I myself hardly go out there at all."

"Wait, why the hell not?"

"Well, there's not much to see. All of the action takes place when I get to talk to souls up here."

"But I mean, you're not even watching the earth or the lives you put there?"

"Not really. Junior keeps a good eye on things for me and lets me know if there is anything concerning going on."

Yeah, nice job you guys are doing up here.

"And, Steven, don't forget: I didn't put lives anywhere. Every soul on earth right now has chosen to be there."

Again unimpressed, I said, "Well, that's a nice story, but all of these rules that you have for the suicides are pretty harsh. I expected … well, at least a little compassion for what I had to go through. I may have killed myself, but did you know that I recycled and had an almost zero carbon footprint right before I, well, you know …"

Frowning, God said, "Steven, you had almost a zero footprint, period."

I was wounded again. "Hey!"

"Okay, okay. Jesus?"

Jesus entered wearing a Japanese Kabuki costume. "Yes, Boss?"

"Do we still have any of those cookies that we used to give out? Steven is upset that he is not being rewarded for what he did in his last life."

"Sorry, Master Steven—we're fresh out of cookies." Bowing, he backed through the doorway.

Smart-asses. "Okay. I get your point. So where were we?"

"We were talking about early life."

"Right. So then, when did things change?"

"Well, eventually, all of the churning in the water and the replicating and the mixing with the materials from below caused the shells we sent life back into to be fortified a bit, and they were very useful as shields in the battle."

I corrected him. "Shields? You mean scales."

"Well, you call them scales now, but the first scales were used as shields against oncoming kamikaze pilots."

"Holy shit! Wait, that one probably doesn't make sense to say, either."

"It really doesn't, Steven."

"Oh, sorry. So holy cow! Hey, cows come up here, don't they?"

"Of course they do."

"Who is responsible for … um, herding all of the cow souls back and forth?"

"Junior is, of course."

"And, you have other animals, right? Like lions and, well, if you have cows, then you must have bulls, and … what about, like eagles and things?"

"All of them."

"And he takes care of moving them in and out of here?"

"Yes."

"Wow! He must be a very busy guy."

"He is."

"But don't you have any other helpers up here besides him?"

"Not anymore. We used to have lots of souls up here to help with the process, but then they all started fighting with each other about the best way to do this and the best way to do that, and so we sent them back down to join the rest."

"Well, it looks like you could use some help up here."

"Steven, the help is needed on earth, not up here."

"Oh, I guess that makes sense. Hey, can we hurry up and finish the story?" *So I can go back to my room and figure out how to get out of here.*

"Finish what story?"

"The story you were … wait, what were we talking about?"

"Scales."

"Oh yeah, the scales. Wait, I think that I know what happened. The scales eventually gave way to fins, and the fins gave way to tails, and the tails, well, what did they do after that?"

"Some of them got fed up with the whole mess and jumped out of the water."

"To where?"

"Well, by then, all of the commotion and the dying and the growing used up a considerable amount of water. So there were little pockets of land all around, and some of the creatures decided that they had had enough of the warring, and they jumped onto land."

"And then what happened?"

"They died immediately, and we had to send them back to the water to start over."

"Shit. That's harsh."

"Steven, new beginnings often are. But eventually, some of the more industrious ones figured out that they had to spend time breathing out of water for short intervals before they could make the full jump onto land."

"And how long did that take?"

"A few billion years."

Hopefully, I asked, "Hey, was I … I mean, was I one of those first creatures who tried to jump out of the sea?"

"Of course not."

Groan.

"Steven, I told you, you have never stuck your neck out for anything. At that point, you were just following the masses, like always."

Getting to my feet, I said, "Okay, that's it. I'm pretty bored and also thoroughly depressed. I think that I need to go back to my room for a while."

"Oh, sure, Steven. I hope that you enjoyed the talk!"

"Yeah, terrific, thanks."

"Steven, by the way, have you figured out yet why you killed yourself?"

"Oh fuck. Was I still supposed to be doing that?"

"Yes."

"Shit. Okay. Roger that, I'll add it to the list, and I'll be back."

XI

Exhausted from the session, I threw myself on the bed and stared at the ceiling. "Fuck. I've still got to come up with this story about killing myself. Why the hell are they making me think about this? With all of those other souls killing each other from the very beginning of time, I can't see how my little act could really be that bad.

"Let's see. I can tell him that I … I wish I could get rid of this fucking suit that still doesn't work … and, why the hell does my stomach still hurt if I haven't eaten anything?

"Hey, I wonder where the zipper is on this suit. Shit, I wish that I hadn't smashed everything in my room. I could sure use the mirror now. Wait a minute, if I can figure out how to unzip this suit or take it off or whatever, maybe I can—"

Jesus suddenly said, "Steven."

Startled, I sat up and said, "Shit. What? Hey, what are you doing here?"

"Nothing. I just came to check on you. How are things going?"

"Oh, fine, just fine. Hey, Jesus, I have a question for you."

"What is it?"

"Does my suit, um, I mean, does my suit have like a zipper or something on it that I can't see? You know, like in the back?"

"No. Anything else?"

"Nope. Everything is shipshape. Thanks." And then he was gone.

"Shit. Now I'll be stuck with this thing forever. I guess I need to come up with a story. Let's see. I tried the whole misery-of-life thing and they didn't buy that. What else can I say that will sound clever and insightful?

"Hey, that's it! I'll tell them that I killed myself so that I could come up here and report on what a rotten place earth has become and that we need a new planet! Yeah, that's it! Surely they must know about all of the global warming and pollution and everything else that's gone on down there. And I can talk about that, because it has nothing to do with me! That's everyone else's fault! Yeah, that's it! I'll go in and ask for a new planet!"

Raising my hand to prematurely cut him off, I said, "Look, God, it's all fine and good to sit here telling history lessons about insignificant amounts of ooze playing Dungeons & Dragons in the primordial soup. But there are some seriously bad things going on down there right now."

Sharply, he said, "Steven, don't give me that. You sound just like the first monkey to climb out of a tree. And before you ask, no, you were not the first monkey to climb out of a tree."

"What do you mean?"

"You got out of the boat, and you did not go all the way."

"Huh?"

"Steven, look, I really don't want to do all of the hard work for you up here. But I can tell you that you set off on an adventure when you were younger, and when your family died, you did not bother to go on with the quest."

"What quest?"

"The quest to find out who you were. Steven. Why didn't you get married?"

"Well, I … um, I guess I never got around to it."

"Oh, bullshit! You didn't get married because you were trying to prove a point."

"I … well … yes, I was! I wanted my parents to know that you don't have to have kids to be a good person."

"And …?"

"Well, I didn't."

"Yes, Steven, but you missed the whole point. You don't have to have kids."

"Wait, wait just a minute. What was all that go forth and multiply stuff?"

"Steven, people were writing that a long time ago, when the human population on earth was much smaller. It made a good deal of sense to say that back then."

Slapping my leg, I said, "Okay, so I was right!"

God nodded and said, "For you, yes. And you missed it entirely. Steven, you didn't have kids, but what did you do?"

"I … well … I had a job, and—"

God frowned deeply. "Steven, don't try to fool me. We've seen the tapes. You sat in your little apartment and only left long enough to go to a job that you hated so you could afford to pay your rent, and then you came home and did what?"

Sweat droplets began forming on my forehead. "I … um … I guess I played a lot of Internet games. I think I remember reading a book or two. And I had a … well, my gym membership had expired by then, but—"

"Steven, you spent nearly all of your time at home watching Internet porn."

Fuck me! Jumping to my feet, I said, "Now I get it! I'm being punished up here for being an Internet porn sinner? Is that it? Does this all have to do with the magazine in my room? Look, it was an accident, and it sucked, anyway. So—"

"Steven, you still do not get it. Do you know why Internet porn is a sin?"

Taking a step back I said, "Because it's … well, I guess it exploits people?"

"Did that shotgun take every bit of sense out of your head?"

"No. I mean … well, why don't you tell me?"

"Steven, you spent the same number of years sitting in your room playing with yourself as you did riding up and down the elevator in your building wanting to talk to Emily."

"So?"

"So why didn't you talk to her? Because you didn't want a real relationship to interfere with your jerk-off sessions? Nice going. Way to think it through."

Slowly sitting down again, I said, "I, well … okay, so Internet porn is a sin, and I'm a rotten individual, and that's why I was alone and killed myself."

"Steven, you are still missing it, and you are not getting off that easily up here."

Hard to do, Chief, without a dick.

"Nothing is a sin by itself."

"Really?"

"No. Do you even know why we call things sins up here?"

"I … um …"

"Of course you don't. Sinning is missing the mark in your life. We do not keep a magic tablet of things that people should and shouldn't do in every single life. But there are things that people generally do down there that tend to miss the mark for the types of lives they are living. In your case, you didn't want to get married because you didn't want to have kids, but you also wanted more than anything to spend your life with someone else, and you didn't bother to do the work to see if you could get it done because there was an easy outlet on your desk."

Leaning back, I said, "So then tell me this, pal. If you don't write down lists of sins up here, what's with the whole Ten Commandments thing?"

"Steven, you should understand by now that the stories people tell down there are about trying to make an earth that works well for everyone. A particular list of rules is just one way of trying to tell everyone that if they do or don't do a certain thing, it is going to make life generally worse for everyone else."

"Well, I didn't see *Internet porn* on the list of the Ten Commandments."

"Steven, Internet porn is the very definition of coveting your neighbor's ass."

"*What?*"

"That person you are watching on the Internet is not yours and will never be yours. That is someone else's ass. And if you want to have one of your own, you have to go out and get it. You can't just sit around in your apartment doing the same things you were doing when you were stuck in your parents' basement."

Throwing up my hands in surrender, I said, "Okay, okay, I get it. I'm a wuss. I should have gone out and gotten my own ass. I'll be sure to write that down and not do it again."

God shook his head and said, "Unlikely. Steven, you would do better to get it tattooed on yourself next time. That way, you wouldn't forget what you were doing."

"Tattooed? Really?"

"Sure, why not? It's the same as moving out of your parents' house and refusing to have kids."

"Wait, those are related?"

"Of course. They are both ways to show the world that you are not going to play by the rules. But, Steven, if you get out of the boat, you have to go all the way."

"I still don't get that one."

"There are generally two paths down there—the one that has been laid by others before you and the one that you will lay yourself. In every life, you have to choose whether to follow the rules or follow yourself. You did not do either, and that is what killed you. That is why you are just like the monkey."

Searching, I said, "Because ..."

"He got bored with everything one day and decided to climb out of the tree and show up his family by walking away. Yes, on two legs."

"Well, that was a good thing, right?"

"I'm not sure. He got killed the very next day."

"Really?"

"Yes. He was out on his own, without the protection of the trees or his family and walking around like an idiot, and a lion ate him."

"Well, the lion survived, right?"

"Yes, and now they are both living in cages. Not a good ending for either of them."

"Oh. Well, so how did we get from there to here?"

"It took awhile, but another primate heard about what the other one did and thought it was a good idea and did the same."

I chuckled to myself. "Funny. My mother always used to ask me if my friend jumped off a bridge, would I do the same. Oh, sorry—go on."

"Well, this one was able to beat the lions to an empty cave and hid out there until they went away. He survived long enough to go off and attract a runaway female, and blammo, a few million years later, humans arrived."

"Well, that was a good thing, right?"

"I'm not sure. You went from living in trees to living in a cave. From up here, we can't really tell which is better." Then God called, "Hey, Jesus!"

Jesus bounded in wearing German lederhosen. *"Jawohl!"*

"Is it better to live in a tree or in a cave?"

"They both suck." And then he clogged his way out the door.

Turning back to God, I said, "What's with him, anyway?"

"Oh, he has a lot on his mind and has a lot to do."

Nodding and rubbing my chin in reflection, I said, "Yeah, and he died for our sins, right?"

"Yes."

"Incidentally, what exactly does that mean?"

"Steven, you killed him."

Defensively, I replied, "I … what? No, I didn't kill him. Oh, you mean the people who were around when he died killed him."

"No, Steven, I mean you killed him."

"Me? What? That's … no … there's no way that's possible."

"Well, you didn't put a nail into his flesh, and you didn't sentence him to death. But, Steven, you were part of the world back then that didn't want to accept his message. You weren't ready for it, and so he died."

Still confused, I said, "And … so … sorry for stretching this out a bit, but you know, this is all new information to me."

"I'll bet."

"But … um, so the sin was killing him? He died so we could kill him? Is that how it works?"

"No, Steven, the sin was that the world judged him and said that they were not interested in the message, in the possibility of the message. The sin was the same one that has always been around."

"And, that was …?"

"Fear, Steven. The fear that things might change if people started to believe in the power of all creation."

"Oh yeah, I guess I can see that. Wow, what a tough racket! I'll bet that getting killed for all life on earth is a hard one to get over."

"It was. At least the first time."

"The *what?*" I exclaimed.

"The first time that he was killed by fellow humans. That one was particularly hard for him to deal with. After that, it got easier."

Throwing up my hands again, I said, "Wait, wait just a minute. Are you telling me that he's been back to earth more than once?"

"Oh, sure. We send him back every few hundred years."

"Wait, who's 'we'?"

"Ted and I."

"*Who in the bloody blue fuck is Ted?*" I shouted.

"He is the guy who takes over up here when Junior is down on earth."

"You are shitting me."

"No, Steven."

"How the hell did Ted—whoever the hell he is—get that job?"

"Well, about a thousand years ago, we were looking for someone to take Junior's place while he was gone, and Ted happened to be around and seemed like a good enough soul to handle the task, and—"

"Wait, who the fuck is Ted?"

"Steven, I already told you. He is the guy who takes over—"

"No, no, I mean, what makes him so special that he gets that job?"

"Steven, I don't know if you would find it so special if you had the task of overseeing all of the souls in heaven."

Coming to my feet again, I said, "Oh fuck yes I would! How long is Junior gone when he goes back down there?"

"Usually twenty to thirty years. Sometimes less than that. He's never made it past thirty-three, though."

"Why not?"

"He gets killed. That's his job. He gets caught up in some strife or another, you know, trying to help people see that they don't have to kill or rob or whatever it is, and he usually winds up getting stabbed or shot. He was hit by a bus the last time he went back."

I said, "Wait, what the fuck is going on? How can you tell me that he can go back down to earth as the Son of God and the most important being in the universe and get hit by a bus?"

God just shrugged. "It happens."

"But how does it happen? And why? And why don't you stop it from happening? I mean, we could use a guy like that around these days."

"Steven, buses run over people. That's the way it goes. The only way to keep that from happening is to get rid of the buses. And I don't think that's going to—"

I stomped sharply. *"No, no, no, no, no!* Look, if you are going to send him back to earth, you need to make damn sure that he doesn't get killed by some fucking bus and that he gets to … you know, do whatever he's supposed to be doing down there!"

"Steven, we don't work like that."

"Why the hell not?"

"I told you. It is not our world to interfere with."

"Then why the hell do you send him down there in the first place? Look, everyone would be a lot better off if you'd let him go down there and either live to be two hundred years old—"

"Steven, people do not live that long."

"Well, for however long it takes to set everyone straight."

"Steven, we've been waiting for that to happen since the very beginning. I hardly think that giving him a longer life span would make much of a difference."

"It would, I'm telling you! You just need to signal to everyone that he's coming, and they'll get everything ready for him, and then he can tell everyone what's what."

"Steven, the last time he did that, he was crucified."

Defeated again, I sat down and said, *"Shit.* You're right. So what's the point of him going back, anyway? And why doesn't he … I mean, even if he only gets to live to thirty or so, why doesn't he go around with his laser vision or whatever superpowers he has down there and just zap all of the assholes off the planet?"

"Steven, first of all, Junior does not have laser vision. When he goes back to earth, he has to play by the same rules you do. Well, almost the same rules. But even if he could zap all of the people you seem to think are so undesirable, all they would do is come up here and complain to Ted that they were zapped out of existence by Junior. Now that wouldn't work at all. We already get enough souls up here complaining about the unnecessary killings going on down there."

"So why the hell does he go back to earth?"

"To get killed. To show everyone that the flesh they cling to down there is only part of the story. To show people that their souls should not be terrified or controlled by the bodies they are stuck in at the time."

In total bewilderment, I said, "Oh. I guess that make sense in a twisted sort of way. Wow. What a load to bear! Why does he even bother to go if all he's going to do is get killed?"

"Steven, it's the only vacation he gets."

XII

Eager not to get stuck with another boring science lecture, I asked, "So what's with Junior and the soccer stuff, anyway? He always seems to be going to a game somewhere."

Chuckling, he said, "Oh, Steven, it is a little-known fact that Junior was the best soccer player in his village. Well, in any village, ever."

"Wow! I had no idea."

"Most people don't."

"Well, if he was such a great soccer player, why didn't he spend more time doing that instead of, you know, getting run over by buses and things?"

In a serious tone, he said, "Steven, the world needs Junior for more than just soccer. Anyway, you show me how to make him spend time doing things other than what he decides to do, and I will show you how to make an Internet porn sinner not shoot himself in the face."

Gulp. "Okay, look. I understand that I killed myself, and that was a sin. Sorry about missing the great potential of my life, and sorry for letting all of mankind down. But look, I already knew that we were living in a shitty place, and now all I've heard is that the souls that you send back do nothing but kill each other and have been doing so since the dawn of time. Then you tell me that Junior doesn't even get to do what he really wants to do. So why don't we just end the whole thing now? I think it's safe to say that we are not going to get the message, and I don't think that my little existence the next time around is going to change things."

"Steven, we can't do that."

"Why not? When does it all end?"

God said, "Jesus?"

Flying through the door, he said, "Yeppers."

God frowned at him and said, "Jesus, are you wearing Mardi Gras beads?"

Backpedaling a few steps, he said, "Oh, um, yes. I had to, well, someone was calling my name down there, and it seemed really urgent, and I had to go see what was going on and, well, it turns out that it was just some lady at the end of a particularly interesting night. No worries."

"In any event, Steven wants to know when it is all going to end."

Puffing his chest, Jesus said, "Steven, life on earth will end when every single soul has had the chance to feel the glowing magnificence of all possibility in creation and when all life is treated with the utmost dignity and respect."

Fuck, we'll never get there.

Jesus bolted through one of the walls and was gone. Settling things down again, God said, "Steven, don't mind him; he's just grumpy."

"But is that right? Is what he said right?"

"More or less. Or if that never happens, we will just end things when life is done living."

Feeling a faint bit of hope, I said, "So then, hypothetically speaking, if I get all of the humans to say that life isn't worth living, we're done?"

Firmly, he said, "No, Steven, all life."

"But I mean, what if humans were to blow up, like, thousands of nuclear bombs, and life itself was wiped out? That would do it, wouldn't it?"

"No, Steven, all life."

"Oh, so we have to pollute the oceans too?"

"No, Steven."

Exasperated, I said, "Well, when can we get the damn thing over with? I mean, I thought that if I died, that was it."

"That was it. For your last life. But that's not the end of the story."

"But I thought that people, you know, followed Junior so that they could get into heaven and see you, and that was the end of it."

"Well, getting here does signify the end of something. But no one ever said when it all ends."

Motherfucker!

Waiving a finger at me again, he continued, "And, Steven, if humans decide to off themselves and destroy the air and pollute the oceans and do the rest of the things in your disturbed little mind, then all we are going to have up here is a giant waiting list for souls to go back as insects, bacteria, and vent worms."

"Vent worms?"

Lightening up, he said, "Oh yes, quite magnificent creatures! They can live at the bottom of the ocean in very extreme temperatures and subsist off of the bacteria created by the energy spewing out of the earth."

Yeah, fucking fascinating.

"We have a whole population of vent worm souls who are very content to keep going back as vent worms. And I don't think that any of them are going to give up their spots in line, so it looks like the rest of you will have to choose something else."

"Wait just a minute! Are you telling me that … well … hypothetically now, and stay with me on this—"

His deep frown set in again.

"Let's say that I go back to earth and survive the next time, which of course I will do, for sure. Are you telling me that I couldn't come back here and choose to be a vent worm?"

"Not likely. They are a stubborn breed, and most of the ones that stopped on that rung of the ladder won't willingly give up their spot for an interloper."

"An interloper?"

"A soul that jumps back and forth between species. We have a bunch of them, but it is always subject to availability. When there are no open spots, you have to choose something else."

"Well, why the hell can't I, as a human, the highest form of life, simply tell another lower form of life to grow up and get out of the way so that I can experience something different?"

"Steven, all life that participates down there—which, based on your last life, did not include you—has the right to participate however it chooses. Some life-forms decided to stop at a certain level; some go on to other levels. Some souls stayed back in the sea when everyone else was jumping ship. To them, the sea is their kingdom, and you, as a human, are certainly not the highest form of life. You wouldn't last five minutes down there with all of the other fish."

Rising to the affront, I said, "Oh, you don't think so?"

"Steven, you are a panicker … and a quitter."

Ouch. "Hey, that's pretty harsh! What happened to judge not … and whatever the rest of it is?"

"Who do you think gets to judge?"

"Oh. I guess that's right."

"And anyway, I am not judging you."

"That ... um ... that sounded pretty close to a judgment."

"No, Steven, in the classical sense, judgment is the final act. I am not saying that you will always be a quitter, but you cannot deny the fact that you quit last time, and if we were to end the world right now—as you seem so interested in doing—that is what you would be. In fact, if we handed out scores right now, you would be in dead last."

"Shit. Seriously?"

"Yes, Steven. But don't worry. By the time it is all over, the last could be first, and the first could be last. We cannot know that right now, so we do not issue a judgment in the final sense of the word."

Sarcastically, I replied, *"Great.* Lots to look forward to. But hey, so if I lose my spot in line by jumping around from species to species, why would anyone ever do it?"

"Why would a monkey decide to climb down from a tree? For a change of scenery."

"Now wait just a minute! I may have, in my most recent life, been a quitter, and I may not be the brightest person in the universe, but I happen to know that life on earth evolved not just because other species wanted a change of scenery."

"That is true, Steven."

"I mean, I was a human last time, and humans exist because only the fittest survive, right?"

"Not really."

"Really?"

"Really. Steven, look at you. You are the sloth of living world."

Again, ouch.

"You basically rolled over on your life, and no one was beating down your door to eat you alive. How do you think the sloth lives, anyway, if only the fittest survive?"

"Well, okay, so maybe that's not exactly it. But the different species down there, I mean, some of them developed speed or night vision or wings or whatever to get an advantage over prey, and that's about surviving by being fit, right?"

"Steven, it is not *just* about survival down there. Life does not subsist on bread alone."

"Huh?"

Brushing my ignorance away, he said, "Never mind. About that 'fittest' business, it is true that some life-forms developed new traits to dominate others. But many, many life-forms grew wings or developed the ability to see in the dark because they were trying to escape being killed by other things, not because they were trying to gain an advantage over the things below them. The sloth survives because other creatures leave it alone and go on to other things long enough for little baby sloths to be born. If every creature developed new abilities just so it could eat everything below it, we would only have one species left. And then you would be stuck as a human for all of eternity."

Shocked, I said, "*Shit.* That's harsh."

"But that is also the reason why we have to send you back."

"It is? Wait, how does that relate to the sloth?"

"If a creature endeavors to develop some new characteristic so that it will have a longer or better, or at least more interesting life, that new characteristic almost never winds up benefitting the one who started the work. Just like the story of the monkey I told you. The first one out on the new limb quite often dies a quick and miserable death."

"So why the hell would anything try to change from what it was?"

"So that the lives that come after it will have a better chance than it did. That is why creatures have offspring."

Yeah, except humans, who have offspring so that they can spend their kids' lives making the kids sorry for ever being born.

"Steven, we have to send you back because you quit and broke the chain."

"What chain?"

"The chain where every being is a part of helping life continue. The chain where every soul participates in the process between there and here. You quit on the children who came after you, you quit on the primates who worked so that you could be down there in the first place. You quit on the first amphibian who showed everyone the path out of the water. Most of all, however, you quit on yourself."

"Wait, how did I do that?"

"You sat here not too long ago and told me that you wanted to go back as a human. That is, after all, why you were down there. And, Steven, you didn't finish the job."

Shit. "Okay, okay, okay, did I tell you that I was sorry about that?"

Ominously, he replied, "Yes, but I am hoping that after enough time, you will actually start to be sorry about it."

Laughing nervously, I said, "Well, time heals all things, right?"

Firmly, he retorted, "Not if you do not get your act together and deal with what you have done."

Grasping, I said, "I just … I mean, I don't understand why I have to be punished for it."

"Steven, what do you mean?"

"Singling me out as the one who has to go back as a human when there are all of those other things that I could be!"

"Steven, that is not *your* punishment."

"What?"

"You go back as a human, because it was the world that failed you. That is the message of a suicide. To pay penance, everyone agreed to give suicides the first available slots to go back as humans so the world can try to treat you better."

"Oh, that's fucking ridiculous! What a lousy gift."

Warming up again, he said, "You are actually quite fortunate. If there was ever a waiting list to go back as a human—which there never is—you would get bumped right to the top of the list. That is pretty lucky."

"Waiting list?"

"Yes. I told you about that earlier with the vent worms."

Fucking vent worms!

"If there aren't enough spots down there for a particular species, and you want to go back as one of them, you get put on a waiting list. Some souls decide to pick a top three or four just to make sure that they are not stuck up here for too long. But you are lucky. When you are ready, there will be no waiting in line for you. If you were going back as a bear, that might be tough. If you were going back as certain types of fish, that might be tough right now too. But there is no line for humans!"

"Waiting list. Holy shit! I had no idea."

"Yes, Steven. And it is a constant juggling act for us. Fortunately, every soul down there, present company excluded, works pretty hard to keep the process going so that we can get souls in and out of here. Seriously, Steven, even salmon are busting their asses down there to help us keep the salmon population up here on the move. You just sat and festered in your own waste and did not contribute at all."

Annoyed, I said, "God, seriously, who cares about the salmon? I don't even like fish."

"Well, we do! And they certainly like being themselves. That's why they go through all of that hard work to keep the species going."

"Yeah, like a bunch of fools ice-skating uphill. All of that work seems completely ridiculous to me."

"I'll bet it does. Most people like you detest hard work. But that's really the only way to get where you want to go down there. Rolling over and waiting for someone else to do it for you won't cut it. And it doesn't help us move things along at all, either."

"So are you telling me that I should have had kids? Or a pet? Or a tree? Or what?"

"Of course not. Steven, life happens whether you participate in it or not. But if you are not going to help us get souls out of here, you could at least do us the courtesy of helping to make the world the rest of the souls inhabit a hopeful place by doing your part."

"And what the fuck was my part?"

Plainly, he said, "Apparently, last time, it was to show the world that it is okay to throw in the towel."

Oh, this all fucking sucks! "Can I go back to my room now?"

Slumping down on my bed, I whined, "Jesus, what the hell am I doing here?"

"Healing."

"I'm not healing! I'm just getting lectured about a whole world that is much more interesting than I ever was. And I still feel like shit. In fact, my stomach is killing me! Are you sure there is no bathroom up here?"

"Steven, you don't have a stomach. That pain you feel is all in your head. And anyway, I can see that you are not getting much better."

"How? Oh, because my face still looks like hamburger meat?"

"Yes."

"Great." Feeling betrayed by everything at that point, I said, "Hey, Jesus, why did you tell him that I had a porno magazine in my room? I thought that my room was, you know, my secret place or something like that."

Frowning at me, he said, "Steven, are you still worried about that? Look, no one cares if you have a porno magazine in your room up here. The point, however, is that you are in heaven, and you are supposed to be focusing on healing the broken parts of your soul so that you can go back down there and make it through your life."

"So why the hell are we spending time talking about all of this other crap?"

"Who knows? Steven, they are your sessions. If you are not interested in what he is talking about, you can ask anything you want. But you are supposed to be figuring out what went wrong and getting better. And along those lines, you could take a lesson or two from nature."

"What, you mean all of that garbage about species trying to improve themselves so that their offspring have a better chance at the future?"

"Well, there's that. But certain things happen in nature just because groups want to separate from other groups."

My ears pricked up. "Seriously?"

"Yes. Steven, blue jays became blue jays not because there is some wondrous difference between them and the other birds. Blue jays became blue jays because they did not want to be robins."

"No shit?"

"No, Steven. And marlins do not want to be sailfish, and monkeys do not want to be chimps. Certain behaviors and traits happen just because souls want to be different from others or because they want to be perfectly alone."

"Wow, I never thought of it that way!"

"Even the planets like to be alone and don't want to be like their neighbors. And, Steven, you came up here wondering about language and whether they spoke your language in heaven—"

Fearfully, I asked, "You heard that?"

"Yes, I was in the room at that time. Steven, certain languages around the world developed because groups didn't want their neighbors to hear what they were saying or because they wanted to differentiate themselves from the group they just left."

"Well, that is all very interesting, but I just don't see how it fits—"

"Steven, you moved out of your parents' house because you were tired of having to hide porno magazines from your mother, so you went out and got your own place."

"I ... um, I guess I can see how that's related."

Blazing his eyes at me, he said, "But, Steven, the part where you fucked up is that you didn't have the courage to finish the game. You just sat there like a pussy and kept doing the same things that you were sneaking down to the basement to do at your parents' house." *Let me tell you, it stings when Jesus calls you a pussy for the first time.* "But you were all alone. You were master of your own universe and could have done anything, and you just kept on fucking around with the same childish things."

Meekly, I said, "So I should have gotten rid of the porn and gotten laid more, is that it?"

"Steven, you should have grown a set of balls and gone out to do whatever the hell it is that you wanted to do in the world. Nothing was stopping you, and you wanted to do things and just sat on your ass and didn't even try. You may have made it to age thirty-four, but you were still behaving like a complete infantile moron. And if that's all you were going to do once you made it out on your own, you probably should have just stayed in the basement jerking off."

"I ... um, I'm sorry about that."

"Steven, don't apologize to me. I am here to help if I can, but I can't make you grow up and *stop fucking off.*"

Completely leveled, I said, "Well, I will, I guess. So … at this point, I think that we're good, and I'll just sit here and think about things and then go back and talk to God some more."

And Jesus flew up through the ceiling and was gone. "Wow, and I thought that he was supposed to be the nice one."

XIII

With slight concern in his voice, God said, "Welcome back, Steven. How are you feeling today?"

"Well, I'm … I think that I'm doing better. Junior and I had a long talk, and I understand a little more where it was that I went wrong."

"That's good, Steven!" he encouraged.

"But he was also pretty pissed off."

God cocked his head and said, "What do you mean?"

"Well, he was cursing all over the place. You should have heard the stuff that came out of his mouth!"

God furrowed his brow at me. "You don't say, Steven."

"In any event, don't mind that. The last time he went back, he was an Irish priest, and we have been trying to wean him off the cursing ever since."

I said, "Man, he sure is … um, energetic."

Nodding knowingly. "Yes, he is."

"And then he gave me this whole big lecture about getting rid of childish things, and—"

God raised a curious eyebrow. "He said that?"

"Yes, he did. And I get the part about not watching porn and going out to, um, you know—"

He grinned. "Find your own ass?"

"Yes. That. And I know that when I was out of the confines of my parents' house, I should have done something. But you know, it's hard to recognize what childish things are and what they aren't. I mean, I guess I still don't understand what a childish thing is or why I have to get rid of it. In case you don't know it, Internet porn is everywhere. So it's a little hard to know that it might cause problems."

"Steven, that is why they call it a temptation."

"Oh. I guess that makes sense. Junior also said that creatures have developed traits just to get away from each other and that some languages developed in the same way."

"Yes."

"But what about that whole Tower of Babel thing?"

He chided, "Come on, Steven."

"That … I mean … that didn't happen?"

"Well, people are always trying to build towers up to heaven, but they crumble and fall down, and then everyone starts back over at the ground floor. But no, that did not happen."

"Do you think that they do so because heaven is too far away now?"

Thoughtfully, he said, "Perhaps."

"Well, should we move it back to where it was?"

Shaking his head, he said, "No, Steven, that is not a very good idea. When you moved out of your parents' house, would you have wanted them to move into the apartment next to you?"

"Oh, fuck no! That would have been awful! Like having the Death Star park next door to—"

"What?"

"Oh, you probably don't know *Star Wars* yet, either. Never mind."

"Well, whatever that is, it is the same problem for us. We are in a good spot now. Humans are free to roam the universe without being disturbed by our little goings-on."

"But then, where did all of those other stories come from? And was I … I mean, was I supposed to be following one of them?"

"Absolutely."

"Which one?"

"Which one did you like the best?"

"I … well, I guess I never really thought about it. My parents were always pretty lax about going to church and all, and … hey, wait a minute. So there's no story that everyone is supposed to be following?"

"Not as far as I know. Steven, from up here, no one has a monopoly on the truth."

"But, well … then why do people spend so much time killing each other over their religious differences?"

"Likely the same reason why they killed each other before there were religious differences to have."

"Fear?"

"Panic, Steven—sheer panic. People are afraid, and when they become afraid, they kill to make themselves feel better."

"That doesn't make much sense."

Shaking his head, he agreed, "No, it really doesn't."

"So what do you do with them?"

"Who?"

"People who kill other people?"

Jesus stomped into the room cursing. God smiled at him and said lovingly, "Hello, Son. How are things going out there?"

Jesus snapped back, "Don't give me that. You want to change jobs? Come on. Then you can see what I have to deal with for a change. Oh, hi, Steven. How are things going in here?"

God said, "Fine, just fine." Jesus stomped back out.

"Wow, he seems pretty uptight! And he was pretty rude to you just then."

Nodding, he said, "He gets that way sometimes. Don't worry about it. He's just mad because of the dinosaurs."

"The what?"

"The dinosaurs. He's still mad at me for making him give them up."

"Wait, you did *what?*"

"I made him give up the dinosaurs. I told him that they had to go. They were taking up too much room and eating everything in sight. There was no way for other lives to grow in that atmosphere, so I told him that he had to let them go.

"And you should have seen him, Steven. Inconsolable for eons. Cursed me this way and that. But as you know, sometimes you have to give up the things you played with as a child in order to move on to more important things."

Now reeling in confusion, I said, "Wait, wait, wait just a minute! You're telling me that dinosaurs were Junior's childish things?"

"Yes. And he used to have a blast with them too. But they were becoming a menace and were stopping all life from moving on. Ultimately, they had to go."

I said, "Well, why did you have them in the first place?"

Waving his hand dismissively, he said, "Oh, Steven, a good childish thing can be a great benefit at first. It was a good way to pass the time while other life started to develop. The dinosaurs also helped Junior to ease into the life he eventually had to live, and they gave him a distraction until he was ready to face it. And it turned out to be a great way to distribute that petroleum that you guys all love so much."

"Wow! Hey, how come you guys couldn't figure out how to keep the dinosaurs *and* have other life move on?"

"You sound just like him. He swore up and down that he could make things work as long as he could keep his playthings. Swore that they wouldn't get in the way, that he had a handle on them, and that everything would be just fine. But everyone says that. And, Steven, you have to get rid of certain things when you are ready to move on. You have to make room for the new, and getting rid of the childish things is the easiest way to do that. It also signals that you are ready to be an adult and deal with your world."

My spirits picked up again. "So, um, are you going to do the same thing to us? I mean, what you did to the dinosaurs?"

God shook his head. "No, Steven. You are not getting out of it that easily."

Still trying, I said, "But you know, we're mucking things up pretty badly."

"Well, that may be true, but you have a lot more potential than the dinosaurs ever did. Don't worry; we are not going to give up on you anytime soon."

Hollowly, I said, "*Great.* So if I have to go back, then I have to be a child again. If I am a child, I get to have childish things. So when do I have to get rid of them?"

"Steven, you do not have to do anything. But if you want to stop being a child, you do have to give up your childish things. In your case, last time you never made that decision. And it wound up killing you."

"So how do I know that? I mean, when I'm ready to stop being a child?"

He simply replied, "If you do not know yourself, you will never find out the answer to that question. Some people, in fact, never stop being children."

"I, um, I'm sure that's right. Now, I asked Junior this question earlier, but are you guys sure that there is no bathroom up here? Since we've been talking, the pain in my stomach has gotten worse, and I, um, I think I need to find a bathroom somewhere."

"Steven, that is all in your head. There are no bathrooms up here, and you do not have any food to digest, anyway."

"Well, okay, if you're sure. But I was hungry earlier, and now my stomach hurts and … hey, why isn't there any food up here to eat, anyway?"

"Steven, food is life. We do not make lives up here sit around to be the food for other lives. Everyone is free to proceed on their own journey."

"Oh, that makes sense. But, what was that about cookies earlier?"

"Cookies are not life."

"Well, then, I guess bread isn't either. Why can't I get any of that up here?"

"Because we don't grow wheat in heaven."

"But you used to give out cookies up here?"

A playful smirk spread across his face. I said, "Okay, okay. I get it. So where were we?"

"Junior. Don't mind him too much. He is also trying to be a bit more forceful with new human arrivals to make up for what Ted did last time."

"What did Ted do?"

"As it turns out, Ted is a bit of a softie. Every time he is up here, he likes to push self-esteem and self-awareness. After his last round up here, humans on earth experienced a wave of self-entitlement, and it ticked Junior off something fierce."

"I can see how that could happen."

"As a result, Junior is trying to be a bit firmer. Don't let it preoccupy your journey up here. Everything will be corrected shortly."

"I won't. But if Ted is so rotten at what he does, why do you let him do that job?"

"Steven, he is not rotten at his job. He is a bit of a softie. So what? A bubble of undeserved self-worth once in a millennium does not hurt anything in the long run. It all evens out in the end."

"Well, that may be. But look, from everything you've been telling me, I get the idea that pretty much everyone is miserable in this whole thing."

"That is not true. There are plenty of people down there who are enjoying their lives, and there are multitudes of other species that are very, very happy doing what they are doing right now. Bears greatly enjoy doing bear things, fish greatly enjoy doing fish things, trees are probably having more fun than anyone, and—"

Exasperated, I said, "But they're all eating each other! You said it yourself. Life eats life. I mean, look, you can't deny the fact that bears eat fish or that beavers eat trees or that lions eat gazelles or that parents feed on their kids or—"

"So?"

"Well, it's all just awful! The whole world is feeding off of itself, and it is very, very frightening and horrific!"

"Steven, that's just the way it goes. Life cannot survive without eating other life. Well, that's technically not correct, but after this much time, I am pretty convinced that even if we were to put you all in a garden of boundless nonlife to enjoy, you would still figure out a way to muck it up."

"Great. And I'm the sucker who has to go back and bear witness to all of the horror down there."

"Why are you so upset about having to go back as a human? Lots of souls up here are delighted to do so. Your father was."

"Oh, fuck that! Look, I don't want to be like my father."

"You don't have to be."

"Well, why would you even bring that up?"

"I thought that you would find comfort in knowing that one of your relatives was back down there voluntarily to witness the horror, as you put it."

Longingly, I said, "Yeah, but look, you sent him to Italy! I mean, if I could go to Italy and paddle a gondola and drink wine and eat sausage all day, I'd be pretty damn happy to go back as well."

"Steven, people in Italy still have to work and struggle and do everything that you are going to have to do."

Staring at the ground and shaking my head, I said, "Yeah, but it's different. I mean, I just know that it's better."

"Steven, no one has it better or worse than anyone else."

I looked up sharply. "Oh, now that's just not true! There are humans down there lying in ditches and being made into slaves and being forced to prostitute themselves, and humans are blowing each other up and killing each other for no good reason. And then there are others living in big fat houses with big fat luxuries, and they don't get stuck in all of the carnage and mess and just sit and watch everyone else have to suffer."

"Steven, everyone spends exactly one life down there, each time. And that is a debt that everyone has to settle with the house at some point."

"Yeah, so?"

"So how you choose to spend your life is up to you. The earth you live on has been there the whole time, as have all of the resources you take from it. The only thing that changes is you and how you choose to participate in what is available down there. However, the conditions you find yourselves in on earth are determined by you, and not by us."

"So?"

"So if you are so upset about how things are going, why don't you go back and make life better for everyone?"

"Oh, fuck that! That's not my responsibility. Look, Chief, I killed myself to get out of there because of all of the shit that was done to me and because there was absolutely no way to pick up the pieces and make any of it better."

"So shooting yourself in the face was the solution?"

"Yeah. Bloody brilliant too! And not soon enough!"

"But now you have to go back and do it all again."

Hollowly, I said, "I ... well, I wasn't expecting that part."

Then he yanked the trapdoor. "Did you think it was going to be that easy?"

Shaking my head and trying to regain some footing, I said, "Well, no. I guess I didn't know what I was thinking. But I still think that it is an entirely unfair rule. I mean, so I shot myself—big deal. There are people down there who cannibalize other human beings and boil their flesh and people who are slave owners and mass murderers and suicide bombers and people who molest little children and lots of other horrible people. Why don't you let them take my place, and I'll go and be a tree or something?"

"Steven, we can't do that. In the first instance, all of the types of people you just named have to go back and live as their own types of life-forms."

"Oh yeah, like what?"

"Well, mass murders, for example, go back as plankton."

"Plankton? Oh, that's fucking lame!"

"Why is that, Steven?"

127

"Well, what kind of punishment is that?"

"Steven, they start out at the bottom of the oceanic food chain. They are eaten by other forms of life down there and eventually deposited on the seafloor as waste. When the souls come back, we send them back as kelp."

"Kelp?"

"Yes. Next in line, so to speak. They are eaten by other forms of life and deposited onto the seafloor as waste. Then we move them up a notch, and so it goes until they have been eaten and digested by everything in the sea. In their own way, they repay the life cycle for what they have taken."

"But what about, like, child molesters?"

"Same thing, different punishment."

"What do you mean?"

"All life that feeds on other life has to go back to help replenish the cycle. The common thing with all of the people you seem to be worried about is that they are in the business of stealing life from others. A murderer steals a whole life, a bomber steals what the bomb can grab, someone who preys on little children takes all or part of that life. In the end, they are all trying to steal something that is not theirs for one reason or another, and so we turn them into food. People who prey on children become deep-sea angler fish. You can spot them by the telltale large jaws and the single light over their heads, used to attract prey just like the things they used to attract prey on the land."

"Holy shit. And how long do they stay down there?"

"The same as the ones who are sent back as plankton. About one thousand years."

"Wow! That's a long time to live as food. Or in the dark, I guess."

"It sure is. But after the lesson finally sinks in and if we are convinced that they are ready to rejoin the human race, we let them back in."

"And what if they're not? I mean, what if like the worst of the worst, you know, all of those evil people who killed millions of others and terrorized the globe, what if those types just never stop being evil?"

Chuckling, he said, "We make them into vent worms."

Furious, I said, "You do what? *Oh, that's just fucking great!* So when humans blow up the world and we're all sitting up here waiting to go back and spend the rest of our existence living like dung beetles or flies or whatever, you're going to let the fucking scum of the earth take up all of the prime vent worm spots so that none of us can get them? That's just wrong!"

"Steven, we honestly hope that it never comes to that."

"Well, Chief, let me tell you, you guys have some pretty screwy rules up here. I mean, if you would just change some of them, this whole life thing might wind up working out better. Can we get Junior in here? I think that if I talked to him with you here, I could convince you both to make some modifications that would really help."

"That won't work."

"Oh yes it will! Wait, don't judge too quickly. I get the feeling that you do that a lot."

God's frown reappeared.

I continued, "Just hear me out. First of all, these suits will have to go. I mean, I think that the one you gave me doesn't work or something, because I still can't get my foot to work correctly, and I can't turn my neck very far. Plus, it's too big and heavy and it's really impeding my healing process. And my stomach is still killing me!"

Trying to halt my progress, he said, "Steven—"

"Wait, wait, wait. Second, you need to stop being so harsh on suicides. I can hardly be blamed for shooting myself in the midst of all of the crap that goes on down there. And regardless of what happens to them in the ocean, it seems like there are other people who were far worse than I was who get a break from being humans and get to relax in the water. Shit, I'd love to just lay on the top of the water soaking up sun. Who cares if I got eaten? It would still be a far better existence than having to compete for jobs and trying to find the perfect mate and saving for retirement and all of the other crap that humans go through."

"Steven—"

"Wait, wait, wait! And you need to get some more help up here. I mean, look at Junior. He's at his wit's end. He has to run around and take care of all of these other souls, plus having to apparently go back down there and check every time someone says his name and … Hey, wait—why does he have to go and check every time someone says his name?"

"Steven, that is his punishment."

"Punishment? For what?"

"For his little reincarnation trick down there. He wasn't supposed to show that to everyone else."

"Why the hell not?"

"Humans work best when they think that they only have one life to live."

Jumping to my feet, I exclaimed, "No, they don't! They panic and shit themselves and make everyone suffer because they think that they have to get stuff done before they die."

Shaking his head, he said, "Steven, people do not do that. They focus and eliminate the waste from their lives and work on things that are really important to them."

"What earth are you watching? Oh, wait. I forgot. I'm talking to the guy who doesn't go out onto the observation deck. Listen, bub, humans panic down there because they think that they have to come up here and have some great big conversation with you in order to justify their lives."

Appearing puzzled, God blinked at me.

Sitting down again, I said, "Okay, okay, so that's what *we've* been doing so far. But I mean, for other people who didn't kill themselves, they should be told that life is eternal and that they can choose what to do and what kinds of lives they'll live next if they just get through it. That way, they wouldn't make their kids pay for their mistakes and wouldn't foist the burden of things that they didn't bother to fix onto their kids, and kids would be free to just enjoy their lives and do whatever it is that they want to do."

Now deeply puzzled, he asked, "Steven, what exactly is bothering you?"

"I don't ... I mean, I don't think I can go through all of that again."

"Why not?"

"Because it is impossible to survive! You can't understand the barriers that are down there that threaten to kill you every day and how hard it is to just keep going and trying to live a good life."

"Steven, based on what we have seen from your last life, I'm not sure that you can understand that."

"Well, I mean ... that's what I'm talking about! Look, I've been doing a lot of thinking about this, and I really do think that I killed myself so that I could come up here and have this conversation with you. *And it has come not soon enough.* If you would spend more time watching from the observation deck, you would know that life has become just too harsh down there, and there's no way that kids are going to survive with the way things are now."

"And why is that?"

Pausing a moment, I said, "Well, for starters, there is nothing to do anymore."

"Steven, do you know how ridiculous that sounds?"

Realizing that I had just stepped into my wheelhouse, I continued. "Wait, let me explain. I was just there, and I happen to know something about this. The world has gotten so fixated on finding answers to things and mapping out everything and coming up with the right way to do this and to do that, and it's all being recorded and televised and blasted across the Internet … and by the way, everything that has ever been thought has been written."

"Steven—"

"No, look, I heard it when I was down there. Someone said that everything that has ever been thought has been written, and so there you have it. There is just nothing for me to do. If someone else already wrote it or spoke it or whatever, then what possible contribution to the world could I have left to give? Hey … *wait just a minute*. I … I know why I killed myself!"

Acting surprised, he said, "You do?"

"Yes! And it wasn't anything to do with all of that stuff I said earlier."

"You don't say?"

"No. And, oh, sorry about that too. I probably said some pretty harsh things."

Intrigued now, he said, "That's okay, Steven. Please, go on."

"I know what it was. I remember. I was sitting there in my apartment and thinking about the fact that my family was all gone and that I had a crummy job and that I was never going to be able to find a porno fantasy that was good enough to match what I was picturing in my head, and—"

The reproachful tone returned. "Steven—"

"Wait, wait, wait. And in the middle of that, I was also watching the rest of the world. I mean, well, watching the commercials and the news stories on the Internet and all of that other stuff. I mean, I was really in tune with all of it, and I got this very real feeling that there was *nothing left to do.* The entire earth has been mapped out, and I think that we've even got a pretty good handle on the whole universe and how it works and where everything is, and these days any fool can buy a travel package and climb to the top of Mount Everest, and I mean, with all of that and all of the stuff that has been written and sung and recorded and everything else, there was just nothing for me to do. There was no frontier to cross, there was nothing to conquer, there was just nothing to hope for."

"And so that is why you shot yourself?"

"*Yes!*"

"Jesus?"

Jesus bounded in wearing a Zulu war outfit. "Yes, Chief?"

God said, "Jesus, we've got another one who killed himself because there was nothing to do."

With apparent boredom, he said, "Great. Big surprise. Anything else?"

"No. Thank you." Jesus bounded back out.

Whirling back toward God, I said, "*What the hell was that all about?*"

God just smiled and said, "Oh, Jesus is keeping record of all of the people who kill themselves and why they do it."

"What for?"

"We're making sure that nothing really serious is going on down there that we need to worry about."

"*What the fuck are you talking about, nothing serious?*"

God said calmly, "Steven, there is no need to shout up here."

"*Well, I'm going to fucking shout if I have to!*"

"But I can hear you just fine."

"Fine. Look, I just told you that I killed myself because there's nothing to do. And I mean, there is *nothing to do*! You tell me that

that's not serious? How the hell do you expect me to survive for another human lifetime if there's nothing to do?"

Encouragingly, he said, "Steven, first of all, I should tell you that it is also an important part of the healing process for you to realize why you killed yourself. Your face has just gotten a little better than it was before! And second, you are just going to have to try harder next time."

"Oh, *fuck that! And fuck you! You try harder!* How about that? And I don't care about healing! This place sucks, and not a goddamn thing works up here!"

"Steven, it sounds like you need to go back to your room now."

XIV

With a deep look of concern on his face, Jesus said, "Steven, what happened in there? I thought that you were making progress."

Stomping around my room furiously, I said, "Progress? Progress? There's no way to do that up here! This whole place sucks! I told him that there's nothing to do down there anymore, and he doesn't care."

"Steven, he cares."

Pausing to wave an accusing finger at him, I said, "Well, sure, *you* think so. You're probably his favorite. But let me tell you, pal, he's working you like a dog, and you should ask for some more help up here."

"Oh, we're doing fine."

"Well, it's shit down there, and I don't see any good reason why I should have to go back. Hey, he told me that you've been back to earth a bunch of times?"

"Yes."

"Why, I mean, why do you do it?"

"To play my part."

"What part?"

Jesus sat down and said, "Steven, I go down there to shelter the weak and get in the way of someone else's fist if I have to. I go down there to help the world see that it is focusing on less important things than it should. Take the last time I went. There was a lot of fighting in Ireland, and I wanted to go back to help them try to get over that."

"And you got hit by a bus?"

"Yes."

"Well, how the hell did that help things?"

"Steven, someone has to get hit by the bus. That is what buses do. And because it was me and not someone else who was playing a role in the skirmishes, people were able to continue working out their differences, and things are getting better now."

Sitting down next to him, I said, "They are?"

"Oh, sure. Things are always getting better."

"But people are still killing people!"

"Yes, but there is less of that than there used to be. Let me tell you, I've been down there during some pretty nasty periods. You can't believe what humans can do to one another. Look, Steven, you have to go back. But on the bright side, you will probably never have to kill your neighbors to establish a political boundary."

"I won't?"

"No, that has all been done by others. And you won't have to be a test subject to find the cure for polio."

"I won't?"

"No, Steven, that has already been done too. You probably won't have to live without access to water, which I can tell you firsthand really sucks, and you probably won't have to eat another human being to survive."

"Well, those all sound like bad things."

"Yes, and other people have already been through them so you don't have to."

"Wow. So when are you going back next?"

Shaking his head, he said, "Oh, hopefully never."

Shocked, I said, "Why not?"

"There's no desert left anywhere."

"What? Of course there's a desert. There are huge deserts down there."

"No, a desert where you can actually get lost."

"Lost? Why the hell would you want to do that?"

"Steven, the best part of going back to earth and starting all over again is finding yourself. Now there is GPS and satellite tracking for everything and cell phone coverage so that it is nearly impossible to get lost in the desert. The world is too plugged in to whatever you guys are doing down there."

"Well, why is that so bad?"

"Steven, you cannot find yourself if you cannot get lost. Nope, I'm not going to be any part of that whole experience."

"Fuck. So, if you're not going back, what the hell am I supposed to do?"

Coming to his feet, he patted me on the back and said, "You'll get through it, Steven. Don't worry. Shit, I have to go."

XV

I stormed in and proclaimed, "That's it! I'm not going back, and I don't care what you do to me up here!"

God said curiously, "Steven, what is wrong now?"

"Well, Junior told me that he's not going back to earth anymore. And if he's not going, I'm not going."

Shaking his head, God said, "Sorry, it doesn't work that way."

Gesturing toward the door, I said, "Well, why should he get out of it if I can't?"

"Steven, you are not the same as him. He has his own work to do, and you don't need to worry about that right now."

I sat down and lowered my head in exhaustion. Looking up, I said, "But why can't we just send him back and make sure that he has enough time to get everyone straight and then things will be fine?"

"Steven, we have been waiting a long time for that to happen."

"Well, how about if we send him back, give him enough time to spread the word or whatever, and then we'll just tell everyone to stop requesting new human lives?"

"Someone already tried that. It didn't catch on."

"Why the hell not?"

"As it turns out, people seem to like life down there and want it to continue. People like having sex. People like to be reminded that we are still up here every time a new baby arrives. And most people are not as interested as you in just getting to the end of things."

"Oh, fuck that! Look, he said that there's no desert left anymore. That's basically what I was saying, that everything is crap because it's all diagrammed and mapped out and the world sucks now."

Dismissing my thought with his hand, he said, "Steven, he's just being overdramatic. There are plenty of new things to discover down there. Don't worry about that. The first step is finding yourself, and you didn't even get that far last time."

Defeated once again, I said, "Well, was I supposed to go to the desert? He did it for, what, like forty days or something. Is that the key to finding yourself?"

"No, but it can help. You do not need to actually go to a desert to discover your true self. You just need to get rid of all of the excess in your life and whittle it down to who you really are. Sometimes doing that means that you have to separate from the things you carried around in your past."

"So, what, I'm supposed to separate myself from everyone and go into isolation? How long do I have to do that?"

"First of all, I told you. You do not have to do anything. Well, we hope that you won't kill yourself again, but aside from that, you don't have to do anything at all."

"Why not?"

He said plainly, "Steven, it is your life. It is your world down there. We do not interfere, trust me. But it does help if you do certain things on earth, and we can give you some useful suggestions so that you don't find yourself in the same predicament as last time."

"Well, look, I won't. I just won't. I'll keep my nose clean and read the right stuff, and … hey, what am I supposed to be reading down there?"

"Steven, that is entirely up to you."

"Really? Where is … I mean … who has … where are the rules to follow?"

"What rules?"

"You know, *The Rules.* The stuff that everyone is supposed to do. Where's all of that?"

"Steven, I'm afraid I can't help you there. The world we see is too big and diverse for any one set of rules."

"Well, okay, but … surely … look, surely even though you say that you don't interfere and all of that stuff, surely there's a checklist or something that you guys keep around here. I mean, you're keeping score, right?"

"Score of what?"

"Of who lives right and wrong, and how many times people have … hey, you said that I've only committed suicide once, right?"

"Yes."

"But you said that if I did it again, something bad might happen."

"That's right."

"And what is that, and why is it going to happen?"

"Steven, you started out as part of a whole. You are one soul in a mass of many, but you are part of the whole. If you do not find a way to live in the glory of all creation and to find the true potential of your life, you could possibly keep everyone else from making it back here at the end. All life as you know it could be stuck in an eternity of hell."

"Holy fucking … How is that possible?"

"You are all in it together. No one comes back to stay until everyone gets to the same place."

Sheer terror ran through me for an instant. "I … well, I find it very hard to believe that we are all going to make it, anyway. I mean, from the looks of the place I just left, I don't think that we are anywhere near that."

"Steven, you may be right. But that is a good thing for now."

"It is?"

"Yes. Why should we end life when you humans are just starting to get the hang of things? After all, the sun doesn't burn out for another billion years."

"Really? Well, who cares about the sun, anyway? Look, I don't think that people are getting the hang of things."

"Sure they are. Life is much better than it used to be. Look at it this way. People aren't burning witches at the stake anymore, the incidents of public stoning are way down from past numbers, people aren't regularly killing their female children anymore, and even suicide bombings are becoming less and less common. Steven, let me tell you, you think you are a mess. You have no idea what we have to do to put a suicide bomber back together up here."

"Well, why can't we stop all of that stuff from happening at all?"

"Who is 'we'? Steven, you certainly can, but you can't do it from here. You have to go down there and make the changes happen. And to do that, you have to live long enough to—"

"That's ... well ... I'm just not sure I'm cut out for all of that."

Reassuringly, he said, "You do not have to be. All we are asking you to do is not kill yourself next time."

"Okay, okay, I will focus on that. But, is that all? Shouldn't I go find a desert somewhere and do what he did?"

Shaking his head, he said, "I wouldn't recommend it to you."

"Why not?"

"Well, Junior is kind of a special case. As you may know, he was the first life I created. He has been around for a long, long time. Don't get me wrong. In terms of his makeup, he is no different from you. But if you had to think of him in familial terms, he is your much,

much, much, much older brother. And like all older brothers, he knows a lot of tricks that you do not."

"So why can't I learn them and be like him?"

"You certainly can. But you have to stop messing around with the childish things you've been playing with and move on."

"Oh, I get it. That's why you go to the desert and avoid all of the temptations and things like that?"

"Yes, that's part of it. Although Junior could have done better if he had slowed down a bit."

"What do you mean?"

"Look at it this way, Steven. You are going to go back down there, and it will take you twenty-five or thirty years to get your act together, to stop screwing around in your parents' basement, and to decide to do something that is meaningful to you. Junior is usually at that point by about age five. By twelve, he can counsel the smartest of people on earth. And that is usually when the problems start."

"Problems? What problems?"

"Imagine it, Steven. You go back to earth and you do not take your life for granted. You actually pay attention to what is going on, and by a very early age, you have the whole thing mapped out and can see where other people are missing themselves and where they need help."

"Yeah, that all sounds pretty good."

"Well, everyone around you will think that is a terrific thing, and your services will be in constant demand."

"Again, not so bad."

"But picture this. You know that humans are capable of so much more, and you have it in you to help teach them something great. However, there is a small problem: your mother keeps asking you to come to her dinner parties to entertain guests."

"Wait, I read something about this. That was the water-to-wine stuff, right?"

"Right. Now again, imagine that you have it in you to do magnificent things and that you want to show the world how to get along a little better and how to start realizing its true potential. When your mom calls you and asks you to come and do parlor tricks for her drunk friends, it is likely to piss you off a bit."

"I can certainly understand that."

"So you do what Junior usually does or what most kids who find themselves well advanced from their peers do. You shut everyone out. You wall yourself off and try to keep your blood from boiling over while you figure out the best escape route."

"And then you go to the desert?"

Shrugging his shoulders, he said, "Perhaps. Or you shoot a bunch of people to try to make yourself feel better."

Shocked, I said, "Hey, you're not supposed to say that!"

"Steven, it happens. In Junior's case, he usually goes to the desert, because he wants to make sure that what he has found inside himself—that is, what he thinks he wants to dedicate his life to—is right for him."

"Wait, why can't he just stay put and do that? Why does he need the desert?"

"Steven, it is nearly impossible to be exalted in your hometown."

"Huh?"

"For many, many people, including Junior, it is necessary to leave the place where you grew up and go to a place which is completely separate. The people you grew up around will only know you and relate to you as you *were*. They usually have a very difficult time accepting you as you want to *become*. So, you have to do a significant part of your own development in a place where you can be given enough room to become you. And you cannot do that with all of the other people around you trying to drag you back into the existence you had when you were a kid."

"Oh. Now I get the desert thing."

"Anyway, so Junior just separates himself. He goes off on an adventure, and he knows that when he does so, he must get rid of all of the things from his past that are going to impede his future mission."

"Well, why is that all bad?"

"I always tell him to slow down a bit, but he never does. He has never made it past thirty-three, because he always rushes off and gets himself killed shortly after leaving the desert. And while he is there, he brushes off some of the temptations that people are trying to lay on him, but he also misses some of the good things."

"Like what?"

"Steven, when you start off on a journey, you will often run into a figure that offers you advice. In Junior's case, he always just ignores it. But the last few times, if he had slowed down long enough to pay attention, he would have realized that one of the people he met along the way was his eternal goddess."

"His what?"

"The object of his physical desire who was there to entice him to slow down a bit and savor the experience. When you embark on a journey, they will always be out there if you know what to look for."

Emily? Shit. Leaning in, I said, "Hey, so you've heard about Emily, but did I tell you what she was like? I mean, she was just terrific. Enchanting smile, great looks, miraculous eyes, and when I first moved in, I could hardly wait to press the elevator button to see if I would run into her. I tell you, that was sure a great feeling to have back then!"

Raising an eyebrow, he asked, "And what happened between you and her?"

Pretending to notice something on the floor, I said, "Never mind. Let's get back to Junior."

Out of the corner of my eye, I saw God's frown reappear.

Looking up and clearing my throat a bit, I said, "Seriously, it's probably important for me to learn from his lesson, right?"

God's frown deepened.

I said, "Come on. I'll tell you the rest of my story later." *No, I won't.* "Just tell me why having an eternal goddess could have helped Junior."

Loosening his face a bit, he said, "Because then he would not get killed so quickly. Steven, why do you think they make objects of attraction in the first place? To help you understand that you need to stick around and savor what is down there. To let you know that life is a good and appetizing thing."

"And that's what his eternal goddess would have done for him?"

"Sure. And she would have also told him to slow down, to not attract negative energy to himself, to taste a bit of what life has to offer. But he universally ignores all of those 'distractions,' even the ones that can really help."

"And why does he do that?"

"That is his lot in life. His mission is to figure out what stage the world is in and to try to help it along. Everything else is an impediment. The only thing he ever tried to slow it down was to tell other people not to talk about him. But you know how that goes. Humans are very bad at keeping secrets, especially juicy ones."

Jumping to my feet, I said, "Well, let's work on him!" *And I will remember not to be such a pussy next time.* "And, hey, weren't we talking earlier about changing some rules around here?"

Skeptically, God said, "Steven, *you* were talking about changing rules."

"Well, let's get Junior in here, and I'll talk to him about slowing down. I mean, I'm the sloth of the world, right?"

"That is pretty close, Steven."

"And we can also work on changing some of these rules. Oh, and by the way, you shouldn't be so hard on that guy. He works his ass off, and punishing him by making him run around every time someone says his name hardly seems fair, and—"

"Oh, that's not my punishment. He does that to himself."

"What? Why?"

"To atone for his sin. Steven, when any being does something that misses the mark in his or her life, it creates a rift in the universe. If something is not done to correct it, it will stay there forever. Junior knows what he has to do, and he does it."

I said, "Wow. Well, I think that we can make things easier on him, and while we're at it, let's think about getting those dinosaurs back into the swing of things too! That would be really cool if we could have them in, like, petting zoos and—"

"Steven, we are not going to bring the dinosaurs back just for you."

"Let me talk to Junior. I'll bet that the two of us can convince you to—"

"Steven, enough about the fucking dinosaurs. We are not bringing them back."

"Okay, okay, but let's get him in here and talk about some of these other things." *And dinosaurs.* "Hey, J—"

"Steven, that won't work."

"Why the hell not?"

"First of all, because he won't listen to you. He doesn't even listen to me. Second, we don't make the rules, so we can't change them."

"You what?"

"We don't make the rules. The rule that says that all suicides have to go back and redo their past lives was made by the other souls up here."

"Who? Which? What do you mean? I thought that it was just the two of you?"

"Steven, all souls on earth come through here in the cycle. A long, long time ago, when the problem of human suicide first started, we got all of them together, and we surveyed them as they passed through and asked them what we were supposed to do with the suicide problem. They unanimously voted to let suicides go back and do their human lives over."

Jumping to my feet with fists clenched, I said, "Oh, that fucking sucks! Where's the committee? Let me at them!"

"Steven, it doesn't work like that. If you want to suggest a change, you have to leave it here, and we will address it with everyone in due course."

"And how long does that take?"

"Usually about two thousand years."

"What?"

"Well, we have a pretty big backlog of requests. Souls are busy when they come up here and are often trying to do other things. So most suggested changes do not get dealt with for quite a while."

"Oh, fuck this! That's the most ridiculous system I've ever heard of!"

Leaning back, he said, "Steven, you just got back from earth. Don't be so quick to criticize. What we do up here has been working for a long, long time."

Stomping my foot, I said, "Well, it doesn't work well enough. In fact, it plain sucks! And I'll bet that I could do things ten times better if, you know, I was given enough time."

"Is that right?"

"Yes! What do you do that's so special?"

"Steven, I am in charge of all life. I created all life, and I created everything in the universe."

"Big deal! Have you seen the things we can do down there? Pretty spectacular stuff!"

"Yes, truly fascinating. Look, Steven, go out and make a sun, and then I will compare notes with you."

"A son?"

"No, Steven, a sun. 'The star that is the central body of the solar system, around which the planets revolve and from which they receive light and heat.'"

"Oh. Well, I'm sure someone will figure out how to do that pretty soon. And who cares about the sun, anyway?"

"Steven, we need to work on your attitude a little bit before you go back."

Leaning in aggressively, I said, "Why? Just tell me why the fuck I should care about anything that goes on up here—or anywhere, for that matter—when this whole fucking place is against me and there's not a damn thing I can do about it?"

Beaming, he said, "Because. There is a family down there right now waiting for the announcement of your arrival. And—"

I froze in my tracks. *"Wait right there, bub. What family?"*

God said, "A family. You know, people who are thinking about having a baby."

"Whoa, whoa, fucking *whoa*! Stop right there! Who is it?"

"Well, Steven, we don't have you reserved for any particular family. But when you are ready, there will be a family down there ready to receive you."

Sitting down to weigh this new information for a moment, I finally said, "Yes, but do I get to pick? I mean, can I be the kid of some rich people or a president's kid, or hey, how about a rock star's kid. Yeah, that would be pretty awesome!"

"Steven—"

"Look, I know that I wasn't a stellar human last time, and I've probably been a bit mouthier than you're accustomed to—"

The frown reappeared.

"But listen, I think that if I can go back as a rock star's kid, I can probably hang on longer and will be able to make it to the end."

"Steven, we don't work like that. Haven't you ever heard the saying 'Give us this day our daily bread'?"

"Yes?"

"Well, that's us. We keep things simple. We just send you back when a couple is trying to conceive, and the rest works itself out."

"It sure as fucking bloody hell does not! Do you have any idea what you're saying? You might as well be throwing me to the wolves!"

"Steven, what is the matter?"

"Do you know how many people are smoking crack and having kids?"

"No, Steven, how many?"

"Well, I don't know, but I think it's a lot. You could be sending me down to be a crack baby. Or a baby with fetal alcohol syndrome. Shaken baby syndrome. I could, I mean, I could wind up being the child of someone who puts me in the oven or the dryer or a kid who is beaten by his parents, or I could be born to parents with bad genes, or—"

"Steven, none of that matters."

"What the fuck do you mean, none of that matters? Look, pal, it's obvious that you haven't thought things through very well up here. If you're going to send me back, you have to make sure that I'm sent back to good, upstanding parents who love their kids and who will give them enough nurturing, support, and guidance to make it through life."

"Steven, we can't do that."

"Why not?"

"Because. All things involving new life are equally good. We do not prejudge what is going to happen. When someone down there gives the signal, and we have a soul ready to go up here, they match up, and everything works out."

Slamming my fist down on the bench and coming to my feet, I said, *"It does not fucking work out at all!* Look, that's the problem. The world is filled with people having kids who absolutely should not, and there is no way in hell that I am going to subject myself to that kind of chance just because you have some stupid fucking rule—a rule which was made by the other idiots up here, I might add—that says that I have to go back to earth as a human! That's it! I quit! I am going back to my room, and when I come out, there had better be a ticket waiting for me to go back as a fearsome tiger in a protected wildlife area!"

God stared ominously at me and said, "Steven, it is too late for that now. You already made your choice."

XVI

Pacing frantically around my room, I said, "That's it! I'm trapped in a nightmare! These bozos are going to send me back, and there is nothing I can do about it. I am trapped on a one-way slow boat heading over a cliff … Okay, Steven, just breathe and relax.

"Breathe? Oh, fuck this! Fuck this fucking fuck shit space suit with the fake lungs and this stupid room and all of the stupid crap up here!

Halting in my tracks, I said, "Hey, wait a minute … Yeah, that's it! Maybe I *can* escape! They gave me this suit when I got here, so it's not really a part of me. I wonder if I can figure out a way to separate myself from it. Then I'll just be a free … well, whatever, and I can get the hell out of here!

Surveying my piled mess, I said, "Let's see. Fuck, I wish I hadn't destroyed that mirror. Show me a new mirror!

"Nothing. Shit. I guess I can't get another one. Okay, how am I going to do this? I can try to just pull my head off; if I stretch far enough, I think I can get my hands around my …

"My arms are too short. What else can I try? Maybe if I lean over my desk, I can throw my body weight down and leverage my head to pop off.

"Oh, fuck me. This is a load of crap!

"Hey, wait, maybe there's a hole in this suit! There's got to be a hole somewhere. If I can find it, maybe I can get out of here. Let's see, when I looked in the mirror the last time, I couldn't see anything from the front. And jerk face said no zipper, but maybe there's a plug or whatever it is that they use. I'll bet that I'm filled with air, and when I get done with the suit, they just deflate it or something. So there must be a valve or a way to let it out. If I can find that, maybe I can deflate the suit and it will let my head go free.

"Yeah! They must make these suits in heaven with assholes, right? I mean, he said no stomach, but there must be the rest of the stuff.

"Shit! But my arms are still too short to feel around the back of my suit. How the hell am I going to do this? Let's see. How would I solve this problem if I weren't stuck in heaven?

"I would start with a verifiable hypothesis. Yeah! Okay. Steven's suit in heaven has an asshole through which he can escape from this awful place. Good. It is well-defined, testable, and … shit, how am I going to test it?"

List research limitations:

+ Arms too short to verify based on tactile observation.

+ Broken mirror, can't turn neck very far, anyway, so impossible to verify with direct observation.

+ Research assistants (namely Junior and the Big Guy) appear to be trying to sabotage my efforts. Bastards.

+ Must go it alone if I am ever to escape this goddamn place.

"Maybe I can back into something and see if I can feel it. Let's see. There's a corner on my desk. Yeah, that should work. Okay, backing slowly now … and I think that I'm up against the side of the desk, but I can't feel anything. Jam it, Steven! See if anything is there.

"Nothing that I can tell. Fuck! How about … yeah, okay, so I'll take this pencil and I'll tape it to the top of the desk … wait, where the fuck is the tape? Let's see some tape.

"There you go. Okay, tape the pencil to the top of the desk with the tip pointing out, and back slowly into it and … shit, I still can't feel anything. Okay, Steven, full speed now, and …" The pencil snapped like a toothpick.

"*Great*. Did anything happen? No, I don't hear any whooshing sound. I don't think that I punctured it. How the hell can I get out of this suit?

"Show me a ballpoint pen!

"Nothing. What the hell? Fuck it, I need to ask for help. Jesus?"

Jesus appeared in a flash of light and said, "Yes, Steven. What is it?"

"I, um, I broke my pencil."

Frowning, he said, "You mean that one on the floor that's wrapped in masking tape?"

"Yes, that one. Can I get a new one?"

"Why? What happened to it?"

"Oh, nothing. I was just, you know, writing a bit and it snapped. I guess I don't know my own strength."

"Steven, you can't poke a hole in your suit. Stop trying to do so."

Then let me the fuck out of here! "Well, can I get a new pencil?"

"No, Steven. You can only have one of everything up here."

"Why can't I get a pen?"

"You only get one writing utensil. Some people are pencil fans, some are pen fans. You made your choice, and now you broke it. Sorry." And he vanished.

"Well, that's a fucking nice how-do-you-do! I can't even get a duplicate pencil or a pen. This place really does suck! What else can

I do? No pencil, corner of desk failed to yield sufficient results … what else can I use?

"Hey, that dance hoop I ripped in two. I can maybe reach around with the curved side of that and … hell, I still can't feel anything. How about that pogo stick I obliterated? Shit, I wish I could sit on it and … wait, that's it! I'll prop it up here next to the bed and climb up on the bed and jump off and …

"Shit. I just broke the pogo stick in two. Well, this bicycle fork is a bit more robust. One and two and jump, Steven!

"Broken too. Still no whooshing sound.

"What am I going to do now? *I have to get out of here.* There's no way that I'm going back to face childhood again, especially when the identity of my parents is left to total chance. These guys just have absolutely no idea what's going on down there, and how the hell could they with God never bothering to go out onto the observation …

"Wait a minute! *That's it!* By God … oh …! Ha! Fuck you, God! I totally forgot! This must all really be a nightmare. I think that the bullet ricocheted off my skull or something, and I am in a coma. Wow! That's a really demented coma.

"Ha-ha-ha, fuck you, Claus!"

XVII

Disclaimer: if you have indeed made it this far, I should warn you that this is the part of the story where I lose my composure a bit ... well, again. I would say that this is where I have a schizophrenic breakup, but that's not really possible in heaven. In any event, I warned you (again).

God welcomed me warmly. "Hello, Steven. How are you feeling today?"

"Much, much better!"

Raising a curious eyebrow, he said, "Oh, so you are starting to come around?"

"Not exactly."

"Then what is it?"

"Well, Big Guy, let me tell you. I really hate to be the one to pull rank on you, especially up in this lofty place, but you're *dead*."

Leaning back a bit confused, he said, "I'm what?"

"You're dead!"

Scratching his head, he said, "That's funny. I don't have any recollection of having died."

Clenching my fists, I said, "Well, pal, let me tell you, you are. I'll bet that I read it in a dozen different places when I was down there.

Dead. *Tot.* Kaput. Pushin' up daisies. Sorry, Chiefie, but you're dead, and this is just a big nightmare. I'm alive right now, probably in the intensive care ward of some hospital with a hot-assed nurse with gigantic jugs taking care of me, and you're dead!"

"Steven, I am not sure where you get your information, but I don't think that I am dead. Jesus?"

Jesus appeared. "Yeah, Boss?"

"Steven seems to think I'm dead. Have you heard anything about this?"

"Nope." Gone.

Clapping his hands together, God said, "There you have it, Steven. I think that I'm still around. So where were we?"

Stomping up and down I said, "Oh no, no fucking way! Look, I don't care what he says, anyway. Everyone down there says you're dead, so you're dead. Now let me out of this fucking place!"

"Sorry, it doesn't work that way."

Steeling myself for the big attack, I said, "Well, okay, I really didn't mean to get this dirty, especially since it seems that you are a bit out of date on developments and the like. But we've found the God particle."

"The what?"

"The God particle. We found the thing that gives mass to everything in the universe. So there!"

Cocking to one side, he said, "Steven, what does that mean?"

"I have no idea! But we found it. The scavenger hunt is over. So even if you're not dead, and even if I am sitting up here in heaven, there's nothing left to find down there, so let me go!"

He glared at me and replied accusingly, "Steven, you couldn't find your own asshole if you had to."

And just then, the temperature in heaven seemed to go up a notch or two.

Backpedaling, I said, "I couldn't … I … what did you just say?"

"You heard me. Now stop fucking around. Life is not a scavenger hunt, and you have to heal and get ready to go back to earth as a human."

Wanting to spit in his general direction, I said, "Oh, there's no way in the fucking bluest of blue hells that you are getting me to go back there! I don't care what you say. I don't care what he says. I'm not going back! That place sucks, and this place sucks, and you did a shitty job of designing heaven and the whole universe and the earth, and if you had been a little bit more foresighted and not just a big, dumb fathead throwing innocent life down onto earth to see what the hell happened to it, you would have planned a little better.

"Hey, Chief, have you ever heard of packing a lunch? Shit, even moms who send their kids off to school for the first time know enough to pack some food for the kids so that they're not forced to eat the other kids on the school yard. I mean, talk about a classic blunder! And sending them down there in the first place … that was a ridiculous idea!

"What the hell were you thinking? Wasn't life good enough … hey … wait … wait, that's it!"

"What's it, Steven?"

Raising a deadly finger at him, I said, *"This is all your fault!"*

"What is?"

"Life! The whole fucking mess! All of the death and destruction and suffering and pain and crap we have to endure down there. It's all your fault. You're too stupid to figure it out, but I have, pally. I'm onto you! I'm stuck in this fucking eternal cycle and forced to go back down into that suffering morass of misery because you were lonely!"

"I was what?"

"Lonely! That's it, isn't it? Junior, that asshole, wasn't enough company for you. You two fatheads were probably just sitting around one day and thought up this great cosmic joke so that you could have

some entertainment. That's it! You're a miserable old fool, and you and he decided to add some jokers to the mix so that you could have something to watch on television in the evening. Oh, nice fucking going, Chief! Well, I'm not going back down there just so you can continue to be entertained!"

Firmly, he said, "Steven, eternal life was my gift to you. Now, if you cannot accept that and accept what you have to do down there, I am afraid that there is nothing I can do to help you."

"Goddamn right there's not! This place fucking sucks, and you suck, and earth sucks, and … *fuck you for starting the whole thing, anyway!"*

Sighing deeply, he said, "Is that all?"

Fuming, I made for the door. *"Goddamn right that's all! Jesus!"*

XVIII

Kicking the side of my bed sharply, I said, "Who the fuck do these guys think they are with this bullshit Boy Scout program up here? There's no way to ever get well with these two knuckleheads running the show. And I'm stuck here. I'll bet that I just have to go back and keep talking to that fucking guy and working on finding my inner child and repenting for this and that and a whole bunch of other stupid fucking bullshit heavenly crap!

"There's no food to eat, no booze, no drugs, no one to talk to, you can't even get any good stuff to play with in your room, and this fucking stupid-assed rubber suit doesn't fucking work and is a ridiculous design, anyway. Hey, geniuses, nice going. Rubber suit with no asshole. Way to go. They probably have no idea what's been going on for the last few billion years of evolution. Idiots!"

Whirling around, I said, "Steven, wait a minute. See if you can ...

"Can I see a shotgun?

"Nothing. Shit. How about a steak knife?

"Nope. Fuck. What else can you use to kill yourself? How about a nice length of rope?

"No? I can't even get a rope in this fucking place? *Oh, heaven fucking sucks!*"

Shouting toward the rafters, I said, *"Hey, Claus, you and your fucking stupid idiot sidekick … Fuck you, and fuck this place! I want to go back to earth right this fucking second, and I don't want to have to deal with another fucking family and childhood, and I want a giant beer and a waitress with huge fucking tits to serve it to me. And another thing, dickhead, I WANT TO TAKE A SHIT!*

…

"Uh oh. What did I just do? I … I think I heard something pop. I … oh shit, oh boy, I'm on the floor, and I can't seem to move anything! Oh, fuck me! Ladies and gentlemen, I think that I just had an accident in heaven. Oh shit! How the hell am I going to explain this one? I … oh crap … I can't move, and now my … my eyesight is getting blurry … and I'm cold … so cold. I … I think that this is bad. I may need to call for help.

"Um, Jesus?"

Jesus wheeled through the door and looked at me in disbelief. "Hi, Steven. *Steven, what did you do to yourself?*"

"I, um, I don't really know."

"Steven, *you blew a hole in the back of your suit!* Oh, oh my. This is serious. Now, don't try to move, and we'll get you to the …"

XIX

Finding myself deep in an impenetrable fog, I said, "Mmmmm. Mmmmm. Aaaaah. Ohmmm. Haaaa. Waaaa. Hel ... eel ... help. *Help*. Hello. Hey. Haaaaa. Hummmm. Whaaa. What the. ... Where am I? Hey? Hey! *Help!* Hello! Hello! Hey! Let me ... let me out of here!

"Oh shit, holy shit, oh my, oh holy shit, where am I?"

"Steven, relax. You're in the hospital."

"Oh, thank my lucky stars! Doctor or nurse or whatever, you have no idea what I've just been through! It was horrifying! I had a nightmare that I was in heaven and stuck in this horrible fucking rubber suit, and God and Jesus were there, and I couldn't talk to anyone or eat or anything and—"

"Steven, you're still here."

"Jesus?"

"Yes."

"*Shit*. Jesus, I don't think that I can go on any further."

"What do you mean?"

My sight slowly returned. I looked at my surroundings and down at myself and said, "Well, look at what I just did!"

Jesus patted me on the head, smiling, and he said, "Oh, you're doing just fine!"

"What?"

"Yes, you are proceeding nicely."

"*What?* Was this … or was all of that … just a test or something?"

Chuckling, he said, "No. Of course not. How could we ever conceive of a test where you actually do what you just did to yourself? Honestly, in the realm of what we usually see up here, that was priceless!"

"Gee, thanks for the encouragement."

"Steven, don't worry about it. We fully expected something like this to happen. Most suicides try something else to escape when they're up here, anyway."

"Seriously?"

"Sure. All of that pressure you put on yourself has to go somewhere, and in your case, it certainly did! But it's okay. It is a good sign. It means that you are trying to find part of yourself again."

"By shitting myself in heaven?"

"Sure! Well, technically, all you did was blow out the back of your suit. But still, it was a pure emotional outburst—and very unique from our perspective. That is perfectly healthy! Anyway, it is better than just sitting there *whining* all the time."

"But how did I do that? I tried every other thing I could find in my room to blow out my suit, and nothing worked."

"Steven, we try not to give suicides objects that they can actually use to harm themselves. We don't want to give them another easy exit to take. However, sometimes suicides can be pretty inventive, and we can't prevent everything. But the power inside of you is enough to do anything, even to … hang on, I'll be back."

Cocking an ear, I said, "Hey, I hear other people. There are voices in here. Holy shit! Wait, Steven, stop saying that. But I can hear voices. It sounds like a group of people talking. I wonder if I get to talk to other people now!

"Wow! All I had to do was blow up my space suit, and I earned the right to talk to other souls in heaven. If I had known that earlier—"

Jesus suddenly appeared beside my bed and said, "Steven."

"Oh, hey, hiya. Wow, you really show up without any warning. Anyway, so I hear voices out there."

"Sure you do. You are not the only one to land himself in the hospital up here."

"So can I … I mean, can I go out and talk to them?"

"Oh, sure."

"But what about that whole rule about not getting to talk to other souls up here?"

"Steven, this is the Suicides' Hospital. This is where all of the suicides we have in heaven wind up when they do something else stupid and destroy their suits."

Disappointed, I retreated under the covers and said, "Oh, great. I get to go out and talk to a bunch of lousy suicides. *Thanks a bunch.*"

"Steven, don't judge them. They are no better or worse than you."

"Okay, okay. But how can I go out to face them? You know, with my face looking like it does."

"Oh, don't worry about that. You've actually healed quite nicely!"

Perking up, I said, "No shit?"

"No, Steven. As it turns out, that little outburst was pretty much what you needed the whole time."

"You're shitting me."

"Steven, you really have to quit saying that, especially now. I told you, we don't do that up here."

"That's what you meant the whole time?"

"Sure. Why, what did you think we were talking about? There is no shitting in heaven, and you just proved it."

"Why the hell didn't someone tell me that when I got here?"

"Steven, we have been saying that *since* you got here. You just weren't listening."

Rubbing my chin, I said, "Wow. Maybe I should pay closer attention to what you guys have been—"

"Steven, that may be the understatement of the millennium. But don't worry about that for now. You look just fine. We've put you into a makeshift suit while your other one is being repaired. You don't have legs on this one, so you can't get up and walk around, but you can stay in your hospital bed and talk with the other souls if you'd like."

Searching my options, I said, "Well, I guess if there's nothing else to do I can ... so there's no television in the hospital up here?"

"Nope."

"No drugs? I mean, you know, like pain medications and the like?"

"Nope."

"Are you ... Wait, let me guess, you are the only nurse or doctor in the whole place, right?"

"Yep."

"So I'm not going to have a large-breasted nurse come in to take care of me?"

"Steven ..."

"Okay, okay, I got it. If there's nothing else to do, I guess I can go out to talk to them for a little while. Hey, how long am I stuck in here, anyway?"

"Well, it takes a bit of time for the suits to be mended."

"What? Why? Don't you just have spares around that I can use?"

"No. Sorry. You get one suit up here, and that's that. Now, if you will let me go, I will start working on mending it."

"What? Why the hell do you have to mend it?"

Almost rhetorically, he said, "Steven, who else is going to do it?"

"Oh, fuck. Never mind. Can you just wheel me out there and get on with it?"

XX

When I entered the room, the prettiest face I had seen since Emily's was just finishing a thought. She said, "And I said to her, 'Why are you shocking me?' And she said, 'Because we don't know what else to do with you.'"

An old, crotchety man frowned deeply at her and said, "Well, that's your fault for getting spotted. You should have known better than to let them get their hands on you in the first place. Me, I got out because I could feel old age coming on."

And a young boy with a face of pure innocence beamed at my arrival and said, "Hey, look, a newcomer! What's your name?"

"Steven. And you?"

"I'm Alex. That girl over there is Mary, and the older gentleman is Roger."

I said, "Hi, all. How's it going up here?"

Mary said, "We're all doing fine." Turning back to finish, she said, "Anyway, Roger, you were stupid to do what you did. You were almost out. Now you've got to go back and do it all again."

Roger snapped at her, "Oh, bullshit. What do I care if I have to do it all over again? I just didn't want to grow old. You're the idiot.

166

You had a pretty cushy life, and you balked on it because you weren't happy with your social condition. You should have had the guts to leave that jerk and get out on your own."

Mary replied sarcastically, "Easy for you to say. Rotten bastards like you are the ones that keep us from being able *to* get out on our own and do what we want."

Roger waved his arms at her and said, "Oh, come on. That is *so* last century. You chickened out, and that's that."

Alex turned to me and asked, "Hey, Steven, what happened to you?"

"I, um, I ..."

Jesus skipped into the room and said, "Hello, everybody."

And the group said in unison, "Hi, Jesus!"

Jesus asked, "How are things going today?"

Alex said, "Oh, we're doing just fine. We were just asking Steven what he did."

And to my everlasting horror, Jesus turned to the group and said, "Well, he shot himself in the face on earth, and up here, he tried to shit himself in his suit and blew out the back of it."

My face heated up like a torch. I tugged on his sleeve and said, *"Jesus!"*

"What?"

"Can you come down here for a second?" Leaning in, I whispered, "Why the hell did you have to tell them that?"

Jesus whispered back, "Steven, relax. This is heaven. Everyone finds out what you did, anyway."

I whispered in reply, "Are you fucking kidding me?"

Jesus whispered, "No. Whatever is hidden is meant to be revealed."

I hissed, "That is the stupidest thing I've ever heard. Can't you see that there is a girl in here?"

Jesus whispered back reassuringly, "Come on, Steven. It's not like you're going to get laid in heaven, anyway."

I whispered, "Oh, right. Sorry about that. Thanks for the huddle."

Patting me on the shoulder, Jesus said quietly, "Don't mention it."

Turning back to the group in his normal voice, he said, "Besides, Steven, don't worry about this crew. They all have their own issues to deal with. Shit, gotta go."

I gripped the covers and chuckled nervously, "Heh-heh-heh. Funny guy. So, anyway …"

Alex exclaimed, "You shot yourself in the face? That must have hurt a lot!"

"I … actually … I have no idea. Hey, kid, what did you do?"

Alex said, "I took all of my mom's sleeping pills. It was a piece of cake. Well, the first three times I tried it were not a piece of cake. I spent weeks in the hospital, and getting your stomach pumped sucks big time. But I got the dosages right the last time, and I was out. The next thing I knew, I was up here."

"And you, Mary?"

Mary said, "I hooked up a hose to the exhaust on my car."

"Roger?"

Roger replied, "Oh, I threw myself down in front of an oncoming truck."

I said, "Shit. That must have hurt!"

Roger said, "Like you, I really have no idea. It did the trick, though."

Mary inquired, "Steven, why did you do it?"

Doesn't anyone ever stop asking that question? Looking down at my bedclothes, I said, "I, um … well, my whole family died in a car accident a few years ago, and that and a whole bunch of other things were just too much to bear."

With a look of deep concern, Mary said, "That must have been tough."

Alex lit up and said, "Are you kidding? Steven, do you know how lucky you were?"

Looking up in surprise, I said, "What?"

Alex smacked the bed. "Oh man, what I wouldn't have given to get away from my parents! You were lucky!"

Skeptically, I said, "Look, kid, it's not exactly that easy."

Alex said, "Well, sure, but you probably had parents that you liked. My old man used to put cigarettes out on me, and when I was five, I heard my mother telling one of her friends that I was an accident."

Whistling in disbelief, I said, "Shit, that's tough, kid."

Alex said, "Yeah, I couldn't really stand it. I just wanted to get it all over with."

Roger butted in. "Well, nice going, kid. You also have to go back and do it all over again."

Alex said, "Yeah, I really wasn't expecting that part."

Waiving a defiant finger, Roger said, "Well, kid, the thing to do next time is to cut your own path and not take shit from anyone. And no matter what happens when you're young, eventually, your parents won't be able to get to you anymore, and you can get out and tell them to go to hell."

Mary chimed in. "Yes, Alex, and if you are brave and strong like Roger here, then when you get to the end of that marvelous path you have cut for yourself, you can jump in front of a moving truck and show the world who is really the boss."

Roger blasted, "Screw you, you stupid harlot!"

Mary retorted, "Fuck you, old man!"

I put up my hands and said, "Guys, guys. Why the hell are you all fighting up here? We're not against each other. We all had the same kinds of troubles down there, and we're all in the same boat."

Roger spun toward me and said, "What boat? I'm not in the same boat with a guy who shit himself in heaven."

I fired back. "Oh, yeah? And what'd you do to get in here?"

Roger said, "Simple. I had a refrigerator in my room and dropped it on myself."

I said, "How the hell did you have a refrigerator in your room if there's no food up here?"

Roger said, "Oh, I just rang the front desk and asked for one."

Shit, I should have thought of that.

Mary resumed her attack. "Roger, it sounds like you have a bit of trouble dealing with the weight of the universe—or perhaps the lack thereof. You seem to be into crushing yourself."

Roger looked up at the ceiling and said mockingly, "Thank you, Dr. Know-It-All. At least I'm not the one who rolled over before I got somewhere in life."

Mary said plainly, "Well, I wanted to make sure that I got myself before the world got me."

I said, "Why, was someone chasing you?"

Mary explained. "No. It's not about someone chasing you. It's about the silent pressure to be something you are not. And I just couldn't take it down there. So up here, I am working on building up my courage so I can deal with dickheads like Roger next time. Steven, what have you been working on?"

Shit. If Jesus comes back, he'll just tell them, anyway. Rubbing my neck nervously, I said, "I ... um ... I've mostly been trying to find the asshole in my rubber suit."

The group roared with laughter.

170

Mary finally recovered a bit and giggled, "Steven, that's okay. We are all on our own journeys up here."

I beamed at her and said, "Wow, you really seem to know your stuff! I wish I had run into you earlier."

And Roger mocked, "Oh yeah, she's brilliant. Steven, do you know what this little minx did to get in here?"

"No, what?"

Roger said, "She swallowed the entire contents of a fire extinguisher."

Mary said innocently, "Well, you can't get an automobile in your room, so I got the next best thing."

I said, "How the hell did you get a fire extinguisher in your room? I haven't seen a fire since I got up here."

Mary said, "Oh, I don't think that there are any fires up here, but I got the extinguisher to appear. And it did the trick."

Scratching my head, I said, "What trick? What's the trick we were all trying to pull? Oh, wait, I know …"

Jesus appeared in a wisp of smoke. "The Great Disappearing Act!"

The group said, "Hi, again!"

I said, "Yeah, that's probably right."

Jesus said, "It is, Steven. You all are trying to jump out of your bodies and disappear. Up here, down there, and it is causing you all the same delays."

Holding up a finger, I said, "Well, Jesus—and folks, stop me if I'm wrong—but I think that we all feel that it is pretty tough down there and up here, and we need to disappear."

Mary said, "Agreed."

Alex said, "Agreed."

Roger spat, "You guys are all a bunch of pussies!"

Mary said, "Roger, did I tell you to fuck off yet?"

Roger said, "Yeah, like seventy-five times since we've been here."

Mary glowed. "Seventy-six!"

And Jesus said, "Shit, I've got to go." And he was gone.

Way to go, pal … bailing out just when the dispute gets heated. I attempted to intervene. "Guys, I still don't see why you are all fighting up here. It is obvious that none of us are better or did smarter things than any of the rest of us. We are all fuckups, and we shouldn't be beating each other up. It's tough enough with the rest of the world against us." Focusing my attention, I said, "Incidentally, Alex, how did you get in here?"

Alex said, "I swallowed 954 marbles."

I said, "Holy … wow! That's a lot of marbles. But wait, how did you get that many in your room?"

Alex said, "I went around to a bunch of the other suicides up here and asked them to each get me a marble. I traded them for things in my room that I didn't want."

I said, "Fuck! That's brilliant! Okay, strike what I said about none of us being smarter than any of the others. But didn't you know that your suit didn't have a stomach in it?"

Alex said, "Oh, sure. But I still feel empty inside. Don't you?"

Jesus sauntered through the door. "You all are, in a way."

It is very convenient that he shows back up just when I've gotten everyone calmed down.

Jesus continued. "But what you need to realize is that the emptiness you feel, the anxiety you are trying to suffocate, the lightness you want to eliminate, the … well, Steven, the need to blow up a little bit, those are the things you need to work on down there. Screwing around with that stuff up here just delays the inevitable and keeps you from experiencing the true nature of this place."

Roger piped back in and said, "Yeah, but it also gets us out of having to talk to that fathead!"

Jesus said, "Who, God?"

Roger said, "Of course. Things are hard enough without someone trying to tell you what's what!"

Mary mocked, "Roger, can you even *hear* yourself talking?"

Roger chided, "Mary, you're not old enough to understand. And besides, you're a woman. I knew everything I needed to know last time, and all I do up here is sit around and listen to stories about how much more he thinks he knows than I do. Seriously, who cares how the first lives became viruses?"

I said, "Wait, he told you that?"

Roger said, "Sure. Why, what did you talk about?"

I said, "Monkeys and sea creatures. Mary?"

Mary said, "Mostly about Mother Earth."

I said, "Why would that come up?"

Mary said, "Because she's bipolar, just like me!"

I said, "Oh, I never even thought about that. Alex, what about you?"

Alex said, "Twins."

I said, "What?"

Alex said, "Twins. You know, twins. Two people born at the same time to the same mother."

I said, "No shit? I didn't even think to ask about that one."

Alex looked down vacantly and said, "Well, I thought that if I had had a brother to take half of the beatings, my last life would have been much easier, so the whole conversation got off on that track."

And upon hearing that, my heart sank. *When someone says something like that, it sure makes you want to take all of your problems and put them to the side for a bit.*

Not knowing what else to offer, I tried to deflect the tension. "Um, wow, Jesus, it sounds like no one really talked about the same things."

Jesus said, "That's typical. Everyone's experience up here is unique, even for a lot like you guys. Steven, your suit is almost done, so we'd better get you back to your hospital room so you can change."

I said, "Oh, okay. Good luck, gang!"

Waving, Mary and Alex said, "Thanks, Steven!"

As we moved toward the door, Roger cupped his hands to his mouth and shouted at me, "Try not to shit the bed next time! Anyway, Mary, what you've got to get through your thick skull is …"

XXI

Back in seclusion, I exclaimed, "Wow, Jesus, that was really great!"

Fiddling with my new suit, he said, "What was?"

"Finding out that I'm not so screwed up!"

"Oh, sure. There are plenty of souls out there who are just as troubled—and perhaps more troubled—than you are."

"Man, that Roger sure is an asshole."

"Steven, I told you, don't judge him. You didn't live as long as he did last time, and you have no idea what he was going through."

"Yeah, but did you hear the way that he talked to everyone?"

"Well, some people are happiest when they have others around them to belittle."

"Boy, I'll say. But that girl, she was hot!"

Raising an interested eye at me, he said, "Really?"

"Oh yeah. I mean, she was wearing a giant rubber suit like the rest of us, but her face was precious! Shit. Are you sure that my face was all healed up?"

"Steven, you look better than you ever have."

"Seriously? I don't feel all that different."

"You sure look it!"

"Well, I wish I could have spent more time talking to Mary. She really had it together. It's a shame that whatever happened to her made her feel like it was better to—"

"Destroy herself before the world could do so?"

"Yes! Oh, shit. Is that what I did too?"

"In a way, yes. But, Steven, think of this. Even a girl in a giant rubber suit in heaven is more interesting than the junk you used to sit around and watch all day long."

"But … well, that's different. I've been up here for a long time, and I haven't seen any, you know—"

"Tits and ass?"

"No, Jesus. Other women. *Man, your language!*"

"Steven, the trick when you get back is to chase your *real* love interests when they cross your path. You can't miss if you do that."

"But, what if I am, like, not attractive when I go back?"

He went back to fiddling with my new suit and said, "What does that even mean? Look, the first step is to find someone who interests you and let that person know that you are there. Signaling and eye contact is ultimately much more important than how you think you look to that other person. And, don't forget—"

"Yeah, yeah, I know. I only see myself as myself, and other people see me in a different way."

"Good. I think that you are going to do just fine down there."

"*Oh God, oh God, oh God!*"

"Steven, what is it?"

"I, um, uh, ho, whooo, ahhhh, I, um, I don't know. When I start to think about going back, I whooo ahhhh, whooo ahhhh, my breath gets short, and I start to, I, um, whooo, ahhhh, I start to panic a little bit …"

Moving toward me with the suit, he said, "Don't worry. You are going to make it next time and—"

"Hoooo, haaaaa, hoooo, ahhhh, I'm, I'm having, whooo, haaaa, I'm having a lot of haaahaaahaaahaaahaaahaaahaaahaaa, having haaahaaahaaahaaa, trouble haaahaaahaaa ... breathing!"

Putting down the suit and resting his hands on me, he said, "Steven, get ahold of yourself."

"It's, haaaa, haaaa, haaaa, hard. I don't, haaaa, haaaa, haaaa, I don't think there's enough aaaah, aaaah, haaaa, air in here."

He started shaking me gently. "Steven, snap out of it. You are having a panic attack and hyperventilating in a rubber suit in heaven with no lungs in it."

Recovering my senses, I said, "Haaaa, haaaa, ha! You're ... you're right! How the hell ... why did I feel like I was hyperventilating?"

"I told you. You can make that suit do just about anything that you did down on earth."

"Really? Well, anything except—"

Shaking his head, he said, "No, Steven, there is still no shitting in heaven."

"Ha! Well, let me ask you this, then. Why do people do that down on earth?"

"Steven, down there, you have to be able to get rid of all of the junk you put into yourself. Otherwise, with all of the life you consume, you would just grow bigger and bigger and bigger until you finally exploded. Up here, things are obviously different, because we don't keep any extra lives around for you feast upon. However, by the time you get here, you're supposed to be over that, anyway.

"And we give you a suit that simulates breathing, because lots of souls up here have freaked out about not being able to breathe the same way they did on earth. But while the digestive system has been evolving for billions of years, and infinite souls have had to deal with that in one form or another, you are the only soul we have ever had up here who was really upset about there being no shitting in heaven."

"No, but … well, hey, that must mean I'm pretty special!"

"Sure, Steven. And just like the famed hero who stole fire and brought it back to the humans, the tale of your victory up here will be the stuff of legend."

Grabbing his sleeve, I said, "Do you really think so? Hey, did that really happen? You know, Mary said that she had a fire extinguisher, but I swore that I had never seen a fire up here. Is that because, you know, that guy *stole* the fire and took it down to earth? Are we not allowed to have fire up here because of what he did?"

"Steven, you really need to get out more."

Bewildered, I said, "Oh. Really? So there are no fires up here?"

"No, Steven. No fires and no shitting, and please feel free to share the news of your joyous discovery with everyone else."

"Hey, that's a great idea!"

Cautioning me, he said, "Wait, Steven, I was joking."

"No, no, I should tell … well, maybe not everyone, but surely someone wants to know this. I mean, in the interest of keeping someone else out of the hospital up here, and for … you know, scientific purposes."

Sitting down for a second, he said, "Steven, while you may have stumbled upon an interesting discovery here in heaven, don't be too sure that anyone else will want to hear about it."

"Why not? Knowledge is power, right?"

"Sure, Steven. But pride is also a folly."

"What?"

"Pride. Being so proud of something you discovered that you run out and shout it to everyone. Don't let that get the best of you. I sure have, and it can really shorten your time down there. When you do things on earth that are really special to you, try not to do them in public for everyone to see. Instead, go inside of yourself and shut the door."

"What?"

"Steven, you don't need to tell the whole world every time you take a shit. There is already enough of that going on down there right now."

"Ha! You're not lying, man."

"Besides, there are certain things that, while they may be breakthrough discoveries to you and may also be true and novel ideas, they might not be interesting to other people, and no one else may ever come across the need for the information."

"I don't get it."

"Well, take atoms. Most atoms never touch. Down there, you never touch anything. You just think you do."

"No kidding?"

"No, Steven. But when you are making out with the girl of your dreams, you really don't care about that little factoid, do you?"

"I, um, well, if I had known it at the time …" *And had I bothered to even say hi to the girl of my dreams.* "No, I don't think that would matter to me."

"Exactly. And for most people, when they are up here, they are working on other issues and don't really care that we don't design these suits with a digestive tract."

"Oh, now I get it."

Standing up again, he said, "Good. Now, let's get you changed, and you can get out of heaven."

Clutching the sides of the bed fearfully, I said, "Wait, wait! I don't think I'm ready for that!"

"Why not? Your face is healed, and you are doing much better."

"Jesus, Who gives a shit about my face? I still don't feel like much of a decent soul."

"Yes, but that is what has healed."

"What?"

"Steven, what did you think you were doing this whole time?"

"Healing my face."

"Steven, that entire ball of energy that you think makes up the head on your suit is your soul."

"You are shitting me."

"Steven …"

"Oh, sorry. I forgot. Really?"

"Yes, Steven. What did you think you brought up here?"

"I, um, well, I guess I left my body back on earth, right?"

"Right. And what is left after that?"

"Well, my soul, I guess. But I've never seen it."

"Yes you did. You saw it in the mirror in your room. Well, before you smashed the mirror."

"But I thought—"

"You thought wrong, Steven."

"But I've never seen my soul down on earth."

"Based on your last life, that's probably true."

"*Thanks*. It's not like it's an easy thing to find, you know."

"Steven, that's ridiculous. If you want to see what a soul looks like, just look at the difference between a live body and a dead one."

"No, no, that's too easy. And that doesn't work. I mean, no one has ever seen a soul. It's not diagrammed in any textbook, and no one can find it when you—"

"Cut open a body?"

"Yes!"

"Steven, think of it this way. If someone were coming at you with a knife, what would you do?"

"I'd run and hide."

"Exactly."

"But … I mean, where is it?"

"What do you mean?"

"I mean, where is it in the body when it's not hiding from a knife?"

Sitting down again, he said, "Steven, down there, your soul is the energy inside of you. When it is in your human body, it fills every molecule, every atom, every nook and cranny of you and keeps you going. When you particularly focus on one part of you or the other, your soul shifts to compensate and help you out. So if a lovesick person describes his or her soul as being in the heart, that is because that is where he or she is feeling the soul trying to burst out. Other people who spend time thinking a lot believe that their souls are in their heads. And they are all correct."

"But I still can't believe that it's there. I mean, up here, you guys do all of your tricks, and that works just fine for this place, but down there, we've looked and looked, and no one in all of that time has been able to find it."

"Steven, believe it or not, your soul is there the whole time. And by now, you should know better than anyone that just because you can't find something doesn't mean that it is not there."

My face turned into a glowing flame again. Jesus simply continued, "However, it is probably a good thing that you can't find your soul down there."

"What do you mean?"

"You would just end up selling it if you *did* find it."

181

"Hardy-friggin'-har! I just … well, I still can't believe most of the stuff you guys have said up here. And I am still very worried about my chances next time. I mean, you say that I'm healed or whatever, but I don't feel all that different. And the same problems are going to be down there, and I don't think that this one little session in heaven is going to be enough to protect me. Seriously, Jesus, what if I try to hurt myself next time?"

"Steven, haven't you heard anything we have been telling you? You have been down there since the very beginning of time. You may not have been the one to ever storm the castle gates, but you were down there nonetheless. And because you have been involved in the whole process of species growing and developing and changing, when you go back, you will have the benefit of billions of years of evolution designed to keep you from hurting yourself."

"What?"

"Steven, the body you will inhabit down there has eons of programming and circuitry all designed to keep you from attacking your inner self. If you cut yourself, your brain will scream at you to stop so that you don't wind up destroying the body you're in. If you tax the body too hard, it will overheat and cause you to pass out so that you can regroup and start over. Steven, even that little panic attack you had earlier would be next to nothing on earth, because if you overdo it during a panic attack, you'll just pass out and wake up feeling refreshed again."

"Yeah, but I can get past all of those defenses with a gun again. There's no warning for that. Just blammo, and then you're out."

"Steven, perhaps it would be a good idea for you to *not* own a gun next time."

"Oh, shit. I could do that! Hey, good idea, Jesus!"

Getting up again, he said, "So now do you understand why things are going to be okay next time?"

"I guess I do. I still worry about finding myself in the same pit as I did last time. You know, where it felt better to sit in my place playing with childish things than going out to … you know."

Gently taking my hand, he said, "Steven, before we put you back in your regular suit, why don't you let me show you something."

XXII

Nearly tripping over my own feet with excitement and still struggling to catch my breath, I ran in shouting. "God! God! God! You will never in a million years believe what just happened to me!"

Turning his attention from something else, he smiled and said, "Hello, Steven. What happened?"

Crashing onto the bench and sucking in giant gulps of air, I said, "Well, see, I was in the hospital, and I met all of these other suicides, and well, they were pretty messed up, but we had a good talk, and then just before I was going to get out of there, Jesus took me on the most amazing trip!"

Acting genuinely surprised, he said, "You don't say?"

"No! And it was, I mean, it was unbelievable! One minute, I was sitting in the hospital in this temporary suit, and the next thing I knew, Jesus put his hand on me, and we were gone. Well, we were still around, but we were gone. Out of the hospital and gone! And flying. Boy, I can't tell you! It seems like we flew all over the universe! We were whizzing past entire galaxies and dipping into and out of black holes and shooting past quasars and ... well, it was like I was light! No ... wait ... *not light*. Light is like a ... like a ... slow-moving bus running on flat tires compared to what we were! We were ... we were ... well, you know how light leaves someplace and then gets to another?"

"Yes?"

"We were outrunning the light! It was like riding on the crest of a light wave that is thinking about becoming itself but isn't there yet. Like I was the message that the light was bringing, and we went, I mean, we went everywhere! It was absolutely incredible!"

God asked warmly, "And, Steven, how did you feel while you were traveling to all of those places?"

"Incredible! Did I say that already? I mean, from the beginning of wherever we started all throughout all of the galaxies and everywhere we went from one end of the universe to the other, I could feel the pulsing energy of everything, and it felt like the things we flew past were ... were ... *calling to me*. Like they wanted me to join them, to fuse with their energy and become part of them. And I felt ... well, for the first time since before I can remember, I felt like I was ... *oh ... my ... God.*"

Raising an eyebrow, he asked, "What is it, Steven?"

Floored with the sudden realization, I said, "*I know why I killed myself!*"

"Really?"

"Yes! I ... I killed myself because I didn't believe that I belonged in the universe. I mean, I didn't believe that I *fit* in the universe ... that I wasn't cut out to be a part of any of it. I didn't think that I was good enough to get the girl I wanted or the job I wanted or any of it."

Supportively, he said, "And now?"

Overcome with sheer joy, I said, "I get it! I mean, I really get it! I am a part of the universe. Everything is a part of the universe. We all are, and we all were, and we all will always be a part of the same thing!

"Oh ... my ... God. I am ... I can't even begin to describe how sorry I am for ... *absolutely everything*—for all of the things I said and for throwing away my life and for ... well, for everything. To think of all of the stupid fucking childish things I played with when I could have been—"

"Steven, don't worry about that. Do you see where the problem was now?"

"Yes, yes, I do! I spent all of that time hiding in my room and having relationships with fake girls and never taking a shot at anything because I didn't think that I was cut out to participate in the world. And I guess I wound up ... well, I don't even know how to describe it."

"Steven, all souls who do what they *don't* want to do because they are afraid that the world will not accept what they *do* want to do just wind up subsidizing the chaos down there."

"What?"

"By accepting the paltry things that you could obtain cheaply and easily instead of going after what you really wanted, you told the world that you would wait on Steven because it was too much for you to actually *be* Steven. You wound up subsidizing everything around you by sacrificing *you* so that the world didn't have to deal with the real Steven."

Shaking my head in disbelief, I said, "Shit! You're right! What a wuss I was! I should have ... I mean, I should have walked out of my place every day and—"

Smiling broadly, he said, "Lived according to Steven?"

"Fucking-A right!"

Clapping his hands in applause, he said, "Steven, congratulations! You have healed."

"I ... I what?"

"Healed."

Puzzled, I said, "I ... oh, you mean because of my face? Jesus told me that that was better back in the hospital."

"No, Steven, look down."

"Holy—! Where did my suit go? I was just wearing it when I came in here. And now it's ... it's gone! And I'm ... well, I'm just ... or I think I am ... or, well ... I look like just one glowing ball of light!"

Beaming contentedly, he said, "Yes, Steven. That is what you look like now."

"But ... I mean ... how did I ... or how is it possible to—"

"You had that in you the whole time. Your soul heals from the inside out, and that suit was just there to hold you up until you were ready."

"Are you serious?"

"Of course. Steven, you fill the suit; the suit does not fill you. Anyway, it's just a rental while you're up here."

"Well, why didn't it work at first?"

"It couldn't until you were ready. When you were willing to let go of the rest of the crap you were clinging to, your inner self came out."

Completely leveled, I said, "Oh my, oh my ... I ... how can I possibly be worthy of this?"

Still smiling, God said, "Steven, you are you. You will always be you unless you decide to muck it up with other things. Once you get rid of those things, you go back to being you."

"Really?"

"Yes, Steven. That is what you are supposed to be doing up here. Finding you again. And, Steven, blessed is he who existed before he came into being."

"But I've ... I mean, I've been so awfully rotten to you and everyone, and I still can't believe that I deserve ... your mercy. How are you not angry with me?"

God laughed heartily and said, "Did you really think that I would get upset about you cursing me and spending all of your time trying to find your own asshole?"

Blushing uncontrollably now, I said, "I, um, well, when you put it that way ..."

"Steven, what would you like to do next?"

And exhaling the first thoughtful breath I had taken in a long time, I said, "I think I need to ... I think I need to go and lie down."

XXIII

Back to bouncing around the room like a pinball, I said, *"Jesus, I don't think I can go on!"*

Sitting down calmly, he said, "Steven, what are you talking about?"

"How can I possibly repay him for what I've done?"

"Oh, it's easy. All he is asking you to do is make it to the end next time. You can do that, can't you?"

"I … um … I will certainly try."

"Steven, for you, there is no trying. You will either make it to the end or you won't."

"Well, I will. I just will. But that hardly seems like enough. I mean, that's not for him. That's about not blowing up the whole universe."

"Oh, we were being a bit overdramatic about that whole thing. We have had souls up here who committed suicide more than once."

Halting in my tracks, I said, "Really? But … so, so I'm not threatening the whole universe if I do it again?"

Chuckling, he said, "Of course not. The actual limit is seven, and no one has come close to that yet."

189

Smacking my fist in my palm, I said, "Look, I'm not going to do it again. I will find a way to make it to the end no matter what I have to do!"

And pumping his arm in encouragement, he said, "That's the spirit, Steven! All you have to do is find yourself, and you will make it through just fine."

Sitting down, I said, "But … where … how … how did it all go so wrong last time? And how can I possibly be given a second chance after all of the horrible crap I said to him?"

"Steven, you have enough energy inside of you to do nearly anything. Power a human for an entire lifetime, blow up your suit in heaven, even endure all of the misery of the world and not let any of it out of you. That is what you never did. You never let that part of you out that made everything worth it. You never took a stand long enough to let the world know who Steven was. Instead, you blew yourself up.

"As for God, well, souls have been blaming him since the beginning of time for this or that or the other. But he has seen his fair share of mischief in the universe, and he doesn't get upset about it anymore. Honestly, you should have seen him ages ago. Fire, brimstone, you name it. But he does not do those things now, and when you scream at him, he does not bother answering you with words. He knows that it is not what you say to him but what you do next time that is the important part. Steven, just try to remember that whatever you do to yourself, you are only doing to yourself. It will not affect us here."

Smacking my forehead, I said, "Wow, you're right. All of the time I spent running around and trying to end myself only wound up hurting me. He never moved an inch, did he?"

"Nope. He doesn't. And when the story has ended, if you are still trying to fight with him, vengeance will ultimately be his. That is a battle that you cannot win, I promise you."

"I, well … and I can see that now, and I sort of see how you do things up here. Wow. I just wish that someone would have told all of this to me before we started."

"Steven, the message comes across much better when you discover it for yourself. Besides, if we had told you everything that was going on, what would you have done?"

"Oh, I would have tried to blow it up for sure!"

Smiling, he said, "See? And by not knowing, you tried to blow it up for you and not for us. That is how it is supposed to work."

"Well, okay. But you have to agree that it's a pretty frightful place down there, and I can hardly be blamed for panicking about the whole situation. And this place is not much better. Shit, I feel like I'm going schizophrenic half the time up here. Stay, go, stay go. It's crazy, I tell you!"

Standing up and smoothing out his tunic, he said, "Oh, Steven, it's not possible to have a schizophrenic break up here."

"It's not?"

"No. All of you is up here right now. You could have a schizophrenic break if you leave part of you up here when you go back there, and then you'd really in for a ride. And then of course if you get down there and someone does something to you to make you wish you *had* left part of you here—"

"What?"

Changing the subject, he said, "Look, Steven, don't worry about all of that for now. You are doing just fine. You came along nicely, and you will make it back to earth in one piece. And when you get back there, you will just have to participate. Life is an activity. It may be gruesome, and it may be hard, but it is an activity. Just dive into it and worry about the rest later. Otherwise, if you spend too much time sitting in your room and shitting yourself, then you're just inviting more misery. And if you don't use your own energy for your own purposes when the time is right, that same energy will turn to stone, and you will wind up drowning because of it."

"Okay, okay, I get it, and I will work on all of that. But why didn't I see any clues that that was the road I was heading down?"

Turning toward the empty spot on the wall, he said, "Steven, did you ever bother to stop and look in the mirror?"

"I, um, well …"

And focusing back to me, he said, "We have actually known for quite some time that you were going to kill yourself."

Floored, I said, *"You what?* Why didn't you stop me?"

Jesus shrugged and said, "How could we? That is something that no one can stop but you."

"Oh, come on. You can do anything from up here, right?"

"Actually, no, Steven. We told you, it is your life, and we do not interfere."

"Shit. Well, how … or … when … or, how long had you known?"

"Oh, ever since your family died in that crash."

Smacking the bed, I said, "See! I told you it was too much to bear."

"No, Steven, it's not that. Millions of people go through the same sort of thing and figure out how to get by and recover. You were gone long before that."

"I was what?"

Pacing slowly in front of me, he said, "Gone, and we could see it happening. Every chance that you had to dig in and make a place for yourself down there, you just let it go by. You never planted a flag and told the world that you were staying. So when something difficult came along, we had no doubt that you would just roll over and give in."

"I … I … well … first off, thank you for ruining what little self-esteem I had built up thus far in heaven."

Jesus smiled coyly. "Don't mention it!"

"But, well, if I missed all of those things and I was heading down a path of destruction, why didn't you at least give me a sign or something?"

"Oh, Steven, there were plenty of signs. You just missed all of them."

Whirling my head around, I said, "What? Where? I didn't see anything unusual."

"That's only because you weren't paying attention. Steven, do you remember the first date you had with that girl in college? The one who made you sick of relationships?"

"Yes, of course! That was the whole reason why I never ... never talked to anyone in a serious way after that."

"Well, if you will remember, the first night you went out with her, when you went to the movies, it was snowing like hell."

"Holy—! I do remember that! I remember thinking, 'Uh-oh, this has to be a bad omen or something, and maybe I should ...' But, wait, you guys don't do stuff like that up here, do you?"

"What? Make snowstorms to let people know when they are getting into a bad relationship?"

"Yes!"

"Of course we don't. But, Steven, you noticed the storm, didn't you?"

"I sure did."

"If you had been as into that girl as you were the eventual object of your affection—the girl in your apartment building that you never bothered to talk to—"

Beaming, I said, "Emily!"

"Yes, Emily. If you had been as into the other girl as you were Emily, then when that storm came down, you would have said, 'Wow, what a great night to stay in and cuddle with this terrific girl!' Instead, you took it as a bad omen and didn't do anything about it."

"So?"

Leaning toward me, he said, "So the writing was on the wall, and you refused to read it. The omen was you. You were the one who saw this or that as a good or a bad thing, but you didn't act on it. You didn't put your whole mind, body, and soul into living according to Steven. And that is when things started to go wrong. Steven, it snows on everyone at some point, and it will snow on you whether you are ready for it or not. What you do when that snow comes can make the whole difference in how you spend your time down there."

Still shaking my head in disbelief, I said, "I just … I guess I didn't see any problems, because I was pretty much doing what lots of other people were doing, and it seemed like it was okay—well, as long as I was left alone and not bothered by anyone about what I was doing."

"Steven, there is a universe of difference between getting away with how you are living and living according to yourself."

Nodding pensively, I said, "I … um … yes, I'll bet that's true. But you can … I mean, certainly after all this time, even you're aware of … I mean, even if you do avoid getting distracted by enchanting figures, like he said … certainly you can understand—"

"Steven, spit it out."

Finally pouring my soul out, I said, "Jesus, you just can't know what it feels like to have something so beautiful sitting in front of you and … well, and you want to talk to her, to reach out and touch her to see if she's really real, and you want to get letters from her and then be nervous about opening them to see what they say and then not be able to not open them and then want to call but not want to seem too anxious and … you get sick and don't want to eat when you think about how good things can be and … well, I guess the complexities of that whole mess are beyond what you've had to deal with, right?"

Stepping back, he said, "Steven, that's exactly how we feel every time we send a new life to earth."

Raising an eyebrow, I said, "No shit?"

"No, Steven. Every single life is a new, boundless, and perfectly wonderful possibility, and we can't know how that is going to turn out until it gets started. The first step is opening the door, and we never hesitate to send someone back down when he or she is ready. When we do, we are just as anxious as you described to see how things are going to turn out."

"Wow!"

"And when you pray down there, that is when we most often find out how things are coming along. Now, those are the kinds of messages I'm always anxious to get!"

Suddenly connecting the dots, I asked, "So that's why you answer whenever you are called?"

Matter-of-factly, he said, "Of course. What did you think I was doing? But, Steven, can you imagine what would happen if, instead of opening that door to new possibility, we just sat here and dicked around like you did?"

"Oh, *now I get it*. What an asshole I was!"

"So do you see how you missed the mark in your own life?"

"Yes, I certainly do." Still reflecting, I said, "I'll say … people pray about a lot of stupid stuff. How do you deal with that?"

"Steven, you seem to have this idea stuck in your head that what one life does is any more or less important than what you do."

"Well …"

"Why don't you try to live your own life and let others do the same?"

"Really? That sounds pretty easy. Huh. Well, I may have to work on that a bit, you know, now that I've gone through all of this. Shit, Jesus, I really wish I could go back and start again. I mean, start again with Emily."

Nodding, he said, "That's regret for you, pal. The good news is that you have a whole lifetime of new opportunities to look forward to."

Dejected, I said, "Yeah, but those same opportunitites are in a world where I'm going to get killed anyway at some point. Or lose the one I love. Or … whatever."

Picking up one of the broken toys on the floor, he said, "Steven, let's end the suspense. When you go back next time, the body you are in will die. It may be squashed like a bug or shot by someone else, or you might just die of old age. But something somewhere is going to send you back to us. Now, Steven, you probably wouldn't care one whit about any of that after having spent a thousand and one nights with Emily, would you?"

Smacking my palms on the bed, I said, "Fucking-A, Jesus! Knowing what I know now, I'd settle for *one* night with her!"

"See? Steven, that crazy, bipolar ball of a mother you live on down there is in reality a treasure trove of infinite possibility. And if you put your whole mind, body, and soul into getting something you want, you can have it. Once you start down that path, everything else that used to bother you will just fade into the background."

Hopefully, I said, "So you're sayin' I got a chance?"

"Of course you do. You just have to get back in the game. And it is waiting for you as soon as you get there."

Shaking my head, I said, "Man, this is some heavy stuff. Thanks for all of the help you put in for us."

"Steven, don't mention it. That's what I'm here for."

"But … hey, why don't you go down there and spend more time playing soccer? I mean, that's what you really like to do, right? This other stuff is … well, I guess it's just what you think you have to do. And I'll bet that you are just totally awesome at soccer too! You know, with all of the tricks you can do and—"

Tossing the toy aside, he said, "Steven, I learned a long time ago that there was never going to be any peace in my own life if I spent it playing games. Most people think that I avoid temptation because I'm a prude or because I'm better than that. In reality, all I do is to only follow those things that are consistent with who I am and what I need to do." Opening a drawer and pulling the magazine out, he said, "Now, don't get me wrong. I do like to watch from time to time, but there really is only one way for any soul in the universe to find peace, even me. And that is by doing what that soul was meant to do. That doesn't always mean doing what that soul wants to do or just doing what comes easily."

"Wow. I get it now! Shit. You really *did* die for our sins. I mean, because we're all such assholes, and we need you to take care of things for us.

"Fucking-A. Well, Jesus, I wish … I wish … well, there are too many things to wish that I had done differently. I wish at least that I hadn't brought all of that crap into my room in the first place. That's probably an awful mess for you to have to clean up after I leave. Sorry about all of that waste."

"Don't worry about it. We expected that to happen too."

"What?"

"Oh, sure. The fake stuff we give souls to play with up here never winds up satisfying them. It's the same as your quest for the perfect Internet porn scene down there."

"What?"

"Steven, when you go for something real down there, most times it will only take one of anything to make you happy. That is what happens when you use your untapped energy to obtain something real. When you use it to chase things that are fleeting and not real, it will just take more and more and more fake stuff to fill the void, and eventually, you will just overload, and nothing will ever satisfy you after that point."

"Shit! I had no idea. I guess I … well, I guess I overdosed on porn?"

Chucking the magazine on the pile of rubble, he said, "Yes, Steven. And one good dose of real contact with a real person whom you fought to attract would have cured all of that. A million of these magazines can never do the same thing."

"Okay, okay, I already know what an idiot I was down there. But why did you let me play with all of that crap up here? I mean, the toys and the poster and that nudie mag?"

"We can't know what it will take to help you rediscover yourself up here. And all of that stuff usually does wind up helping in the end. But don't worry, it will get reused."

"How? I destroyed everything in there."

"Oh, we take all of the stuff people bring into heaven and smash it all together. It will eventually be turned into a new star somewhere in the universe."

"Wow! Wait, where did you get the stuff that's in my room now?"

"From old stars, of course."

Surveying all of the carnage I created, I said, "Holy shit! Well, I still feel bad about smashing everything."

"Steven, we knew that you would do that the minute you brought the mirror in."

"You did?"

"Sure. Most people will do anything to avoid really looking at themselves. And like you and the rest of the group in the hospital, we get a lot of people up here who think that if they defile themselves or their rooms or whatever, we will just give up on them and kick them out of the universe."

My excessive blushing problem seemed to come back just then. Jesus continued, "But, Steven, as you know, we cannot get rid of you, because you are part of everything else. There is no such thing as being thrown out of the universe."

"Incredible … What a ship you guys run up here! Hey, can I … I mean, could I go and visit it? You know, the star that is going to be made out of the crap in my room?"

"The way you guys are going now, I doubt it. You will have to all get your acts together before you can take a trip that far. But don't worry, Steven. You have a perfectly good planet to work with already. Just learn to get along with her, and you will be fine."

Slowly accepting that truth, I said, "Yeah, I guess so. But hey … I would … I sure would feel better if you were going back with me."

"I know, Steven. But you don't need me to make it through next time. Besides, I have work to do up here. You can understand that, can't you?"

"Yes, I guess I can. But what if, I mean, what if I get lost again, and I can't find my way out of it?"

Sitting back down, he said, "Steven, people get lost all the time. It is part of the process. And as I said before, it is my favorite part. Fish need to get lost in water. People need to get lost in themselves. Don't worry. What you are really seeking is within you, so you can't miss it if you try. And if you do get lost and can't find your way out, you can start by looking at other people and how they have gotten past their own demons."

"Demons? What demons?"

"The forces that try to drag you away from who you really are."

"Well, I can see that. But I think that people have figured out that there are no real demons down there. I mean, no dragons, no evil witches, no nine-headed monsters. Just other people who … Oh, wait, now I get it. Who needs demons with evil grandmothers? And … well, I guess we do most of the rest of it to ourselves, right?"

"Now you're getting it, Steven. Just try not to let anything block your energy down there, especially you. That is the best way they have to make you fly off the handle and miss your own mark. Remember Mary from the hospital? That was her problem. She let others block her energy and keep it from going where she wanted it to."

Shaking my head regretfully, I said, "Yep. Real shame too. Gosh, she was a sweet girl. Anyway, so is it time for me to go now?"

"Not just yet. You still have a little bit of time before we'll be ready to send you back, so you can stay here and think about what you want to do next time."

My bewilderment returned. "What I want to do? I … well, I haven't even given that any thought."

Rising and crossing the room, he said, "Don't worry too much about it now. I have to go for a while, and if you want to go back and talk to God again, you don't need me to take you there."

"What?"

"Look."

And Jesus opened the door to my room, and I could see out onto the whole expanse of heaven, and it was … it was …

"Holy—! Okay, I *will* stop saying that from now on. Where did the walls go?"

"What walls?"

"*The walls!* Every time you and I went from here to where God was, there were walls and corridors and everything, *everywhere!*"

"Steven, they were never there in the first place. But you couldn't see past that until you found yourself."

"Wow! And all I had to do was blow myself up?"

"Well, that and then learn from it. Steven, despite all of your bellyaching, we do things pretty easily up here. Ask, and it will be given to you. Seek, and you will find. Knock, and the door will be opened. And once you have done the work of finding yourself, everything looks entirely different up here."

Leveled with surprise, I said, "Absolutely incredible! And I can see, well, I can see *everything!* And I can see exactly where he is and … oh, Jesus, what a wretch I have been!"

"Steven, don't worry about that. You'll do better next time."

"But I … I … *I even fucked up my trip to heaven!*"

"No, you didn't. You did just fine up here. You did exactly what you were supposed to do."

"I did?"

"Yes. You behaved according to Steven, and it was flawless."

"Well, okay, so yay for me, I guess. But ... but, look at all of the things I could have been doing! I ... well ... I spent all of my time in this room just shitting myself, and look at all of the glorious things I could have been ... Jesus, can I just start over with the whole process up here?"

Resting a hand on my shoulder, he said, "Sorry, Steven. One trip through per soul. Don't worry about it. This will all be here when you get back, and you can spend time focusing on other things next time."

"I don't even know what to say."

"That's okay, Steven. I have to go now."

Breathing a deep sigh, I said, "I understand. Thank you. Thank you again, for everything."

XXIV

God beamed at me when I came back in. "Welcome back, Steven! How are you feeling?"

Throwing myself down on the bench, I said, *"Horrible!"*

"Why is that?"

"Well, I am supposed to be healed at this point and on my way back down to earth to live as a human, and I don't understand how all of this fits together."

"Steven, that's not a problem."

"How can you say that? How can I possibly get through another round with all of these unanswered questions in my head?"

"First of all, it is not necessary to understand how the entire universe works or even to know much of anything about anything in order to have a long, happy life."

Surprised, I said, "Really?"

"Of course not. Humans have functioned for eons with some information, wrong information, or without even looking for information, and everything turns out just fine. The trick is to focus on one thing that you really want to make a part of your life and to stick with that."

"Huh. Well, that hardly sounds like it could lead to a satisfying life, especially now that I know all of these things."

Dubious, he said, "Steven, what do you know?"

Counting on my fingers, I said, "Well, I know for example that … that life is eternal."

God said, "Good for you."

"And … um, that I have to go back and finish what I started … and, that we're all in it together, and that I *am* a part of the universe, and …"

"Steven, those are all very good things. But most people can figure those things out very early on, and it won't be difficult for you to relearn them, either."

"Relearn? Oh shit, I almost forgot. I'm going to forget all of this, right?"

"That's right. Well, not exactly right. Your soul never forgets itself."

"But why can't I keep the knowledge too?"

"Steven, do you honestly want to remember what you did in your last life?"

Pausing for a second, I said, "Um … most of it, no. But I don't want to forget myself."

Smiling, he said, "After all of the work you have done here, I don't think that will be a problem."

"Well, it still seems like such a waste of great knowledge! I mean, can you imagine how far I could get if I could remember this stuff for, like, seven or eight lifetimes? Or if I didn't have to eat or sleep or—"

"No. How far, Steven?"

"I don't know, but pretty darn far, I can tell you that!"

"You sound like so many people we have seen up here. Everyone claims that if things were just different or if they could live longer, they could master the universe or find their great lost love or build a tower to the stars. Let me tell you, fighting against the way things are turns out bad in most cases."

"Yes … but … I … well, I'm also worried about forgetting all of the good things I learned up here, and I'm worried about losing myself again and, you know, failing."

God raised his hand in reproach. "Steven, there is no such thing as failing. Whatever you do, you do, and you will have to deal with that on the return trip. And didn't Junior tell you? If you get lost, just look for other people to help you out of the woods."

"Yeah, he said something like that." Perking up, I said, "But hey, wouldn't it be great if all of this were written down somewhere?"

"All of what?"

"Well, all of this. You know, the infinite nature of the universe and life and those things?"

Wrinkling his forehead, he said, "Steven, I am pretty sure that someone has touched on all of this before. Haven't you read this anywhere?"

"Not as far as I know. Well … you could say that I haven't looked very hard, but I am quite sure that nothing I came across last time would have kept me from killing myself. As a matter of fact, can I go back to my room for a while?"

"Sure, Steven. Why?"

"Well, I want to look up some things. What I mean is, am I on a deadline to get out of here?"

"Not exactly. You are ready to go. We are just waiting for the right family to come along for you."

Exclaiming, I said, "Right family? See, I knew it! You do pick who I go back to!"

"Only in a very minor way. We are waiting on a couple that wants to have a child named Steven."

"A what?"

"A child named Steven. We can't very well send you back to a family that wants a Mark or a Larry or a Joe. Then you'd really be lost! No, you are Steven, and so we have to find a family looking for a Steven."

"Why the hell does that matter?"

"Steven, you are Steven. You have always been Steven, and you will always be Steven. That has not changed since the beginning of time."

"But, what if … what if I don't want to be Steven anymore?"

Shrugging, he said, "Well, if you still feel the same way, then when you get old enough next time, you can always change your name. But, Steven, why would you want to be anyone else?"

Scratching my head, I said, "That's a good question. I guess I don't even know what it means to be Steven."

Nodding slowly, he said, "That's right. The world has, in fact, never seen the true Steven. And if you have the courage to go back and hang on, then the world will have yet another great mystery to ponder."

"Mystery? What mystery?"

"The mystery of Steven. The mystery of a soul who endures and does not give up. Who participates and accepts the adventure he is given. Steven, you will eventually have to realize that the world you will live in next time actually has more to do with accepting your own circumstances than it does with fighting for survival."

"Wow, I never really thought about it like that! I spent so much time pissed off because I thought that the world had already figured everything out and that I didn't fit in it that I—"

Cocking his head, he said, "Steven, how can the world already have all of the answers when they haven't seen you yet?"

"Holy—! You're right! I mean, I am part of the universe, and I am an answer in the universe too! Right?"

"Right."

Shaking my head in disbelief, I said, "Wow. This is *deep stuff.* But you know, we are never really told down there to ponder our own mysteries. It's always about someone else's life or product or whatever it is that they're selling or what I should be doing or not doing or thinking or not thinking. Shit. I spent years down there just destroying myself, because no one ever gave me the option to be me. No one has ever told me before that I have the right to just *be Steven!*"

"Well, you do. That is your gift in the universe."

"And no one has ever told me that I was on an adventure. Everything seems pretty boring down there. Well, outside of what you see on television and the Internet."

"Steven, you do not need to go off on a quest to slay a dragon or sail to an unknown land to have your own adventure. You don't even need to get circumcised."

"What?"

God flipped his hand and said, "Oh, people have been circumcising males for eons to remind them that they can no longer go back and be the children they used to be. But you don't have to have an experience like that to know that you need to grow up and be your own person. And if you live the questions in your own heart for you and only you, then every single day of your life can be an adventure, no matter where you are. The trick is to try to make the world you see inside of your head match the world you see on the outside too. How you do that is entirely up to you, and no one can ever know what it is that you are seeking, except for Steven."

"Incredible. Just incredible. Thank you again for letting me be, well, I guess, me."

"Steven, don't mention it. That is the gift you get with every new lifetime. And besides, you did all the work, not us."

Skeptically, I said, "But … so I'm basically going back exactly as I was? No changes?"

Resting his hands on each other, he said, "Well, things could change. We certainly can't predict what you will learn from your parents or what will happen to you during the reentry process or—"

"But all things being equal, minus the genes and whatever else may happen while I'm in the womb or on the way out or whatever, I'm still going to be pretty much the same, right?"

"Pretty much. Why do you ask?"

Smacking my knee, I said, "Because I want to go back and find someone like Emily!"

Leaning in, he asked, "Well, Steven, why don't you just go back and find *her?*"

Shocked, I said, *"What?* How can I do that? I mean, I shot myself, and she was still down here. That was … hey, how long ago was that?"

"About five years ago."

"What? How can it take that long to get in and out of here?"

"Well, you were out of commission for over six months when you first got here. We put all suicides in a mandatory six-month detox program, and then—"

"Wait, why did it take that long? I wasn't even addicted to anything when I got here."

Frowning, he said, "Steven, you know that's not true."

"Okay, okay, fine. I was. But they were just for recreation, and I could have quit at any time."

Leaning back, he said, "Sure, sure. Look, Steven, it doesn't matter. You should know by now that if you spend your time living in a pseudoreality, you're not actually living. But souls have real work to do up here, and we need them to be clear and free. We get so many souls up here that are addicted to something that it's just standard protocol these days. And anyway, your soul was pretty scattered and traumatized when you got here. Steven, trying to destroy yourself is an addiction in its own right. We had to keep you under while you were fitted into your suit and got over the whole experience of blowing your face off. Seriously, you were screaming for the first month you were up here, and it was horrible to listen to."

"Screaming, really?"

"Oh yes. It is quite typical with gunshot victims. I tell you, you should see the souls that set themselves on fire down there. They get here still smoldering from the flames. Nasty stuff. The smell is impossible to get off the sheets."

"But then why has everything else taken so long?"

"That was completely up to you. Some souls are in and out of here in a jiffy. You spent lots of time asking questions and looking for your own asshole and then in the hospital and out and … well, you get the idea."

"Huh. Well, I guess my real question is, why didn't you just tell me all of this instead of making me go through it? You know, a nice stern lecture followed by a pat on the butt, and a 'go and get 'em, tiger.' That sort of thing."

Frowning, he said, "Come on, Steven. You should know by now that there are no magic words or magic pills or anything that we could do, even up here, to change how you were feeling. When a soul is set on destroying itself, the change can only come from the inside. Nothing anyone says or does is going to change that. But once you find the meaning of you—for *you* and not for someone or something else—then you can get over anything, even despising your own existence."

I said, "Shit. You're right! Oh, that probably sounds stupid to say to you too. I'll bet that you hear that all the time."

Grinning coyly, he said, "Once in blue moon. But I don't let it go to my head."

"Well, so next time, if I don't have to recover from killing myself, and don't … you know, do those other things, how long will it take me to get through heaven?"

"That is again up to you. If you were to answer every single question you might have for yourself on the next round—which no one ever does—and you don't dillydally while you're up here, you can be back on the ground in as little as six months."

"Really? That short?"

"Sure. After all, you probably won't have to wear a suit and—"

"Wait, what? *No suit?* Why did I have to go through that this time?"

"Steven, we give those suits to souls who need extra protection while they are recovering. That includes all suicides. Sorry, but it was for your own safety."

"Well, shit. I wish I had known that I could have skipped that part if only I hadn't—"

With a mild rebuke, God said, "Tried to end yourself?"

My eyes found the floor. "Yes. And again, sorry about that."

"Steven, it's over. You are past that now. Anyway, like I said, if you don't get lost up here again, we can have you back on the ground pretty quickly. We even used to be able to turn souls around so that, if you wanted to go back as a human, we could almost send you back to your same family."

Looking up repulsed, I said, "Ewww! Why would anyone want to do that?"

"Believe it or not, some people actually like their family members."

Shaking my head, I said, "Weird. Okay, okay, I get it. But what were you saying about Emily?"

"Oh, we just sent her back."

"No kidding?"

"No."

"How on earth did that happen?"

"She spent a few more years down there after you checked out, and then she fell down an elevator shaft."

"Wow, *that's great!* Oh, I mean, no, that's *tragic.* But it's fortunate for me … or I guess I should say … maybe that's an interesting coincidence!"

"It was an interesting coincidence. She was on her way to see a counselor in an office building because she was depressed about being single—"

"You have got to be shitting me!"

"No, Steven. As it turns out, she was just about as lonely as you were and was having a hard time dealing with it when she accidentally died."

"That is awesome! Oh, I mean, you know, not awesome in the classical sense, but awesome that she was … well, no, that won't sound right, either. Oh, wait. If I hadn't killed myself, we might have … oh my God!"

Nodding slowly, he said, "Yes, Steven, that's right. But you are lucky. Most people don't get a second chance this close in time to find their great love."

Disgusted, I said, "What a waste I am! What a colossal waste of a life! I mean, mine. How can I ever live with that knowledge?"

God smiled and replied, "The good news is that you do not have to. Or the knowledge of shooting yourself in the face. You just have to start over and try to do better next time."

"But, well, look, even you can see that it's tough. It's so incredibly tough down there and … well, if I knew then what I know now, of course I wouldn't have done it. I would have done everything exactly the opposite. But it was so hard. I mean, problems like this, like suicide and people falling down elevator shafts and death and destruction and disappointment with your family and everything ... I mean, nothing ever gets fixed down there, and the shit and misery just pile up."

"Steven, how about if we start with you? Don't kill yourself next time, and get the girl, and that will be two wrongs that have been righted. And to boot, why don't you go crazy and try to make it to, say, forty? That will be a huge improvement!"

"Forty? How is that a huge improvement?"

"You didn't make it that far last time. That is something to shoot for. Steven, wonderful things will happen to you every day if you stick around and keep exploring your own mysteries. And don't worry about all of that other stuff. If you spend too much time worrying about things that you cannot control, you run the risk of developing agoraphobia."

It is amazing how easily he controls the thermostat in this place. Blushing again, I said, "What?"

"You know, that thing that you were going to tell us all about earlier? Look, Steven, if you spend too much time living in your little bubble, then when you actually experience the world, it could cause you to just blow up."

"Oh ... er ... you know, that agoraphobia thing was ... that was nothing. It was just a thing that I was experimenting with as a ... you know a cause of—"

"Steven, start with you, and worry about the rest later."

"Right! Focus on Steven. Got it. And Emily! Hey, wait, did she go back to the same town?"

"Pretty close. The next town over. You'll be able to spot her if you try."

Oh, you can bet your ass I'm going to find her!

"Steven, I should tell you at this point that, when you *start talking like this, everyone can hear what you are saying.*"

"You are shitting me."

"No, Steven, I am not."

"Everyone? You mean *everyone?*"

"Of course. Well, most souls up here are busy tending to their own affairs, but what you say can be heard by anyone who wants to listen."

"Oh, fuck me! Hey, why can't I hear everyone else?"

"You can; you just have to listen. Listen."

Cocking my ear, I said, "Oh, shit! I can hear it! I guess I could hear that the whole time; I just thought it was like background noise or singing or something."

"Well, some of it is."

"*He's got the whole world, in his hands; he's got the whole world, in his hands …*"

"*Oh fuck!* Is this the place where they learned that damn song? Is that what you do in the other parts of heaven? Teach songs and crap like that?"

"No, Steven. We did not teach them that song. That is coming from the Children's Ward. They just sing whatever they feel like singing."

"Well, I can't stand that song!"

Frowning, he said, "Steven, don't be such a sourpuss. But I can understand what you are saying. It is not a very good song."

"What? Really?"

Shaking his head, he said, "Oh, it's completely inaccurate. It would be more appropriate to say that I have the whole universe in my hands, but I don't technically have arms anymore."

"*What?*"

"Oh yes. How do you think I made everything in the universe? I used my left arm to make the stars and galaxies and my right arm to make life."

Surveying his form in disbelief, I said, "But, I mean, as you sit in front of me, you have two arms."

"Steven, I am just a projection here. You cannot see me, because I am vaster than the entire universe. You could never look upon my actual form and ever see all of me. So I just show you a part that you want to or can handle seeing."

Incredulous, I said, "But you gave up your arms for life and the stuff in the universe?"

Smiling broadly, he said, "Of course. Steven, you cannot make something from nothing. But don't worry. When it is all over, everything will return to become one with me again. And then the universe will truly know itself as it was and is."

"Fuck me. This is some deep stuff. Well, I'll work on getting that song changed next time as well."

"Steven, I wouldn't put that on the top of your priority list. Don't pay too much attention to what other people are doing. Just focus on yourself, and let the rest go."

Slightly wounded, I said, "What? You don't think that I can teach the world to sing a new song?"

"Of course you can. You can teach a choir to sing just about anything. But you need to stick to the basics first. Find yourself, get the girl, and make it to the end. Worry about your singing career on the next trip around."

"Okay. I will. And I have no inner monologue in heaven, which means that I need to get out of here fast!"

"Well, the others can't hear you in your room. And don't worry about everyone else. They just think that you are talking to yourself, which is quite common up here."

"Oh, good. Speaking of that, can I get back to my room now? And how much time do I have left?"

"Steven, you're just fine. Don't worry about it. Life will wait a little longer if need be, so take your time."

XXV

Patting the arms of his chair tentatively, God said, "Welcome back, Steven. Are you ready to go?"

Waving my hand at him and clutching my notes, I approached with a determined step and said, "Not quite yet. I have a few problems we need to take care of before I go."

"Problems? What problems?"

"Well, can we get Junior in here?"

"Sure. Jesus?"

Jesus skipped in whistling and said, "Hello, Steven! Are you ready to go?"

"No. Hey, sorry to disturb you in the middle of whatever you were doing, but—"

"That's okay, Steven. What is it?"

"Well, I read ... okay, so this time I actually read the Bible, and I especially read all of the things you said when you were down there last time, and—"

Shaking his head, he said, "Steven, that wasn't from the last time."

"Well, okay, I know that, but I guess from the last time that you were down there talking to people and it was being written down."

Nodding, he said, "Okay. Go ahead."

"Well, I didn't see anything in what you said that would keep me from killing myself next time. I mean, you didn't mention any of this stuff or about suicides having to do it over again or any of that."

Jesus shrugged. "Steven, I apologize, but I was pretty busy, as you know."

"Oh, of course."

"And I couldn't touch on every little subject in the short time I had. I had a lot of tax collectors and prostitutes to deal with, if you recall."

"Yes, I do. And by the way, they're still down there."

Chuckling, he said, "Well, see, so there *is* something for you to do next time!"

"Very funny. Listen, seriously. I am very concerned about this whole getting lost thing and killing myself again, and I didn't see anything that would have helped. I mean, if you would have just said 'All of life is energy, and it is indestructible, and souls can support all forms of life on earth, and don't panic and shit yourselves in heaven,' that might have been a big help to me."

Going over the teachings in his head, Jesus said, "I think I pretty much covered those things."

"No, you didn't!"

"Well, I may not have said all of the words exactly like that—"

"Look, it didn't even come close."

Showing his palms to me, he said, "Sorry, I was busy. And I didn't get all that much time. Between carpentering and the wine parties and the tax collectors and prostitutes and the crucifixion and execution and the desert … let's not forget the desert … I had a lot on my plate."

I pleaded, "Well, could you please just go back one more time and say all of that?"

"What for?"

"So I don't kill myself and wind up shitting my space suit in heaven again!"

"Oh, Steven, it's easy. Just don't do it."

"Well, can you at least go back and correct the part about a woman being made from a man's rib?"

Skeptical, he said, "Come on. No one takes that seriously."

"Yes, they do! Women have been mistreated for centuries because their husbands believed that they were made from the man's rib."

Dismissing my thought, Jesus said, "Steven, that was all corrected ages ago."

"No, it wasn't!"

"Well, maybe you're right, but people are working on it. And anyway, we are still waiting for you all to stop eating each other and—"

"Oh, like that's ever going to change. Look, just go down and fix that one thing and don't forget to mention something about being careful with your space suit in heaven and—"

Firmly, he said, "Steven, there are bigger problems to worry about."

I stomped my foot in opposition. "No there are not!"

Jesus shrugged. "Agree to disagree. Look, Steven, if you want to change something down there, you are just going to have to do it yourself. I'm done getting crucified for spreading messages."

Defeated, I said, "Well, why didn't you at least tell them about the light stuff?"

"You can't cover everything in one lifetime. But I think I did mention that one a time or two."

"No, but you said *light*. I am faster than light, I am lighter than light. I am … shit, I still don't know how to describe it."

Jesus shook his head and said, "Steven, when you are trying to spread a new message, you need to use terms and concepts that are familiar to your audience. It would not have done any good for me to talk about things that no one understood or related to back then. They would have thought that I was a crazy person or something! But don't worry. Everything works out just fine in the end."

"Well, why didn't you include things about blue jays and dolphins and things like that?"

Jesus said firmly, "Oh, I did."

"Really? I didn't see that anywhere in there."

"Steven, do you remember the parts in the Bible where it said that I stopped speaking in parables and spoke plainly to my disciples, and they immediately understood me?"

"Yes."

"Well, what I said at that time was that your soul is lighter and faster and more powerful than any particle you will ever discover in the universe. And we can make it into a tree or a bear or a dolphin or a blue jay, and watch out, because it is hard to find the asshole in your rubber space suit in the Suicides' Ward, and there is no shitting in heaven."

"*Really?*"

Smirking at me, he said, "No, dummy. Blue jays and dolphins do not need therapy sessions, either up here or down there. They already know what they are doing. And the rest of the planet does not need everything spelled out the same way you do! Shit, I have to go. Sorry."

And he vanished. God clapped his hands together and said, "Anything else, Steven?"

"Well, I am still very worried about my chances and about all of these things that apparently *I* have to take care of because he's not going back anymore."

"Steven, you will do just fine."

Shaking my head and sitting down finally, I said, "I don't know. It all sounds pretty insurmountable." Patting the bench, I smiled hollowly and said, "Hey, it would ... it would just be so much easier if we could sit and talk like this all the time and fix everything that way."

"Sorry, Steven. It doesn't work like that. Your idea has to become the energy inside of you, and that energy has to turn into action. That is the only way to make changes down there. T-shirts and bumper stickers will not do it."

"I still can't understand, I mean ... with all of the incredible things you guys do up here and how good I feel right now, why did it take so little for my life to feel rotten last time? I mean, I'm sure that I was a happy baby, right?"

"You were."

"And then what happened?"

"Somewhere along the line, you became disappointed in what you encountered. It happens all the time."

"Well, how do we stop that?"

"I honestly don't know if you can. So many souls start out trying to duplicate how they felt when they were up here or even how they felt at the very beginning."

"What do you mean?"

"I told you. When this all began, we had an infinite number of souls up here pulsating with energy and hope and eagerly ready to experience the world, for whatever that meant. At that time, there were regrets, no killings, no vengeance, no losses, no disappointment, and yes, Steven, no shitting."

Perking up, I said, "See! I told you that you should add that in up here. Seriously, that would be one thing to help people deal with—"

"Steven, we probably won't make that change up here anytime soon. Get over it. Anyway, even if we did, it wouldn't stop people from giving up down there because they can't duplicate how they feel up here or because they think that it is hopeless to even try."

"Shit. Well, what do I do?"

"Endure, Steven. That is the first step. If you just throw in the towel like you did last time, you will never get anywhere."

"Well, I will. I swear on my life, I will!"

Smiling contentedly and rocking back in his chair, he said, "Now, Steven, that is the kind of swearing we like to hear in heaven!"

I may have a persistent blushing condition to deal with in the next life. I said, "Heh-heh-heh! Sorry about all of that!"

"That's okay. Don't worry about it too much. Do what you can next time, and let the rest go. And do not try to do too much. The soul that tries to do more than it can in a lifetime is a fool."

Jesus stormed back in and said, "Yes, but the soul that does not find out what it can do in a lifetime is *a fucking garden slug!*"

God said, *"Jesus!* Steven does not need to hear that right now."

"Well, do you know how many souls I wind up talking to who say that they would have done this or that or the other if only … I tell you, some people just need to have the balls to sock someone else from time to time."

I said, "See, this is what I was talking about! But, Jesus, what about turning the other cheek and things like that?"

Shadowboxing, Jesus said, "Steven, the best way to deflect a punch is to turn the other cheek. Then, what you do is you follow up with a haymaker—"

"What?"

"Or a kick to the shin works well too. Uppercuts won't usually work, because the other person's arm will be blocking your view, but—"

God snapped at him, "Jesus, go to your room now! Steven does not need any more of your encouragement at this point."

"I'm just saying—"

"Good-bye, Jesus." Jesus stomped out mumbling under his breath.

I said, "What was that all about? I thought that guy was supposed to be meek and mild."

God said, "Most people do, Steven. But that's not Junior, not in the least bit. Don't forget, he is the same guy who said 'If you don't have a sword, sell your cloak and buy one.' But he was also in some respects the world's first tai chi master."

"Wow! So what do I do? Dodge a punch or buy a sword?"

"Steven, that is entirely up to you. As long as violence remains in your hearts down there, it may at times be necessary to buy the sword and deal with it rather than hiding in your cloak. But don't worry about it for now. You have come a long way, and you will do just fine next time. Take each day, and do what you can with it. Strike when the time is right, and let the next day take care of itself."

"I will! But how do I know when the day is done?"

Frowning, he said, "Come on, Steven. We gave you a perfectly good sun to help you with that."

I laughed nervously. "Heh-heh-heh! Sorry about what I said earlier."

"That's okay. The sun does not need you to thank it for doing its job. Now go back to your room, and finish up whatever you need to do. When you are ready, we will send you back down."

"Okay, thank you."

XXVI

God said, "Welcome back, Steven! Are you ready to go?"

"Not just yet. How am I doing on time? Where is Emily?"

"Oh, she's still developing. Not quite out yet."

"Good. Just wanted to make sure."

"Don't you want to get back down there so you will both be the same age?"

"Not really. I'm hoping that she will have a year or two on me. Older chicks are hot! Hey, so, and again, I'm just trying to clarify, but I'm going back as Steven, and she's going back as Emily, right? I can find her in the next town if I look for a girl named Emily?"

"Well, that's pretty much right."

"What do you mean, 'pretty much'?"

"Steven, we don't decide whether you turn out to be a boy or a girl. That all happens down there. You happened to be Steven last time, but you could just as easily be Stephanie next time."

"Oh, fuck me!"

Spreading his arm up high, he said, "Think of it, Steven! You could become a vessel for potentially helping us get life out of here!"

222

"Oh, fuck! I'm really not sure I'm ready for *that*."

Settling back down, he said, "Well, don't worry. It's your choice, anyway."

"But what about Emily? Is she 'Emily' yet?"

"We still can't tell. She might turn out to be Emilio."

Deflated again, I said, "This all sucks! I don't … I mean, I don't even want to think about what happens if I turn out to be a girl. That may be more than I'm cut out for next time. But what if I go down there and she happens to be a boy and I do too?"

"So?" he said dismissively.

"Well, then what do I do?"

"Steven, you can do whatever you would like. We don't make rules about stuff like that."

"Well, what if she's one sex, and I'm the same one, and both of us aren't gay?"

"That happens too. Steven, look, you're just going to have to go down there and give it a shot. I can't guarantee any of it one way or the other. There is no safe word for being born."

"Well, why can't you just make sure that I am Steven and she is Emily?"

"I told you, we don't make that call from up here. We can't. And anyway, it could all change down there at some point. That is up to you."

"Oh, now I feel totally hopeless again. Hey, they'll still have Internet porn when I get back, right?"

Stomping a foot, he scolded, "Steven, stop that! Why would you even open that wound back up?"

"What wound?"

"The one you gave yourself because you didn't believe that you were good enough to participate in the world. Steven, it is one thing to play around giving yourself black eyes when you are trapped in a bubble and the world won't let you out. It is quite another to do the same thing when you are completely free and can make your life into anything you want to."

"Oh, I get it. But if the love of my life is going to be a boy, and I wind up being a boy, then everything gets screwed up, anyway. So why should I even bother?"

"Steven, she will still be a real person, whether the same sex as you or different. What you choose to do with that is up to you, but finding out the *real* answers to the *real* questions in your life is the only way to go. You will never get that playing around with a plastic box."

"I guess I still just don't understand why I can't keep my fantasies *and* get to live the way I want. You know, without it causing me to fall apart."

Frowning, he said, "Steven, listen to yourself. How can you live in a world where you want to do certain things but tell yourself that you're only good enough to have an artificial existence and then call *that* living?"

"Wow, you're right. I never thought of it that way."

"Most addicts go through the same thing, regardless of what they're addicted to. They hit bottom and decide that they want to live, and then the reality of living sets in, and they decide they want to die again. It's a vicious cycle. The only way to stay out of it is to let the wound close and confront life face-to-face."

Nodding slowly, I said, "Okay, I get it. But hey, what about the whole Sodom and Gomorrah thing and the sin of masturbating and all of that?"

"What about it?" he asked dismissively.

"Well, if you're telling me that I can go and find her, even if she is a he or whatever, and just live as I see fit, then I don't get it all."

"Steven, we are in the life business up here. You have to understand that, for us to get you back down there, we need people who want to come together to make a new human life. That's just the way it is. When all of those people were writing that stuff back then, they were just trying to help the process along."

"What do you mean?"

"We can't very well get you back down there if someone is just sitting around jerking off. That won't do it. And contrary to popular opinion in some epochs, you cannot gestate a human life in the large intestine. So people write stories in an effort to encourage the process up here, and it works quite well."

"So why don't you just write that everyone has to have kids and no one can do any of that other stuff?"

"First of all, Steven, I told you. We are not in the book-writing business up here. Second, what good would that do? We don't need for *everyone* to have a child. We still manage to move the population of souls that want to become humans along very well with the current set of people who do want to have kids. The rest of it is up to each individual to decide. Besides, if you make the rules too rigid, then wayward teenagers who are disappointed in their parents will have nothing to do for fun."

"Okay, okay, I get it."

"And besides, they are already making things easier for us to get lives out of here without us having to write or say anything."

"What do you mean?"

"Well, Steven, people are doing better down there. Education is better, nutrition is better, standards of living are becoming better, and as a result, humans are finding themselves more attractive than they have been in a great while. And with breast implants and other forms of plastic surgery, physical attraction is at an all-time high. Frankly, I'm surprised that you left the place with all of the gigantic racks. I would have thought that was right up your alley."

Shocked again, I said, "Hey, you're not supposed to talk like that!"

"Steven, do you think that we don't see everything that goes on? If you do it, we know it. But don't be ashamed. It is all a part of the marvelous process of life down there that we get to observe up here. And thank goodness for silicone too!"

"What?"

"Oh, that was one of the greatest by-products of the creation of stars. That little element has sure calmed things down a bunch."

"Ha! Hey, while we're on the subject, how come I didn't have any private parts in my suit?"

God frowned at me. "We *weren't* on that subject."

"Well … oh … you're right. But, anyway."

"Steven, everything we do up here is planned."

"Really?"

"Really. We don't make suits for you with private parts, because you can't use them up here. Reproductive life only flows one direction. And besides, it is hard enough to get you out of your room up here without giving you an excuse to sit around playing with yourself. Anything else?"

"Well, I'm sure that I have a million questions, but if we go through all of them, Emily will be long gone by the time I get back."

"That's right, pal."

"So I guess if I had to ask one more, it would be … why did you first appear to me as my grandpa?"

Reproachfully, he said, "Steven, that is hardly a good last question to ask. We already went over this."

"Yeah, and I get the whole 'familiar face' thing. But why not my dad?"

"We were aware when you got here that he was not the person who meant the most to you down there."

"Okay. But I mean, I didn't hate the guy."

"Oh, most people do not hate their parents. But most people do struggle with their parents at one time or another, and it is tough. It's just part of the process. With grandparents, most people wind up loving them very much."

"But why does that happen?"

"Because by the time you are born, your grandparents, if they are still around, have already fought the battles in their own lives. In most cases, they are already retired or at least no longer struggling to make their way in the world, and they are at peace. So you don't feel the same need to compete with them as you do with your own parents."

"Okay, I get that part. But—and this is the thing I've been wondering since I got here and you told me that I had to go back—I mean, my grandpa lived a pretty good life, and he got old, and we all thought that he came to heaven."

Nodding, he said, "He did."

"No, but I mean, we thought that he came here to find release from the burdens of, you know, living."

"He did. You all have that coming to you."

"What, death?"

"No. Rest. I told you, Steven. This is a haven between worlds. But you will eventually have to put on another suit and go back down there."

"Well, shit. I still don't know if I'm ready for that. I'm pretty exhausted. Come to think of it, I haven't slept since I got here. How the hell is that possible?"

"Steven, you do not need to actually sleep to rest your soul. You just need to get rid of the garbage that is weighing you down. But don't worry. You will get plenty of sleep when you are on earth."

Sarcastically, I said, "*Yeah, right!* With fucking early development videos playing all day long by the time you're three years old and all of the other shit they put you through—"

"Steven, if you fret when your mother puts you down for a nap, that's not our fault."

"Okay, okay. But with my grandpa, I mean, we thought he came here to rest for good. You know, that he had lived a good, long life and deserved to be here."

"He did. But we have never had a single soul up here who, upon finding out that they were going back—and in your case after a lot of therapy—who was not ready to go back and join the effort. Life takes participation, and everyone who leaves here goes willingly. Your grandpa just said, 'Thanks for the ride,' and we sent him back."

"Where did he go?"

"He is currently living as a great redwood tree in the Pacific Northwest."

"Wow! That must be awesome! Hey, I'd sure like to do that when I go back, you know, the next time!"

"Sure, Steven. And we can talk about that when you get back. But first—"

"I know, I know, I need to get through my life."

"Well, there's that. But, you also need to work on firming yourself up a bit."

"What do you mean?"

"Steven, not just any soul can be a great redwood tree. You have to be able to sit in one place and grow and not be bothered by things going on all over the place, and it takes a tremendous amount of character to do that."

"So?"

God raised his hands and framed a scene. "Well, Steven, picture this in your mind. There is a giant great redwood sitting there."

"Okay."

"And on the side of the redwood is a man hanging down from a rope."

"Okay."

"And on the man's shoulder is a gnat."

"Okay."

"Right now, your soul is just about calm enough to be that gnat."

"Shit. Okay, now I'm just depressed again."

"Steven, I'm just giving you a hard time. Hey, you've had it pretty easy up here!"

"Easy? You call all of this *easy?*"

"Well, we used to have a much more strenuous program for suicides."

"Really?"

"Sure. In the early days, we would boil you in oil and string you up from a tree in front of everyone and feed you to the eight-headed lorax and—"

"Wait, there's no such thing as an eight-headed lorax!"

Matter-of-factly, he replied, "Well, we got rid of it when we changed the suicides' program, but we used to have one here. Anyway, we learned over time that the things you will do to yourself are much more instructive than anything we could think of. So—"

"So you just let me sit in my room festering until I shit myself?"

"Exactly. And it worked out great. Anyway, we had to let you do something to get rid of all of the leftover energy you had."

"What do you mean? I thought that I only had a fraction of my life left when I got here."

"Steven, most souls who have lived out their entire lives come up here with a very small portion of their remaining energy left. You still had 60 percent of yours."

"But then how did I die?"

"You didn't. You just blew your head off, and as a result, your body lost the ability to contain your soul. Just like a burst air bubble. But you had enough energy left over to cause a great deal of ruckus up here. And, Steven, you would have been better served to cause the ruckus down there."

"Well, I know that now. And again, sorry for causing all of the trouble."

"Oh, it's fine, Steven. Most other souls are pretty peaceful, anyway. But you suicides are difficult lot to deal with. The really hard part is keeping all of the sharp objects away from your rooms."

"Yeah? And how do you do that?"

"Up here, we have everything—everything that you have ever had down there. Most souls get access to anything they want. But for you suicides, every time you think of something dangerous, Junior grabs it before it gets to you and locks it in a safe until you are gone."

"Holy crap! I'll bet that keeps him plenty busy!"

"That and the other things. In the end, all we really try to do is to give you enough time to find yourself and try to keep you safe along the way. They pretty much do the same thing down there."

Not falling for that one, I said, "Yeah, right. But on earth, everyone is also stuffing their version of who you are down your throat."

He said, "Steven, the thing they miss down there is remembering that finding yourself is the most important part of the process. People are too busy finding answers, and they forget that the questions are much more valuable in the long run. From up here, *you* are the answer. We don't supply that, you do."

"Well, that is very nice of you. But I still don't understand how I could blow up my suit if I couldn't poke a hole in it."

Shaking his head and laughing, he said, "Oh, Steven, you silly rabbit. The valve on your suit only goes one way! We changed that years ago, because people spent so much time poking themselves and trying to escape."

My face and the rest may have healed, but my cheeks were threatening to fall off with all of this blushing. "Heh-heh-heh. Well, now that I know what I know, I wish I hadn't wasted so much time! Isn't there an easier way to get suicides through all of this?"

"That is entirely up to each individual. You took longer because you were still full of a lot of crap when you got here. Other people's programs take less time. In fact, when we first started the suicides' program, it used to only take twelve months."

"Seriously?"

"Yes. Well, hell in general used to be a twelve-month program. It didn't start, of course, until the souls got rid of the things that landed them there in the first place, but—"

"What? I thought you said that there was no hell."

"Steven, I told you. Hell is the place where your soul is being torn in two, and heaven is the place where you rest and regroup. Both places can be anywhere, if you know—or perhaps *don't* know—how to use them."

"But did you used to have a separate *place* called hell?"

"Sure. But with all of the things that souls do to themselves, up here and down there, we decided to do away with it. Everyone had already voted, anyway, and they decided that it was too frightening."

"So why did you have it at all?"

"Oh, hell was a very useful idea when it first started. There was a certain mob satisfaction we got by chaining a particular soul to a rock for a while or feeding a soul to a hairy-legged beast or whatever the particular punishment might have been. But the interest just dwindled after a while, so we got rid of it."

"Well, what if souls come up here and they still need to learn from something like hell? What do you use for that?"

God turned his head toward the ceiling and called, "Jesus?"

Jesus' voice echoed in. "Yes, Boss."

"What do we use for the hell program up here now? You know, for the nonsuicides?"

"Absence of light."

"Oh, that's right. Thanks, Son. Yes, Steven. What we do is we put the souls in a dark room and don't let them talk to anyone or play with anything, and Junior dresses up in a white sheet and howls outside the door. It usually does the trick."

"And if it doesn't?"

"We turn them into plants."

Shaking my head, I said, "Amazing. You guys really run an amazing ship up here."

"Steven, it's really not too hard. Most souls are fulfilling their purposes and do not require much from us. Some souls cannot let go down there long enough to heal up here, and those are the ones that usually give us the most trouble. And with the ones who cannot let go of the life they used to have … Boy, I could tell you some stories … Seriously, Steven, you should see what poor Geoffrey has to go through."

"Who in the hell is Geoffrey?"

"He is the camel we keep up here to educate the wealthy."

"What?"

"People who think that all that they have gained is theirs. They come up here and boast about their wealth and revel in it. When they get here, they are always trying to buy their way into a longer stay or better accommodations or whatever it is that they are looking for. And we tell them, 'Well, we can grant you an exception to the rules, but only if you can get Geoffrey here through the eye of a needle.' Poor little guy has to endure quite a bit just because people can't seem to let go."

"Wow! I never even thought of asking for a better room. Probably because I died with ten dollars in my checking account and ... Hey, wait a minute. I thought that you said it was just you and Junior up here full-time. You keep a camel on staff too? Man, I'd like to get that gig!"

"Steven, eventually you will have to get over the fact that you have to participate down there. It really is a magnificent place."

"Yeah, yeah, sure, sure."

"And anyway, we don't keep Geoffrey up here full-time. He has eight siblings, and we rotate them so that he gets to go back to earth and do camel things."

"Wow, eight siblings. What are their names?"

"Well, there's Donner and Blitzen, and Comet and Cupid—"

Shaking my head and laughing, I said, "God, those are Santa's reindeer!"

Scratching his head in confusion, he said, "Oh, really? Well, hell, I can't remember what they're called. I think that we just call all of them Geoffrey. Do you want me to get Junior in here to ask him?"

"Never mind. I'll find out later. Hey, Roger said that he rang the front desk and asked for a refrigerator."

"Yes, he did. Roger is one of those interesting cases who killed himself *and* had a lot of money. But we knew what he was doing the whole time, and it worked out in the end."

"Well, where is he now?"

"Already gone. On his way back to continue his adventure of self-discovery and mutilation."

"He's kind of a dick. Maybe you should have turned him into something else."

"Steven, under ordinary circumstances, we would have made him into a turtle for the way he was before he died."

"A turtle?"

"Yes. All wealth one earns is transitory, so people like Roger who die without having realized their true selves and their right desires find no permanent happiness in any world to which they go. So we ordinarily turn them into turtles on the return trip so that they can slow down a bit and get to know themselves better. But rules are rules. He killed himself, so he has to go back as a human."

"Well, if I run into him again, I'm going to punch him in the nose."

"That's fine, Steven."

"Really?"

"Sure. As long as you are not upset if he punches you back."

"That's the whole do unto others thing, right?"

"Right, Steven."

"Well, okay, I'll have to consider how to deal with him. But for now, I have bigger things to worry about. How are we doing on time?"

"Fine. She's just been born. It was a girl, after all."

XXVII

1. There is no shitting in heaven.
2. ~~Try to~~ make it to the end next time.
3. Get the girl.
4. We are all in it together.
5. Be kind to birds.
6. Do not own a gun.
7. You can only have one of anything. Trade for the rest.

Jesus entered with a surprised look and said, "Steven, what are you still doing here?"

"Oh, nothing. Just writing down a few things before I go."

"Steven, you're not writing a book, are you?"

"Of course. I'm … well, I guess I'm writing the book of … me. And I'm working on a few other things. Why?"

Doubtfully, he peered at me and said, "Are you sure that what the world needs is another book?"

"Why? Could having one more harm things?"

Jesus backed away and said, "I guess not. And if it keeps you from killing yourself again, that's fine. But you know that you can't take it with you, right?"

"I … well, oh, of course. Who has ever heard of a baby being born with a book? Heh-heh-heh. That's just silly, Jesus!" *Shit.* "But if I can't take this with me, how will I know what to tell everyone else?"

"What do you mean?"

"Well, I've got to tell *someone* about this!"

"Steven, I told you about pride already. Some things are better kept to yourself. If you make it through next time and you find what you are looking for, don't be an asshole and splatter it all over the front page. Everyone is entitled to seek their own truth."

"Okay, fine, fine."

"Good. Now hurry up. Time is running short."

"What do you mean? I think I'm fine on time. I talked to God not too long ago, and everything is shipshape."

Seemingly pondering the mess he was going to have to clean up, he said, "Well, but the Johnsons get here very soon, and we need your room."

"*What?* Who are the Johnsons, and why do they get my room? Are you … are you going to *kill* them?"

"No, no. I told you, we don't do that. But it is highly likely that they will be committing a double suicide in the very near future."

"Why?"

"Oh, it looks like joint debt problems. They'll probably be here in the next few days."

Exasperated, I said, *"Well, can you stop it?"*

"What, the debt problems or the resulting suicides?"

"Both!"

"Not from up here. Things like that can only be changed from the inside."

"*Great.* So they're coming, and you're going to give them *my* room?"

"Well, you know, space is a bit limited in the Suicides' Ward, and so we were just going to put them in here, assuming that you were gone already. But—"

"But I thought that this was *my room!*"

"Well, it is. Was. You know, when you needed it."

Scowling at him, I said, "That's a pretty crummy thing to do, after all I've been through."

"Look, Steven, the circle of life has to move on. When a house is torn down, the grass grows back. When you heal, the Johnsons get your room. That's just how it goes."

"Fine. I'm almost done, anyway. Hey, do I get the same room the next time I come back?"

"Steven, we are hopeful that you will be in a different ward next time and—"

"Oh, right. Heh-heh! Sorry about getting upset about … never mind. There are just a few more things I need to work on, and then I'll be out of here."

Curious, he said, "Hey, where did you get the pencil, anyway? I thought that you broke yours."

"I did. I traded with one of the other suicides for his. Little trick I learned in the hospital."

XXVIII

God put his hands on his knees as if ready to get up and said, "Hi, Steven. Are you all set to go?"

I motioned for him to stay put. "Not yet. How am I doing on time?"

Settling back down, he answered, "Not bad. She's just learning how to smile."

"Okay, so she's a few months old?"

"Something like that."

"Why does Junior go all over the world visiting all of these different cultures when a lot of them don't even believe in him?"

"Steven, I tell him the same thing I tell all souls. If you believe in yourself, what others think of you doesn't matter. The greatest trick the world can in fact play on you is to get you to believe that you do not exist or that you do not fit somewhere in the universe."

"Boy, I know that feeling."

"Besides, most everybody does believe in him."

Dubious, I said, "Oh, I don't think that's true. I mean, so many cultures believe that—"

"Steven, every culture on earth has a belief in a spiritual helper who aids them along the way. We call him Junior up here. But other people call him by whatever name they want. The particular details of who he is and what he does do not matter. It is the role he fills that draws him down there."

"Wow! You're right! But there are a lot of people who don't believe in anything."

"Steven, everyone believes—or wants to believe—in something outside of themselves. They just use different terms to describe what they are seeking. The real amazement I have is that people rarely think to look inside of themselves first."

"Huh. I'll bet that's right. Man, what a crazy universe."

"It is, Steven. But we wouldn't have it any other way."

Thumbing back through my notes excitedly, I said, "Well, to make up for what a shit I have been, and to hopefully help you guys out a bit, I have been in my room working on a few things, and I think that I've found a pretty big solution to a lot of the problems that have been going on."

With piqued interest, he said, "You have?"

"Yes. We need to get rid of the vent worms."

He said disapprovingly, "Steven—"

"Wait, wait. Just hear me out. Those little bastards sit on the bottom of the ocean and, well, as far as I can tell, they don't provide any benefit to anyone. Yet they take up all of the prime spots, you know, in the event of an eventual Armageddon. And most of them are probably just mass murders, anyway, so I think that the world would be much better off if we got rid of them."

"Steven, we are not going to do that."

"*Why not?*" I shouted.

Shaking his head, he replied, "I can see that your parents are still going to have to work on that yelling problem when you get back.

Steven, vent worms are doing exactly what they should be doing, and you don't need to worry about that right now."

Continuing my campaign, I said, "But they're lazy, and they don't contribute to life on earth, and they're just in it for themselves and probably sucking up more oxygen from the water than they're entitled to based on how little they give back to us. That much is obvious, even to me."

Still shaking his head, he said, "Steven, I will never understand how people can equate what we do up here with eliminating other groups down there."

"Well, if you had fewer things to focus on, especially like those scheming devils on the bottom of the ocean—"

"Do you know how many souls have sat up here and said the same things about innumerable other groups on earth? Everyone has someone else to blame for their problems."

"Yeah, but I think that I'm really onto something here!"

"Okay, Steven, then let's get rid of the sloth too."

Horrified, I said, "Hey, what did the sloth ever do to hurt anyone?"

"Now do you see what I mean? Are you done throwing stones at the little vent worms? Why don't you hit the mark in your own life next time and *then* come back and tell me if you still think that the vent worms are the problem."

"Shit. Okay, okay, I get it. Idea number two. We need to get rid of Ted."

"What?"

"Yes. Ted has to go."

"Why?"

"How can I go back and live on a planet knowing that there is someone else down there who gets a thirty-year vacation when I don't?"

"Steven—"

"How can I? That's just ridiculous and unfair!"

"Well, Steven, Ted's tenure comes up in a few hundred years."

"Really?"

"Yes. And around that time, we will be looking for a replacement for him."

"Wow, cool! Oh, wait, does everyone else know about this?"

"Everyone who asks, sure."

Dejected, I said, "Oh, then it's hopeless. I'll bet that I am at the bottom of the barrel, and there must be like, what, a hundred thousand other people in line already. I'll never make it."

Encouragingly, he replied, "Actually, Steven, the line of applicants is pretty short."

"Really?"

"Yes. I told you, the job of caring for all of the souls in heaven is a difficult one, and most souls just want to go about their business and let someone else do it."

"Really? That's great!"

In a hushed voice, he said, "And, well, then there are *the others*."

I leaned in. "The 'others' who?"

He laughed. "Oh, the ones who are busy trying to sabotage the others who are trying for Ted's spot."

"Bastards!" I shouted. "How can you let them get away with that?"

Dismissing my thought, he said, "Steven, that is just how people behave. Honestly, every day, we get tons of souls up here who actually want to boast about *how* unqualified they are to do Ted's job—or Junior's for that matter. And some souls are perfectly content just keeping you from getting what *you* want. All they really care about is that someone else is worse off than they are. I say, the things people hold onto as trophies are sure amusing!"

"Amusing, my ass! That seems downright unfair! I mean, that just sucks. And Ted's job … well, it's a good job, and everyone should have a shot at it!"

"Oh, Steven, it's just tyranny."

"What?"

"Tyranny. The same as the dinosaurs who were running around and keeping life from becoming what it wanted to. The tyranny of people trying to keep you from getting Ted's spot, and the tyranny of people trying to keep you from being who you want, and the tyranny of the urgent who do not have the patience to let the world play out, and the tyranny of the old and the young, and the tyranny of parents who make you go to bed too early, and … well, you get the picture. Down there, you will run into numerous people who are trying to throw you off whatever course you are on.

"But if you find yourself and stick to that, nothing can touch you if you don't want it to. Imagine it, Steven; you can even live in your own tyranny!"

"Wow, that sounds great! But I still have no idea how to do that."

"The trick is to get rid of everything that is not *Steven.* We had a guy up here years ago who was a master sculptor. He did not have very many questions about other things, so we spent time talking about his work. He could create the most incredible sculptures using nothing but his mind and his tools. And I asked him one day, 'How is it that you can stand in front of a block of stone and whittle it into such an amazing statue of an eagle?' And, he said, 'It's easy. I just look at the block of stone and take away everything that is not an eagle.' Steven, your life is the same process. Everyone who has known the self within sees it in everything he does."

Wanting to spit on the floor again, I said, "Yeah, and when some asshole comes along and steals your tools or defaces the project you are working on?"

"Steven, that is bound to happen. Try not to get too angry about it. If the person you become really means something to you, you can still get to your goal despite all of the obstacles. Don't forget—knowing yourself is the first step, and if you rejoice in that fact, you will become the master of yourself and the master of your world down there. And the others who would steal from you do so because they do not know themselves and are in fact slaves."

"Well, I can understand that. But, what if … I mean, what if I'm afraid to ever cut into the block?"

"Some people are. But whether you yourself cut into it or not, the block will eventually fade to nothingness. While you are down there, you will just have to decide whether you want to shape your own life or let the world shape it for you."

"Okay, I will think about that. But it still sounds like a lot of tyranny to deal with. Can't we just get the dinosaurs back? That would be much easier."

"No, Steven. You have to learn to find yourself and rise above all of that. Otherwise, you will just spend all of your time up here complaining about everyone and everything that kept you from living according to Steven. Just try to hit the mark in your own life. If you do your best at that, *then* you can come back here and tell me whether you are still worried about the tyranny of others."

"Shit. I guess I can live with that for the next round. But, hey, what do you have to do to get Ted's job?"

"Not much. You can't cause any tyranny."

"Seriously? How do you do that?"

"Do unto others as you would have them do unto you."

"Wow. That sounds simple. Okay, what else?"

"You can't get married."

"What? Why not?"

"Because, Steven, when Ted is up here, he can't play favorites with anyone. His soul must be pure so that he can advise and help souls along in a fair and unbiased manner. If he had a spouse up here who died around the same time as he did—"

"Okay, okay, I get it. No marriage. I may have trouble with that one the next time around, but after that, no problem. What else?"

"No kids."

"Oh, right. Same reason?"

"Yes. And no drugs. No alcohol. Must have a compassionate soul. No cheating on fellow humans. No traffic tickets. No Internet porn. You have to have been an orphan."

"Wait, an orphan? What's that all about?"

"Same thing, Steven. Favorites. We ran into that problem a long time ago with Junior and his brother. It created a real mess, and we have been trying to straighten it out ever since. Ted must be able to assess each individual life and help it find what it needs."

"Why doesn't he help them find what they *want?*"

Shaking his head, he said, "Steven, you can't always do that. Some souls may want to go back as this or that or the other, but it is not always possible. Sometimes there is a waiting list problem. Sometimes a soul thinks that it should be one form of life but really it needs to be another for a while. That sort of thing."

"Oh, you mean like suicides who want to go back as tigers or dolphins, but they really need to go back as humans to finish the job?"

"Something like that. And for people with a lot of violence in their hearts, we usually recommend that they go back as trees for a while. The solitude and focus of a tree is often good to help them calm down a bit."

"Wow. That's a lot to consider. Who could ever qualify for that job?"

"Not many, as it turns out. But, Steven, if you had not *completely missed* yourself last time, you would have been on your way to becoming a viable applicant."

"Hey, you're right! Other than the … well, I guess everything that I actually did, I was pretty close!"

"That's correct, Steven."

"Well, next time, can I get credits for the tyranny I have to put up with?"

"What?"

"You know, credits for all of the people who try to drag me down and get me off course and keep me from getting Ted's job? Can I get credits on my application score for all of the shit I had to put up with down there?"

Another lightbulb went off. I said, "Hey, I have a great idea! I can spend my life down there making a list of all of the people who are getting it wrong, and then we can go over those when I get back here and—"

Frowning, he said, "That's fine, Steven. Just don't forget to write down your own shortcomings along the way."

"Shit. I'm not supposed to be casting stones at people, right?"

"Not unless you want them cast back at you."

"Crap. Okay, maybe I'll forget about Ted's job for right now. But when I come back next time, we're going to talk about me being a tree, right?"

"Of course, Steven. Look, don't try to analyze things too much. If you remember to do unto others as you would have them do unto you, you will go a long way next time."

"Right. Shit, that does seem to work for a lot of these issues. What a good idea."

"We often tell people that it is the most important 'rule' of all."

"Well, what about all of the other stuff? You know, like forbidden foods and all of that?"

"Oh, Steven, those were just from a time when interlopers up here wanted to go back and make sure that they were safe from everyone else. It was a way to have their cake and eat it too, so to speak. But nowadays, all souls who go back as food know what they are getting into. Your sister did."

Smacking my forehead, I said, "Shit! I almost forgot about her! What if I eat a can of tuna and my sister happens to be in it?"

He replied, "That's a possibility, Steven."

"Okay. No fish. Got it. And I will work on the rest. But do you think I can be a great redwood tree next time?"

"We'll see. You may do better to start out as a nice weeping willow or something small."

"Okay, now that just sounds insulting."

"No, no, Steven. Don't count them out. Willow trees are very important to life on earth, just like all other forms of life. But, Steven, anything can happen in a lifetime. You will just have to do your best to cultivate a sturdy and patient soul. Do you have any other bright ideas for today?"

Tentatively, I offered my last ounce of brilliance. "Well, do you think that we should cancel Christmas?"

Shaking his head and laughing, he said, "Strike three, Steven."

"What? Look, I'm just saying. If it's not the only day for his birthday, you know, because he's been back more than once—"

"Steven, if you people had any sense, you would have Christmas on *more* than one day, not cancel it. In fact, if all of the humans on earth would just take an actual day of rest once per week, you wouldn't be worrying about global warming and a whole host of other problems. But you are all in a great hurry to get something done, so you had better start making friends with the lower forms of life. You might need to borrow someone's spot in the future."

"Shit. Okay, I'll make note of that. And no need to keep any of those other suggestions permanently on file for right now."

XXIX

God said, "Hi, Steven. Ready to go?"

"Not quite yet. How is she doing?"

"Still rolling around on the ground. Four months old. Not bad."

"Okay, thanks. Hey, why didn't I get along with my mother?"

"You were different people. It's hard to do."

"Yeah, but I was disgusted with her always wanting to have a big, happy family and have everyone smile for pictures and all of that junk."

Leaning back, he said, "Steven, that is mostly your fault."

"Really?"

"Yes. Your grandmother pressured your mother into having an abortion before you were born."

"Seriously?"

"Yes. And it traumatized her for her whole life. But your mother originally became pregnant with what would have been your big brother when she was very young, and it was just socially unacceptable at the time. So she spent her whole life trying to make up for it. And after you, it took ten years before she could work up the courage to have another child."

"Wow, I had no idea. Wait, why is that my fault?"

"Because you judged her for who she was."

"I ... I ... shit, you're right. Now I feel bad about all of the pictures I tried to ruin and all of the, well, as you can imagine, I said some pretty harsh things to her."

"I know. Junior has the same problem when he's down there. It is very difficult. We tell people to try to love and honor their parents because it is hard to remember that they were the ones who helped to get you out of this place."

"Wow! An abortion. That's tough!"

"It is, Steven. An abortion hurts the world about as much as a suicide does."

"What?"

"They are almost the same thing, but for different reasons. A suicide, like you, is a soul who does not believe that there is any place for them in the world. An abortion is the world saying that it is not ready for a new life. It is just a different side of the same coin."

"Man ... Hey, wait, that could happen to me, right?"

Nodding, he said, "Sure. But don't worry. You don't lose your place if that happens. We will just send you back to a different family who wants a Steven and skip all of the talks."

"Oh, great, thanks. So, um, if I get sent back down there, and you know, I am a developing new life, how long does it take before I can survive without my mother?"

"About thirty or so—"

"Weeks?"

"Years, Steven."

"Wait, come on."

"Well, it can take less time. Some kids move out on their own at sixteen, seventeen, twenty-five … but you really don't have to be anywhere until you're thirty. So—"

"No, no, that's not what I was asking. How long—"

"Steven, you want to know how long you can go and still kill a human life before it becomes life?"

Backing off, I said, "Well, when you put it that way …"

"Steven, as far as I know, you can kill a human life for the entire time that it is alive. Does that make you feel better?"

"Um, let's just forget that this conversation took place. Thanks."

XXX

"Do you think that I can find my dad when I get back? I mean, the last guy?"

God raised an eyebrow and said, "Ah, the old father quest! Perhaps. If you get to a certain age and still want to try, you can. But you will have to learn Italian."

"Oh, right. I almost forgot. Well, people learn Italian every day, so maybe I can do it too."

"If you want to, you probably can. It may surprise your new parents if you suddenly express an interest in Italian, but that too happens all the time."

"Shit. My new parents. I almost forgot about them."

"Well, Steven, they are going to be very important to you, at least for a while. Don't forget, we need them to get you out of here. Even Jesus needs parents to get back in the game down there."

Bracing myself for the task, I said, "I know. I just wish there was an easier way than having to get to know a whole new set of people."

"Sorry, Steven. For now, you are stuck with parents in one form or another. Perhaps the next time you come around, we could send you back to be a clone—"

"Oh, fuck that! Having to inherit part of your parents is bad enough. I'd rather just take my chances with the old-fashioned process than become a laboratory byproduct."

"That's probably right, Steven."

"I just, you know, I feel bad that he and I—you know, my old dad—never understood each other."

Nodding in acknowledgement, he said, "It's hard. A lot of people go through the same thing. Parents have the responsibility to bring new life into the world, but sometimes they are still working on their own journeys. Sometimes they're not much more than kids themselves. And don't forget: you have to deal with your parents, but they have to deal with their parents and everything they have been through before that and before that, and … well, you get the picture."

"I do. It was just strange that my last dad always seemed more interested in some other culture than he was in me."

Curious, he asked, "Do you know what that was all about?"

"No, not really."

"Your dad lived in Italy when he was a kid. His parents dragged him there and then brought him back. All his life, he wanted to go back there to live, but it would have been too hard on you and the family. So he just took your mom on a lot of short trips."

"Well, he sure was gone a lot. I guess I always resented him for that."

"You may find out that having a parent who is gone is better than having one who hovers over you and micromanages everything you do. Parents spend so much time raising you at the start that they often forget that when a child comes of age, it is impossible to both know *who* they are and *where* they are at the same time."

"What?"

"The inevitable uncertainty of finding your own path. When you go out to find it, you will be by necessity no longer at home. You may even be perfectly lost somewhere. But that's where you will be becoming you. So it is impossible to both know where you are and know who you are at the same time. If they know where you are, then you are not being you. If they know who you are, then you're probably off on an adventure somewhere."

"Wow. That's tricky stuff."

"It is, Steven. Very hard for anyone to manage or predict. People also tell me that the worst thing is having parents who are both gone *and* try to micromanage."

"Yeah, I'll bet that sucks. But can't you just find parents that I will get along with?"

Shaking his head, he answered, "Steven, that could be a very bad thing for you personally."

"What do you mean?"

"Some souls are very good at accepting what comes to them down there and are perfectly content to follow their parents' lead. They may never go out on their own and may never need to add uncertainty into their lives. As a result, they will tend to get along with their parents in all respects. That is not and was not you, Steven, and your last dad knew enough to leave you alone so that you could find your own vision of the world. You just didn't take the opportunity."

"Crap. So if I don't get along with my new parents, what should I do?"

"That is up to you, Steven. However, no matter how bad it gets or how miserable you may be as a child, do not make the mistake that most kids we see up here do."

"Which is?"

"Hurting yourself just because you happened to draw people who were like that first soul and his clone. People who have children for their benefit instead of for the possibility of new life. Remember Alex from the hospital?"

"Boy, do I. I felt so bad about that kid and what he went through. I hope that he'll be okay next time."

"Oh, he will. It is just sad that some people can make a kid like that think that all of their problems were his fault. But his own mistake was not waiting long enough to grow up and get out on his own. If he had done that, then he could have made them pay."

"What?"

"Steven, parents can also forget that doing unto others means that you can do unto them."

"Wow, you're right! So if my parents put cigarettes out on me—"

"Yes, Steven. You have my permission to do the same. Just make sure that you can get away with it when you do."

"Oh, I will."

"In actuality, Steven, young people often forget that living well is really the best revenge against anything, and that can apply to the place in which you grew up as well. Fortunately, most people we see up here were just severely annoyed with their parents, like you were. Which is, of course, just payback for how much your parents had to go through when you were a little baby and shitting all over the place."

I tell you, rosacea in heaven is tough to deal with.

"And that annoyance can be a great impetus to get you out of the house and onto your own adventure. That is why we generally advise all people that they should get married and leave their parents when they are ready. That usually covers all bases."

"Yeah, and then their parents wind up moving next to them, anyway."

God belted out, "Just like the Galactic Empire coming in for invasion!"

"Hey, you learned *Star Wars*!"

"Oh yes. While you were busy shitting yourself and getting repaired, I had a nice talk with a lady who had a photographic memory, and she told me all about the books."

"Seriously? Why don't you just read them yourself?"

"Steven, we are not much in the book-*reading* business up here, either. There is too much activity to spend time reading. But people with photographic memories come in handy for lots of different things."

"Wow! Hey, so when I make it to the end and don't kill myself next time, can I get sent back to Italy? You know, if I learn Italian and everything?"

"Steven, you would have to live there and participate in the culture for us to do that."

"Why?"

"Your soul is programmed to only go places where it has belonged before."

"So why can't I just visit a bunch of times?"

"Steven, being a visitor is not the same as belonging somewhere. Tourists do not build bridges."

"Huh? Oh, so I have to build something? Wait, that doesn't make sense."

"No, Steven. But you do have to participate and let your soul become part of the place where you are. Otherwise, there is no way to get you back there."

"Well, so maybe I'll look into living abroad next time. God, do I really have to go back to the same place where I was when I killed myself?"

Frowning, he said, "Steven, you already know this."

"Yeah, but I don't get it."

"You cannot redo your life in a different place. You have to go back to reexamine the issues that caused you to harm yourself. And they do not think the same or talk the same or tell the same myths in different places than they did where you were."

"Are you talking about my country or my state or what?"

"Steven, I was talking about your apartment building."

"What?"

"Every neighborhood on the planet has its own culture. You may not know it while you are there, but they do. And they all tell stories that are different from anyplace else. You have to go back and finish the story of Steven—"

"Or Stephanie?"

"Yes, or Stephanie. And to do that, we have to send you back to basically the same postal code. Those are actually quite useful to us! They make for handy coordinates for sending suicides back."

"Yeah, great. The wonders of the modern world. Anyway, I'm not going to fret about it. I will do fine next time. And besides, that's where Emily is going to be."

Nodding, he replied, "That's right, Steven."

"So if I can find my old dad, and if I get along with my other family, and if I find Emily and marry her, then that will be like, well, it could be like five or six people who get me. That's pretty good!"

"Steven, you will be lucky if you find one. And if you do, don't fuck that up."

"Oh, I won't. You can bet that I won't. But what about Junior? He had, that one time, like what, twelve disciples or something?"

"Yes, and twelve turned out to be too many."

"Oh … right."

"Steven, if you can find one other soul on the planet with whom you can share your entire self, that is all you will need. If you find one other person who wants to share your vision of the world, you will be the luckiest soul on the planet. Once you have that, you won't need twelve, or eleven, or even six of those. You'll just need one."

"Oh yeah, I get it. That's why you tell people to honor the commitment they make for marriage for their whole lives, right?"

"Something like that. But you know the tale … people are prone to panic and think that they chose wrong or are going to miss something or that they are expiring too soon, and so they have to go out and grab something else to feed off of."

"Yeah, that's the pits. Hey, how are we doing on time?"

"She just started learning to grab objects. Five months or so."

XXXI

"What if I get back there and my parents say that I was a mistake?"

Shaking his head gently, God said, "Steven, you should know by now that that is not possible. You have accepted that you are going back, and at this point, you have just as much of a choice in the matter as they do. You can't be a mistake."

"Wow! But what if they say, like, that I'm not what they wanted? You know, that I'm a disappointment."

"Steven, it is all a very risky business. They risk on you, you risk on them."

"Man, what a messy universe. Hey, what if, I mean, what if I hadn't come along while I was up here? You know, what if I hadn't accepted what you were telling me and all of that?"

He answered, "Oh, we would have just vaporized you."

"*What?*"

"Steven, relax. I'm just fucking with you."

"Well, thanks for not saying, 'I told you so.' I think that I'd really hate it if you said that to me, after all that I had to go through."

Knowingly, he said, "Steven, I'd hate that too. Anything else?"

"Well, what if … what if my suit down there doesn't work the way I want it to? I mean, what if I'm like, you know—"

Waving his hand dismissively, he answered, "Steven, don't worry about that. You are not ready for that yet."

"What do you mean?"

"You are not ready to be a special messenger."

"Huh?"

"Steven, it is only the strongest among you who can endure to go back with real challenges. The weak ones would never make it. You are not ready for that, so it probably won't happen. Souls who go back to earth with markings, or what you would call imperfections or even disabilities, are the messengers for everyone else. The differences help to identify what they are there for. But the last thing you will need next time is a reason to doubt your existence. You are not ready for that yet, so you will most likely go back as an ordinary participant, just like everyone else."

"Wow. So what if I'm participating and I get hit by a bus?"

"That happens. If you survive it and are in need of assistance, hopefully you will find someone great down there who is willing to help you out and be your servant along the way. After all, that is why we send helpers back in the first place. Before buses, we hardly needed them down there."

"Ha-ha. Very funny. Thanks. Time?"

"Still doing fine. She's started playing peekaboo. Six months old."

XXXII

Flying back in, I said, "Do you know what kind of incredible stuff is up here?"

God said, "Hello again, Steven. Yes, I certainly do."

"I mean, wow, just wow! You guys have everything up here. Well, at least from what I can see looking in on everyone else."

"Steven, you would be surprised to know that you had everything down there too. However, the rules are the same in both places. If you don't participate, you can't play."

Settling down, I said, "Okay, okay, I get it. But what the hell is with the pinball tournament?"

"What do you mean?"

"Why is there a pinball tournament in heaven?"

"Well, you've heard about the deaf, dumb, and blind kid who could play pinball, right?"

Chuckling in disbelief, I said, "God, that was just a made-up song."

"If it was made up, then why did so many people follow along?"

"That's just what they do."

"Well, everyone up here wanted to have it, so we do. Steven, even that guy found a reason to go on, despite his shortcomings. And his parents were absolutely awful to him."

"Okay, okay, I will remember not to get hung up on things that I cannot change and that I may have it better than someone else, no matter how bad things seem."

Swinging his arm, he said, "That's the spirit!"

"But, hey, I've never seen a pinball machine quite like that one. It was amazing!"

"Well, it's a copy of one that is down on earth."

"Serously? Oh, wait, is this ... is heaven the place where all of the forms come from?"

"The what?"

"The forms! You know. Is heaven the place where the form of every chair that can ever be thought up on earth, or every bed, or every ... whatever, comes from?"

"Quite the opposite, Steven. Before life started constructing things on earth, we didn't have anything here. I told you that earlier. So the only way that we get stuff up here is if you think of it first down there."

"Wow!"

"So, when you go back to earth, if you want to create something new, just be sure to make it really spectacular, and then you can have it up here."

"Too cool! Hey, so does that mean that you guys have nuclear bombs up here?"

"No, Steven. We have you instead!"

"Ha! Sorry again for ... never mind. How are we doing on time?"

"Seven months; she's learning how to sit up. Still doing okay."

XXXIII

"What if I set out to do something and I can't do it? What if I come up with a really great idea and someone else does it first?"

God said, "Those are the risks you take. Some people say that life is suffering, and you should do nothing. Other people tell me that they let their energy go and just rode the wave. In the end, it is largely a pacing problem, and it is completely up to you. What I can tell you is that you may win at something you try, or you may lose at it. But if you are acting according to Steven, you cannot lose no matter what."

"Well, what I really want to do is to do something really spectacular and something daring and that the world has never seen, but I want to make sure that I get out of it safely and that I make a lot of money along the way."

"Good luck with that. Steven, don't overtax yourself on this next round."

Suspicious, I lowered my gaze at him. "Wait, are you telling me *to* sit around and do nothing?"

"No, Steven. You can do whatever you want, and you can risk your life on something big. But you are just healing from committing suicide. You will want to proceed a bit slowly and cautiously next time. You wouldn't want to run off and get yourself killed right out of the gate, would you?"

"Probably not. But there seem to be so many things to do and to fix and—"

"Steven, remember what I said about you being a bomb? You are pure energy that is put into a human suit down there. You are the same as a ticking bomb with the power to blow up anything, even yourself. However, if you learn to pace yourself and to wait for that big thing that you want to conquer to come along, then you can use your energy before it winds up using you. If you can, then you will unleash the true potential of yourself down there."

"Well, I will have to think about that. I've just never considered myself in terms of energy."

"Steven, it is all around you. Under normal circumstances, you are no different from an atom that decays at a predictable rate—except that you do not decay at a predictable rate. You decay at whatever rate you set. And as you know, that same atom can be used to unleash all of its energy at once, and that can produce miraculous as well as horrible results."

"Yes, I have seen that firsthand. I guess that I'm better at blowing things up than using my energy for a meaningful purpose."

Nodding, he said, "Steven, you and lots of other people."

"Well, I will think about that. How are we doing?"

"Nine months. Learning to crawl."

"Great, thanks! I'm almost done."

XXXIV

"No, Steven, you cannot switch from one form of life to another down there. People try it all the time, but if you eat too much bacon, you will not be able to turn into a pig. If you smoke too much, you will not become a tobacco plant. Your body may think that is what you want, but it just isn't possible. In the end, consuming too much of anything that is not you will cause your whole body to revolt, and you will wind up back here to face me."

"Of course I like to play dice. I've played twice, and both games are still going."

"I told you, life is not a scavenger hunt. Life is an adventure. The difference is whether or not you have predetermined what the outcome will be."

"Just took her first step. You'd better hurry, or she may get away from you."

"Steven, you are the only creature in the universe that can believe that it has survived billions of years of evolution and countless wars, plagues, and other disasters, but you fall apart when you think that someone won't like what you brought for show-and-tell. Get over it."

"With all of the stuff going on up here, why do people spend so much time trying to live forever?"

"I don't know, Steven. Perhaps because they don't want to talk to me anymore. But I don't take it personally."

"Well, the good news is that I may live to be 120 or so next time. At least that's what I heard them saying before I left."

"Steven, if it takes you 120 years to get your shit together down there, we are all in for a lot of trouble."

"Yes, Steven, you can still jerk off when you're married. Don't be such an asshole. But you might consider sticking to things that are real when you do so."

"Oh, don't worry. I'm going back to lingerie catalogs!"

"Steven … well, never mind. That's a start."

"No, Steven, we cannot give you your own planet. We could send you to Mars, but there would be no one else there with you, and you would survive for less time than it took you to ask that question. Besides, Mars is cold as hell."

"Where did I come from? Steven, if you can find out the answer to that question, I will let you take Junior's place at my side."

"Eight? What did you do with the ninth planet? Jesus, now you're even discriminating against planets!"

Jesus entered and said, "You rang?"

"Oh, shit. Sorry, Son, I didn't mean to do that."

Shuffling noisily toward the door, Jesus mumbled, "Great. Now he's doing it too. I wonder what Ted is up to these days."

XXXV

Jesus knocked and said, "Okay, Steven, time to wrap it up. This couple has been trying to conceive for a while now, and we should announce your joyous arrival to the world."

953. Try to respect all of the planets that we have been given.

954. Learn about deep sea life (just in case).

"There. I think that I'm finally done. And I'm ready to go."

Glancing at my stack of notes, Jesus said, "Steven, there is no way that anyone is going to be able to follow all of these rules. When you get back, you might want to consider whittling it down a bit."

"Oh, don't worry. These aren't rules for other people. They are just for me."

"Oh, good. You're probably safe, then. But you forgot to write down the most important rule of all."

Looking down I said, "I ... what? Shit, you're right. I did. But I seriously doubt that I will forget that one the next time around."

"Let's hope not. It can sure make your life easier. Look at it this way. Even if you only remember two of these rules and you make it to the end next time and don't have an accident in heaven, you will have come a long way."

"Well, I guess that's a good start. But it does seem like an awfully slow way to progress."

God said, "Steven, don't worry about that. Learning these things can take lifetimes. You are doing just fine."

"So how am I going to find these materials I get back here? You know, to see how I did?"

God said, "Oh, we'll bind everything together and put it in the library for you."

"There's a library up here? Oh, wait, let me guess, suicides can't go in the library, either."

"Of course they can."

"Well, why didn't I get to go to the library?"

"You didn't ask. Don't worry, Steven, you can do that next time. We'll put your book in the library under your name so that you can find it easily next time."

"Huh. A book about ... Steven. Well, I guess I'll be in good company between Shitting and Suicide, right? But ... so does that mean that anyone can read it if it's in the library?"

"Yes, Steven. We do not censor anything up here, even the story of a journey as strange as yours. Are you all set to go?"

"Well, whether I am or not, you have been more than fair."

"Jesus?"

Jesus raised an eyebrow. "Yes, Steven?"

"I am so, so sorry about everything."

Smiling, he said, "Steven, don't worry about it. That's what we're here for."

"And, God?"

"Yes, Steven?"

"Thank you, for everything."

"Don't mention it, Steven. Just remember, your life will be better spent down there if it is an activity that results in a story, and not the other way around."

"Right. Got it! So how do we do this?"

God said, "All you have to do is pass through that door behind me."

"Door? Wow! I never saw that the whole time I was here. But don't you have to code me or zap me or something to make sure that I wind up as a human?"

"No, Steven. We don't have to do anything to you at all. You are the one who makes that happen."

"Amazing. Absolutely amazing. Hey, God?"

"Yes, Steven?"

Moving toward him with my arms outstretched, I said, "The whole time I've been up here, I never touched you. Can I get a hug before I go?"

God folded his arms and said, "No."

"Why not? Oh, wait, let me guess. You are, as the Great Creator, not allowed to touch souls up here, right?"

"No, Steven. As the Great Creator, I have touched all life in the universe. If I were to touch you now, even in this form, you would be reconnected to all of that life and thus would have the choice to go back in whatever form you chose. I cannot do so, because you have to go back to where you started."

Taking that all in for the last time, I said, "Fuck. That's a pretty heavy burden to bear."

"It is, Steven. But you are the only one who can carry it in your next life. No one else can do it for you."

"Okay. But all of this not touching stuff can make you a bit crazy, you know."

"Steven, don't worry. Your parents will be sure to hug you when you get there."

"Okay. Deep breath, Steven. Well, guys, I will do my best next time and look forward to seeing you again. But not too soon!"

God said, "Good luck, Steven. We'll be up here watching. And, remember, if you need anything—"

"Don't worry, I know."

Then I said, "Shit. I almost forgot to ask. What is *the Word*? I have been up here this whole time meaning to find that out."

God said, "Love, Steven. Love."

"Oh, right. That should just about do it. Mom and Dad, or wait, I guess it could be Dad and Dad, right?"

"That's right, Steven."

"Well, Mom and Dad, or Dad and Dad, or Mom and Mom, or whomever is helping to get me out of here, buckle up! Here comes Steven!"

EPILOGUE

Jesus said, "Do you think that he got the message?"

God said, "Oh yes. He will do just fine. He will provide shelter to people and help take pollutants out of the air and develop strong roots that will keep him stabilized when tough winds blow by."

"No, Dad, you forgot. We sent him back as a human."

"I know, Son."

"Oh. Right. Anyway, I'm going to go and work with the Johnsons. I think that they understand what went wrong, and I have a great deal of hope that they will start to come around pretty quickly. After that, I think that I will drop down to the Middle East and see how the peace process is working. And after that, I think that I'll ... hey, why are you laughing?"

"I just get a kick out of it every time that you start to make a plan."

"Oh, right. Well, I hear someone calling, so I guess I have to go."

"Good luck, Son. I will see you for the next adventure."

Postbook Legal Disclaimer

Everything you just read is a story. It was written by a human on earth. Please do not take any action or inaction based on what you have read in here. The opposite of everything in this book could equally be true. Or the converse. Or the contrapositive.

In the end, the truth may be buried somewhere in the quarks, or leptons, or in a cave, or whatever, and it will not accessible to us until someone tells us it is.

Whatever you do from this point forward, do not do anything based on what you read in a book or learn from anywhere else. If you are going to act—or not act—do so because it comes from you and you alone. In the end, that may be the only real truth you can find on this physical plane.

This book was also not intended to offend or disparage any one particular thing. No offense was certainly intended to buses or Internet porn. When used properly, both can be very enjoyable and get people to where they need to be.

Printed in the United States
By Bookmasters